PRAISE FOR THE FIRST CAROLINE RHODES BOOK
A DEADLY LITTLE CHRISTMAS

"HIGHLY RECOMMENDED... CHARACTERS ARE WELL DRAWN...ABSOLUTELY CHARMING. FOR A FIRST NOVEL THIS ONE HOLDS MUCH PROMISE, THERE IS SO MUCH TO LIKE INCLUDING THE HEROINE...A DELIGHT."
LINDA HURST, UNDER THE COVERS BOOK REVIEWS

"A KNOCKOUT CHRISTMAS COVER GIFT-WRAPS A DEBUT HINGING ON A CHRISTMAS TREE...SO BEGINS A DEVILISH PLOT."
THE POISONED PEN, DEC. 1998 BOOK REVIEWS

"ONE REACHES FOR AN AFGHAN AS THE AUTHOR DESCRIBES THE WEATHER."
KATHIE LAWSON, BOOKBROWSER REVIEW

"BRING ON THE NEXT CAROLINE RHODES MYSTERY-- THIS IS A BELIEVABLE CHARACTER IN HER MIDDLE AGE WITH WIT, INTELLIGENCE, AND ROOM TO GROW. WE NEED MORE LIKE HER."
PAM WEINBERG, CHICAGO PUBLIC LIBRARY

"A DEADLY LITTLE CHRISTMAS IS A PLEASURE NO ONE SHOULD DENY THEMSELVES. THE CHARACTERS ARE FUN, EMOTIONAL, AND ENGAGING. ALL WILL HAVE YOU WANTING TO TURN TO THE LAST CHAPTER TO FIND OUT IF THEY ARE THE 'MAD BOMBER'."
BENJAMIN POTTER

ALSO BY MARY V. WELK

A DEADLY LITTLE CHRISTMAS
ISBN 0-9665157-0-6

ABOUT THE AUTHOR:

Mary V. Welk's first full length novel,
A DEADLY LITTLE CHRISTMAS, merited an award in the
1996 Hemingway First Novel Competition
under the title *FOUR TO GO.*
It was released by Kleworks Publishing Co. in fall, 1998.
Ms. Welk resides with her husband and family in Chicago,
and is currently at work on a third
Caroline Rhodes mystery novel,
TO KILL A KING.

FOR INFORMATION ON THE AUTHOR OR HER BOOKS,
CONTACT KLEWORKS PUBLISHING COMPANY,
OR VISIT OUR WEBSITE AT
WWW.MYSTERYKLEWORKS.COM

A CAROLINE RHODES MYSTERY

SOMETHING WICKED IN THE AIR

MARY V. WELK

KLEWORKS PUBLISHING COMPANY
CHICAGO, IL.

SOMETHING WICKED IN THE AIR
Published by Kleworks Publishing Co.
First Printing April 1999

Publisher's Note: This is a work of fiction. Names,
characters, places, and incidents either are the product of
the author's imagination or are used fictitiously, and any
resemblance to actual persons, living or dead, events, or
locales is entirely coincidental.

ISBN 0-9665157-1-4
Library of Congress Catalog Card Number: 99-94020

Printed in the USA by
Morris Publishing
3212 East Highway 30, Kearney, NE 68847
1-800-650-7888

For my husband, Fred,
who's still crazy after all these years,
with all my love and gratitude.
I couldn't have done it without you, Derf.

You're still the one.

Caroline Rhodes is a fictional character, yet she is
patterned after the many fine nurses I've been
privileged to know. Their strength, intelligence, and
tenacity, both on and off the job, are attributes I've
tried to duplicate in Caroline. To these men and
women of nursing I dedicate her existence.
In a very special way, I dedicate Caroline to
Sue Stuebe,
an exceptional person,
and the finest nurse I've ever known.

Special thanks to Martha Eicker
for her editorial assistance,
and to Jim Grundy
for his input on police procedures.

CHAPTER 1

"What a glorious day to be alive!"

Professor Carl Atwater, roly-poly chairman of the History Department of Bruck University, Rhineburg, Illinois, threw back his head, expanded his lungs, and sucked in the fragrant scents of a midwestern spring morning.

"Just look at those clouds, Cari. A few minutes ago they were little more than powder puffs on the horizon. Now they're magnificent mountains tumbling across the sky."

Caroline Rhodes, a woman who knew thunderheads when she saw them, looked up from her handiwork and rolled her eyes in mock despair.

"It's a good thing you don't teach meteorology, Carl. You'd have been sacked long before reaching tenure."

The Professor ceased his deep breathing exercises and feigned indignation.

"And what's that supposed to mean?"

"That means your 'magnificent mountains' are jam-packed with magnificent raindrops," Caroline snorted. "We'll be lucky if we aren't drenched before long."

She surveyed her surroundings from a tall-backed cedar bench parked strategically in the center of Bruck Green. The grassy oval separating St. Anne's Hospital from the campus of Bruck University was riddled with puddles from previous storms, and the cobbled walks criss-crossing the lawn still glistened with dampness.

"As if we needed any more rain," she added with a grumble.

Carl turned his back on the approaching cloudbank and waggled his bushy white eyebrows at his friend.

"Come now, Caroline. Your pessimism is an affront to this beautiful May weather. Besides that, it's affecting my mood, which is exceptionally good considering I've just had breakfast with Professor Littlewort."

"Dr. Eccentric? You've got to be kidding, Carl."

Andrew Littlewort stood out like a sore thumb at conservative Bruck U. The Captain Kirk of English Literature, Littlewort boldly went where no other teacher dared go. His required reading list included both William Shakespeare and *Rolling Stone* magazine, a combination not unreasonable except for the professor's attempt to prove a similarity between the two. Had his opinions been restricted to the classroom, Andrew might have fared better in the eyes of his colleagues. Unfortunately, the man had a way of turning one and all against him. He publicly sneered at his peers, calling them 'educational cowards' whose 'slavish attachment to the status quo' reneged on their commitment to advancing the quality of education at Bruck. His acerbity cost him both respect and friendship, still few professors dared criticize him to his face. Rather than deal with Littlewort's explosive temper, the faculty simply avoided him like the plague.

"Andy's impossible at times," Carl conceded, "but at least he's sincere."

Caroline groaned.

"Pul-lease! As the good folk of Rhineburg would say, that man is downright squirrely in the head." She twisted an imitation rose onto six inches of wire and tied a bit of red ribbon to the stem. "At least I know why you're acting so weirdly today. You've been infected with Littlewortitis." She tossed the flower to Carl. "Would you put this in the basket with the others? They're for the Maypole."

Carl purposely ignored her comments as he twirled the plastic posey under his nose.

"Ah, yes. The haunting fragrance of synthetic polymers. Robust, yet not intense. Redolent of...of...achew!" The Professor dropped the rose and grabbed a handkerchief from his pocket.

"Redolent of dust," Caroline remarked while rescuing the decoration from the grass. "And so bleached by the sun that they're practically colorless. These flowers belong in a Dumpster, not on a Maypole, Carl. Can't the university afford to buy some new ones for the Festival of Knights?"

"Take it up with the Emperor," Carl grumbled between sneezes. "He owes you one."

That's true, thought Caroline. Garrison Hurst, the President of Bruck University scornfully dubbed 'Emperor' for his dictatorial style, was deeply indebted to her. The FBI had invaded his college over the Christmas holidays after a bomb exploded at nearby St. Anne's Hospital. Hot on the trail of a student terrorist, they'd disrupted the equanimity of both faculty and parents before Caroline's snooping flushed out the true killer and saved the university's reputation.

Of course Caroline hadn't been driven by purely altruistic motives. A nurse by profession and a newcomer to Rhineburg, she'd attracted the attention of Tom Evans, lead investigator for the FBI, after witnessing both the explosion and a subsequent murder. Evans didn't believe in coincidence, and when he learned of Caroline's recent emotional breakdown following the hit-and-run death of her husband, he began to suspect she was Rhineburg's infamous 'Mad Bomber'.

It was only with the help of Carl Atwater that Caroline had

extricated herself from the mess. Thirty years younger than the septuagenarian professor, she now considered him a close friend. Over the course of their investigation he'd reintroduced her to life as she'd known it before Ed's death. For that she'd be ever thankful.

Despite her fondness for him, Caroline recognized one alarming trait in Carl. He tended to go ballistic whenever Hurst's name was mentioned. The two men were engaged in a decade-long feud rooted in jealousy on Hurst's part over Atwater's considerable literary success. All attempts at civility had vanished last winter after Carl led a faculty rebellion against the President's proposed curriculum changes. Currently, the pair conversed only when university protocol or unavoidable circumstances dictated the necessity. Sensing the Professor was building up to another anti-Hurst tirade, and unwilling to be the cause of his next hypertensive crisis, Caroline quickly changed the subject.

"Tell me more about the Festival of Knights. How did it get started?"

Atwater sank down on the bench and pulled out his pipe.

"The first Festival was held back in 1967. I remember it well because I was thrown by my horse during the opening ceremonies." Carl chuckled at the memory before catching sight of Caroline's upraised eyebrows. "Don't look at me that way, woman! It may be hard to believe, but I weighed a hundred and sixty pounds back then."

"That must have been before you discovered the pleasures of Rhineburg's restaurants," Caroline quipped. The Professor's adipose tissue had more than doubled over the years, and his present girth resembled that of Santa Claus, the mythical figure he portrayed each year at the town's Winter Festival.

"Now you're going to badger me about my diet," Carl growled. "You may be a nurse, Caroline, but must you always think like one?"

Caroline threw up her hands. Although she tried not to nag the Professor, her instincts sometimes proved too strong to resist.

"I'll save my lecture for the day you land in ER. Getting back to the Festival of Knights, tell me why the university started sponsoring it."

"Call it a dose of preventive medicine. Even staid old Bruck fell victim to flower power during the '60s. We weren't overrun by hippies, mind you, but we did have our share of unwashed bodies littering the dormitories."

"Amazing. And here I thought you'd survived that period unscathed."

"Let's not get nasty, Cari," the Professor warned. "You Chicagoans weren't the only ones living in the age of Aquarius." His tone turned lofty. "It's just that we Rhineburgers coped with the times better than most people."

"I'll bet you did! Who was running Bruck's security department back then? The Archangels' father?"

Caroline referred to the present day guardians of Bruck University, Michael, Rafael, and Gabriel Bruck. The triplets wore their nickname for obvious reasons and had a unique way of dealing with troublemakers. Those who violated the rules and regulations of Bruck U. shoveled snow in the winter and cut grass in the spring. Apparently a few hours of hard labor had an enlightening effect on most students, for few ever served a second sentence.

"Their grandfather, John Bruck. The Festival of Knights was actually John's brainchild. He figured if the students had to work together on one huge school project, they'd be forced to put their political differences aside and get to know each other as individuals. Nehemiah MacCardy, the university's President back then, saw the wisdom in John's thinking. Nehemiah's background was in history, so hosting a Renaissance Faire was a natural for him. He persuaded the Student Senate to go along with the plan, then bullied the History and Art Departments into assisting with sets and costumes."

"I suppose the Festival has evolved over the years."

"Sure has. In '67 we had a two-day tournament with a couple of food booths on the sidelines. Today the Festival lasts a whole week. It opens with an evening banquet here on the Green followed the next day by a Grand Parade of Knights and preliminary jousting trials. Along with the games there are exhibitions of falconry, candle making, weaving, and other crafts. And of course there's the archery competition. That always draws a huge crowd."

"Sounds like a lot of fun. How exactly are the students involved?"

"Each booth and event is coordinated by a different student group," explained Carl. "The kids start planning their parts as early as September. Some of them even attend fairs during the summer, then they incorporate new things they've seen into our celebration."

"I didn't realize the Festival was such a big deal."

Carl shrugged. "It takes a lot of work to put on a decent show for the public, but the students reap the rewards. Each group or club gets to keep fifty percent of the proceeds from their booth or event. That money funds their activities for the next year. Besides that, the students enjoy this week of merrymaking prior to final exams. It gives them an emotional boost before they settle down to serious studying."

Caroline thought of her forty-two charges in the nursing school dorm. In addition to her job as a float pool RN at St. Anne's, she'd taken on the duties of dormitory housemother in exchange for a rent-free apartment and a minimal stipend from the hospital.

"Considering how my gang burns the midnight oil night after night, I admit they deserve a little fun." She placed the last rose in the wicker basket beside the bench before stretching both arms skyward. "I can't say I'm sorry to be done with this job. Next year find me something to do besides plaiting ribbons on plastic flowers, OK?"

"They'll look very nice hanging from the Maypole," Carl assured her. "Speaking of which, those boys should have finished digging the hole for it by now."

Carl half turned on the bench and gazed across Bruck Green. A group of young men were gathered at the north end of the grassy oval, two of them wielding shovels while the others supported a tall wooden pole on their shoulders. As Carl watched, one of the diggers threw down his spade and began scrabbling in the dirt with his hands. The pole bearers let their burden slide to the ground and encircled their companion.

Carl frowned. "What in the world are they up to?"

As if in answer, the fellow kneeling by the hole jumped up and waved in their direction.

"Hey, Professor! Come see what we've found!"

Atwater clambered to his feet. With Caroline hard on his heels, he circled the fortune teller's tent and headed towards the boys.

"What's up, guys?"

"Look what was buried here!"

The erstwhile digger extended his hands. Cupped in his palms was a large gray rock, its surface smoothed by contact with the earth.

"Let me see that."

Carl took the stone and wiped it clean of dirt. He frowned as he examined the rectangular shaped rock.

"That's a pretty hefty chunk," Caroline commented. "It must be at least five or six pounds."

"This is impossible," Carl muttered. "It can't be real."

"Let's ask Professor Littlewort," one of the boys suggested. "He's the expert on this stuff, isn't he?"

Caroline was lost. The students were all talking at once as they crowded around Carl, craning their necks for a better view of the stone.

"What's so special about that rock?" she finally asked. "It looks quite ordinary to me."

The Professor turned to face her. He cradled his prize in one hand and with the other pointed to a series of nicks and scratches on the stone's surface resembling a triangle bisecting a straight line.

"I'm no archeologist, Cari, but if these boys' suspicions prove true, there's nothing at all ordinary about what I'm holding. You may be looking at an ancient Viking rune stone."

"A what?"

"Atwater! Tell me I'm not dreaming!"

From the direction of the university ran a dark scarecrow of a man. His thin arms flapped in the air like the scrawny wings of a starving bird as he swooped down on the group. One oversized foot tripped over the other until he finally stumbled to a halt, completely out of breath, beside Carl.

"Is it...really...a rune...stone?" Professor Littlewort panted excitedly, his eyes behind horn-rimmed glasses flicking from face to face before settling on Carl's in hopeful anticipation.

Professor Atwater slowly shook his head as he handed the rock to his colleague. Logic, that bane of all dreamers, now dampened his initial enthusiasm.

"I know what you're feeling, Andrew, and I admit that when I first held it, the thought that it could be genuine... But no. We both know they couldn't have traveled this far inland."

Littlewort ignored the doubt in the Professor's voice.

"Look at the markings! If this isn't a letter from the futhork..."

"Hold on, Andrew." Carl's tone registered gentle reproof as he touched the other man's arm. "I wish for your sake you could prove your theory, but don't go jumping to conclusions. Those scratches could have been made by anyone at any time."

Littlewort pulled away from Carl's grasp. He cradled the rock to his chest and covered it with both hands.

"You're jealous!" he thundered. "You can't stand sharing the limelight with anyone else at this university, and when I use this stone to prove the Vikings actually visited Rhineburg, I'll be the famous man on campus, not you!"

"Andrew, Andrew," Carl said softly. "This has nothing to do with jealously. I'm only urging you to exercise a little caution."

But Littlewort was beyond pacifying. His hawk-like nose quivered with indignation and the veins on his thin neck bulged rigidly. He extended his face to within inches of Carl's.

"I'll send it to Chicago for verification," he snapped. "The Field Museum will be honored to confirm my find." He turned his back on the Professor and suddenly addressed one of the students. "Thank you, young man. Informing me of the stone's existence showed great intelligence on your part. Others, I fear," -- and here he glared accusingly at Carl -- "would have dismissed your report as sheer nonsense."

The youth, a stocky fellow with forearms twice the size of Littlewort's legs, stared at the ground, his face reddening in embarrassment. His companions said nothing, but they also appeared

uncomfortable with the situation. Caroline sensed their relief when Littlewort turned on his heel and strode away with the stone.

"I think you'd better get that Maypole up," she told the boys. "It's going to rain any minute now."

The group went back to work quite willingly. Caroline and the Professor left them to it and walked back to where the basket of roses lay unattended by the bench.

"Now tell me what that was all about."

Carl shook his head in disgust.

"I think someone's played a practical joke on old Littlewort. And unfortunately, he's fallen for it." He sank down on the bench and reached for a flower. "We know these roses are fake, don't we? Up close anyone could tell they're plastic. But from a distance, say twelve feet up on the Maypole, most people will assume they're flowers newly picked from the university's gardens."

"I don't think anyone will mistake these old things for live roses, Carl."

Carl waved aside the objection.

"Folks believe what they want to believe. Wait and see. Tied up with greens and ribbon, even these decrepit blossoms will appear real to some."

Caroline grimaced. "So what's your point, Carl?"

"Andrew wants to believe he's found a treasure, an actual runic relic left behind by ancient travelers. Common sense says it's impossible, but Professor Littlewort lacks common sense. He's going to make himself the laughing stock of the university."

"Back up a minute, Carl. You lost me on the 'runic relic' part. Just what are 'runic relics'? And that other word Littlewort mentioned; futtock, or..."

"Futhork. The Norse alphabet."

"Norse like in Norwegian?"

"Sort of," Carl replied. "The early inhabitants of Scandinavia -- our present day Denmark, Norway, and Sweden -- were called Norsemen, or Northmen. They were a fierce people skilled in warfare and seamanship who made a living as pirates and invaders. The Norse word 'vik' means 'harbor'. Norse warriors would 'go a-viking', sailing into bays along the European coast and raiding the villages."

"So that's how they got their name."

"Correct. The Vikings attacked as far east as Russia, and for a time they occupied parts of Britain, Ireland, and France. They plundered Sicily and even made it to Constantinople, the capital of the Eastern Roman Empire. That was way back in the 8th and 9th century, but their influence was felt all the way up to 1050 A.D."

"Pretty powerful guys, those Vikings! But let's get back to Andrew Littlewort and his futhork. What was he talking about?"

Carl shifted on the hard wooden bench.

"We sometimes call our alphabet the ABC's, right? Well, the Norse called theirs the futhork. The letters of the futhork were known as runes. Norse children learned to cut runes on stones much as our kids learn to write on paper. Early Norsemen used runes for scratching their names on personal belongings or on memorial stones. Over time, the memorials became more elaborate, runes intertwining with pictures and designs like stories told in rock. Today the word 'rune' also means a Norse poem or oral story."

"And these memorial stones still exist today?"

Carl nodded. "Thousands have been found on the Scandinavian peninsula, and one was also discovered in Greenland where Eric the Red, a Viking explorer, established a Norse colony in 986 A.D. Eric's offspring, Leif Ericson, was a seaman like his father. He sailed as far west as Newfoundland, which he called Vinland the

Good, off the coast of Canada. A Norwegian expedition uncovered the remains of a Norse village there in 1963."

"So Ericson reached the North American continent some four hundred years before Christopher Columbus."

"It appears that way," Carl agreed. He ran his hand through his thick white head of hair, then shook his head. "And that's exactly why the rock those students found is so important to Andrew Littlewort."

"How so?" Caroline asked.

"You know how Andrew is always arguing obscure points of academia with anyone who will listen to him."

"He's fanatical in his beliefs, Carl. I remember overhearing him lecturing a group of people at the faculty Christmas party last year. He wouldn't give an inch. In fact, he got downright ugly with one of the younger professors who disagreed with him."

"Andrew's got a temper, all right. I've seen it in action a couple of times, which is why I won't let him bait me into an argument. Much of what he propounds is just plain hogwash, but occasionally the man makes a valid point. About three weeks ago he brought up the subject of Leif Ericson at a faculty luncheon. We history buffs agreed the Viking deserves more recognition, but most of the other professors pooh-poohed the entire idea. Of course that really angered Andrew. If there's one thing he can't stand, it's to be rebuffed by his peers. In retaliation he began a one man campaign to replace Columbus Day with a holiday honoring Leif Ericson. He's been writing to congressmen and state officials trying to persuade them to take up the banner. In fact, that's why he invited me to breakfast today. He wanted me to join the cause."

"Tell me you didn't agree to help him."

Carl rubbed his jaw. "I sympathize with Andrew's point of

view, but he's gone way overboard this time. I suspect he's less concerned with Ericson's rightful place in history than with spitting in the collective eye of the faculty."

"This campaign is bound to fail," Caroline reasoned. "The Italian-American community would declare war on Congress if they even considered dumping Columbus Day. And it's sheer idiocy for Littlewort to take on the entire Bruck faculty. He'll only make more enemies for himself."

"Nobody ever credited Andrew with wisdom, Cari. But I agree with your thinking. There are plenty of folks at Bruck who would like nothing more than to cut Professor Littlewort down to size. Given this latest bit of nonsense, this rune stone charade, they just may have the chance to do it."

Caroline gathered up the loose bits of wire and ribbon and discarded them in a container next to the path.

"Let's hope nobody else gets hurt along the way," she said as she finished cleaning up the area. "After all, Andrew Littlewort may deserve his comeuppance, but settling a score can sometimes get out of hand."

Little did she know how right she was.

CHAPTER 2

The first raindrop fell amid a low rumble of thunder. Caroline grabbed her basket of roses and together with Carl hurried off towards Bruck Hall, the university's administrative center lying just west of Bruck Green. Since the Professor's version of hurrying differed greatly from Caroline's, his shorter legs and rotund body negating any actual attempt at speed, the two of them were moderately soaked by the time they reached shelter.

"Snow all winter and rain all spring," grumbled Caroline as she shook the dampness from her short ash brown hair. "Don't you Rhineburgers ever have good weather?"

"Just wait until summer," laughed Carl. He brushed water droplets from his shoulders, then peeled off his windbreaker and hung it on a rack near the door. "I guarantee blue skies and sunshine from June to September."

"I'll hold you to that," replied Caroline, passing Atwater her own lightweight jacket before turning to gaze out the lobby window. "Looks like the students aren't fazed by the rain. They're still cordoning off the jousting field." She pointed to a group of youths nailing wooden rails to fence posts at the south end of Bruck Green.

"Take a look at old Branch. He's watching those kids like a hawk." Carl gestured towards the side of the field where the university's head gardener stood scowling at the boys. "It must try his patience to see his tulip beds threatened each spring."

Caroline studied the stocky gray-haired man who was supervising the activity on the Green.

"I don't see why he should be nervous," she said. "There's a good-sized patch of grass between the field and the flowers. I doubt the spectators will overflow that large an area."

"It's not the spectators that worry Branch, Cari. It's the horses." Seeing Caroline's bemused expression, Carl explained. "Jousting takes place on horseback. Unfortunately, we don't have a place to stable these nags between events. The riders are supposed to hitch their horses to lines strung between the trees, but sometimes they let them free to graze on the lawn. Many a noble steed has nibbled one of Branch's blooms to the bare root."

Caroline burst into laughter.

"I'd hate to be the owner of any horse who foraged on the flowers at Bruck," she chuckled. "Branch is as fanatical about his gardens as Andrew Littlewort is about Leif Ericson. I once saw him tear into a student who picked a daffodil from alongside the path on the Green. Talk about tempers!"

"Actually, I'd like to," Carl replied. "Talk about tempers, that is. But first, how about a bite to eat? It's almost noon."

It was closer to eleven-thirty by Caroline's watch, but she knew better than to argue with the Professor. She'd learned early on in their relationship that food was never far from Carl's mind. As a result, over the winter she'd gained not only a friend but also six pounds and an extra inch around her waistline. Exercise and diet had finally banished the unwanted weight. Still, any time they were together, Caroline was forced to discipline herself

"Nothing for me, " she said firmly as Carl headed down the hallway towards the kitchen. "I'll meet you in the faculty lounge."

The lounge looked nothing like it had that evening last

December when Caroline first met Carl. She'd been invited to the faculty Christmas party ostensibly because her son Martin, a PhD candidate at Bruck U., was Carl's teaching assistant. But Caroline suspected she'd been included on the guest list for an entirely different reason. As a witness to the bombing at St. Anne's, she'd achieved an odd sort of celebrity status, a position she'd shunned from the start. As it turned out, her very unwillingness to discuss the matter had branded her a troublemaker in the eyes of the killer.

Caroline shook off the memories of last winter and let her eyes wander about the room. Instead of Christmas poinsettias, outdated magazines now littered the wide windowsills bracketing the far corner of the room. To the left of the windows the enormous stone fireplace stood empty of logs, a tarnished screen drawn across its open mouth. Tartan plaid easy chairs were still grouped in pairs in front of and to the right of the fireplace, but to the left, on the spot once occupied by three beautifully decorated Christmas trees, there now stood a brown leather couch and a small oak side table.

"Are you sure you're not hungry?"

Carl entered the lounge with a tray of sandwiches and beer that he placed on the massive oak table in the center of the room. He scooped two sandwiches onto a paper plate, flipped the cap off a bottle of beer, and settled himself at one end of the leather couch. Caroline sank into an easy chair opposite the sofa and shook her head. She refused to be enticed by the sight of rye bread piled high with thin slices of tender roast beef and cheddar cheese.

"Tell me more about this rune stone the boys found," she said, diverting her eyes from Carl's plate. "Why are you so sure it's a fake?"

"To tell the truth, Cari," the Professor answered between bites of his sandwich, "When I first saw those scratches, my heart beat a little faster. The thought of finding a genuine Viking relic completely overwhelmed me. But then my common sense took hold. Rhineburg's over a thousand miles from the Atlantic Ocean. How could a seafaring people, even those as adventurous as the Vikings, make their way this far inland? And why would they want to?"

"How about the St. Lawrence River?" Caroline suggested. "They might have sailed into the Great Lakes, then come ashore to explore."

Carl wrinkled his nose. "The colony in Newfoundland lasted only three years. I doubt those settlers had enough time, energy, or resources to mount an expedition as ambitious as the one you suggest. Besides which, no physical evidence of Viking exploration has ever been found west of the Newfoundland site."

"So you think the stone is a hoax."

Carl nodded. "Somebody's putting one over on Littlewort. It may be a faculty member who's sick and tired of Andrew's temper tantrums. Or maybe a student heard about the ruckus and decided to play a practical joke on him. It really doesn't matter who's behind this little prank. The important thing is the Professor's going to heap scorn both on himself and on the university if the press gets wind of this."

"As it surely will if he sends the stone to the Field Museum," mused Caroline. "Maybe he'll come to his senses before he does anything rash."

"I've never known Andrew to back down even when he's been clearly proven wrong. He just gets angry, and his anger is something to behold. Before, when you were talking about Branch reaming out that student who picked the flowers, all I could think about was Andrew and his temper. Branch is a lamb compared to old Andrew."

Atwater set his plate on the side table and stared moodily out the window. Caroline could tell he was troubled; he'd left half a sandwich uneaten.

"You really mustn't worry about this," she said soothingly. "You did try to stop Professor Littlewort. Now if he continues to act like an obstinate fool, it'll be President Hurst's problem, not yours."

Carl's face brightened. "Serves the Emperor right! He's been glowing like a light bulb ever since he pushed through that deal with the Town Council. Littlewort's scheme ought to jar him back into reality."

Caroline chuckled. Carl was still furious over Hurst's plan to field a football team at Bruck. The school had no reputation for athletics, but the President firmly believed football would attract more students to the university while luring the sports-minded alumni into donating more cash to their old alma mater. It was a plan with potential except for the fact that Hurst had no seed money to hire a coach or even buy uniforms. He resolved the problem by firing several untenured teachers, cutting a few courses, and increasing the student-teacher ratio in the classes that remained. His move had of course angered a good portion of the faculty, and they were fighting the changes tooth and nail. Dictating the order of battle was no other than Hurst's greatest critic, Professor Carl Atwater.

"Your esteemed leader will suffer many a headache if Andrew Littlewort publicizes his find. You'll have treasure hunters digging holes all over Bruck Green in search of The Next Great Find!"

Carl's eyes narrowed. He began to stroke his snowy beard in slow deliberate motions as a grin spread across his wind burned face.

"Oh no you don't!" Caroline sputtered, correctly guessing what her friend was thinking. "You encourage Andrew Littlewort and you'll be as much to blame as he when all hell breaks loose!"

"Now, Cari," Professor Atwater purred. "I'm just going to have a bit of fun at the Emperor's expense. I won't let it get out of hand, and I promise not to involve you in it." He levered himself upright and smiled down on her in a benevolent fashion. "In fact, I was thinking more along the lines of Martin as an accomplice."

At the mention of her son, Caroline jumped to her feet. "Listen to me, Carl Atwater! Martin is your teaching assistant, not your partner in crime. He's a year away from earning his PhD, and you'll not get him expelled from Bruck." She paused to draw a breath, then continued a bit more calmly. "Just think what Nikki would say if she got wind of your shenanigans."

"Martin's wife won't mind his helping me. She detests the Emperor." Carl's confidence cooled under Caroline's steady glare, still he tried to smooth her ruffled feathers with a hearty laugh and a show of bravado. "Come on, Cari. You know I'd never jeopardize your son's career. Marty will graduate with honors and probably earn a teaching post right here at Bruck. Eventually he'll take over my job as chairman of the History Department, and then won't you be proud!"

"I should live so long," Caroline muttered. "I think you're as mad as Andrew Littlewort, Carl. You're both obsessed with stupid vendettas, and you're both heading for trouble."

"I promise to be careful." The Professor placed his right hand over his heart and raised his left hand in the air. "On my honor, Cari. I intend to do nothing more than tweak the nose of Emperor Hurst."

With that said, Atwater suddenly remembered he had a faculty meeting to attend. He mumbled an apology to Caroline, escorted her to the door, and then beat a hasty retreat in the direction of the Liberal Arts building. Left standing on the stairs of Bruck Hall, Caroline could only stare at Carl's vanishing backside and wonder what the man was up to.

CHAPTER 3

The storm had been short lived. Only a few puddles dampened the road encircling Bruck Green and Caroline avoided them when she approached the parkway. She could see the Maypole standing tall in the center of the grassy oval, but the students were nowhere in sight. She found herself wondering if they'd unearthed anything else in the wet ground of the campus.

"Like Leif Ericson's bones," she muttered aloud.

'Enough!' she told herself. Carl's mischievousness was a worry, but Caroline forced it out of her mind and savored instead the warm spring sun beating down on her shoulders. The air was fragrant with the scent of newly mown grass and raindrops glistened on the daffodils lining the cobblestone path. She stopped in the shadow of a towering oak to drink in the day and admire the flowers' varying shades of gold.

"You like my daffodils, Mrs. Rhodes?"

The gardener had appeared out of nowhere. He stood with his head cocked to one side, his dark eyes narrowed as he observed the expression on Caroline's face.

"I do indeed, Mr. Branch." Caroline had been caught off-guard and her voice betrayed her surprise. Branch was quick to notice.

"Didn't mean to creep up on you," he said in apology. "I guess you're wary of that sort of thing since that business with the bomb last winter."

Caroline blushed. "I admit the murders left their mark. Still, it's time I put the experience behind me."

"Some things you never get over, Mrs. Rhodes." Branch's gaze fell on the daffodils. He shrugged his muscular shoulders before drawling somberly, "Bein' careful ain't such a bad idea. Gotta protect your backside, my daddy always said."

"Hmm." Having no such pearls of wisdom to offer in return, Caroline simply joined the gardener in admiring the flower beds. After a few moments of uninterrupted silence, the man spoke again.

"You garden?"

"What? Oh! No, not any more." Caroline bent over and flicked a raindrop off a drooping petal. "My gardening days ended when I moved here from Chicago. It's a pleasure I miss, living in an apartment like I do. You have so many varieties of daffodils here, Mr. Branch. Did you plant them all yourself?"

"My daddy was head gardener before me, but he was a rose man. When he died, I took over the job. I figured the walks could use some dressin' up, so every fall I planted a few more daffydil bulbs. Now all my paths are lined with gold." Branch threw back his head and uttered a loud guffaw. "That's what I tell all the boys who work for me, but none of 'em understand. Not even Mr. Smartypants over there." He pointed a callused finger at a young man lounging against a tree some twenty feet away and hollered, "Get back to your raking, Burke, or I'll report ya to the Archangels."

Caroline hadn't noticed the youth before. He was a tall good looking boy with curly black hair and an insolent manner who motioned rudely in Branch's direction before strolling off across the Green. Only Caroline witnessed the gesture; the gardener had already turned away.

"I saw you here earlier today. You and Professor Atwater were helpin' the students put up that Maypole."

"We weren't really helping them. We only walked over there to see what all the excitement was about." Caroline explained about the rune stone. "Professor Littlewort intends to send the stone to Chicago for verification. It's probably a fake, but I'd advise you to keep a look out for strangers carrying shovels. I'd hate to see your flower beds dug up by fortune hunters when word of this gets out."

Branch's jaw dropped. "You think people will come looking for more of those stones?" he asked in horror.

"It's possible," Caroline answered. "I don't mean to worry you, Mr. Branch, but it's only fair you're warned."

Branch shook his fist in the air. "They come diggin' here, and they'll get a load of buckshot in their pants. I won't tolerate no strangers messin' around on these grounds, ya hear me?"

"I hear you loud and clear." Caroline was taken aback by the sudden fury of Branch's response, but then it came to her that the gardener's passion could be put to good use. "Perhaps you should tell President Hurst how you feel about the situation," she slyly suggested. "After all, he's the only one who can put a stop to this business."

Branch rocked back on his heels and stared at Caroline.

"That's a darned good idea," he growled. "Problem is, you can never find the man when you need 'im."

"There's a faculty meeting going on over in the Liberal Arts building," Caroline murmured. "I'm sure the President will be presiding. And I'm equally sure he'll want to hear what you as a valued employee have to say."

"He'd better!" Branch replied heatedly. "I thank you for tellin' me all this, Mrs. Rhodes. You've been one real helpful lady."

"I try to be, Mr. Branch. I really do."

Caroline smiled smugly as the gardener loped off across Bruck Green. She watched him disappear around the corner of one of the buildings before she turned and made her way back to the nursing dorm. Knowing Garrison Hurst, she was sure he'd cringe at the thought of rock hounds digging holes all over Bruck Green. Archeologists were one thing, but an uncontrolled public hunt for rune stones on his beautiful campus? No way! After hearing from Branch, he'd quickly crush Littlewort's plans. And if there was a sledgehammer handy, he might even crush the stone itself.

Carl would be disappointed, she mused. But at least Martin wouldn't be dragged into his little farce. And that's what really mattered. Martin was altogether too fond of the Professor. He'd follow Carl to hell and back if asked. And probably be expelled from school for doing so.

"Not while I'm around," Caroline muttered grimly. To paraphrase Branch's daddy, a mother had to protect her son's backside.

CHAPTER 4

Caroline pulled into the driveway of the Blue Cat Lounge precisely at 7 p.m. The last rays of the setting sun filtered through the green-gray boughs of the Ponderosa pines guarding the graveled parking lot, illuminating it just enough for her to see Martin's old Chevy parked halfway down the left hand aisle. Professor Atwater's 4x4 stood near the entrance of the roadhouse, and she braked beside it when she saw him standing there.

"Better late than never." Carl opened the door and waited as Caroline switched off the ignition.

"Kerry called," she said with a smile. "She was bubbling over with news about school and her new boyfriend."

"Another one?" Carl had yet to meet the entire Rhodes clan, but Caroline had regaled him with stories of her daughters. Krista was a teacher in Chicago, Kerry a theater major in college. "What happened to the last guy? She only met him a month ago!"

Caroline shrugged her shoulders. "Maybe she was just too much of a challenge for the poor boy. Anyway, Kerry says this fellow is the real McCoy." She locked the Jeep, and together they headed for the tavern. "Am I so late that you had to come looking for me?"

"Shiloh sent me out to check the gutters. He claims one of them is leaking."

Carl was part owner of the Blue Cat Lounge, a roadhouse outside of Rhineburg specializing in home brewed beer and jazz music. It was a decrepit looking building with brown paint peeling off the warped windows and ancient wooden siding. A jumble of mismatched shingles covered the roof, and a blue neon cat flashed erratically over the sagging entranceway. There was no sign on the door; the cat said it all.

"It's hard to believe this place is structurally sound," Caroline remarked with a shake of her head.

"I sank a lot of money into the Blue Cat after Shiloh and I became partners. We put in new support beams, new floors and ceilings, new electrical wiring and plumbing. All the appliances in the kitchen and bar area are new also."

"And you preserved the exterior of the building in its original state so tourists wouldn't find it attractive."

Carl nodded. "You're darned right we did. Rhineburg's becoming too quaint for its own good, Cari. Every week there's another grand opening for an antique store or some high brow artsy-craftsy joint. I tell you, this town is losing its character. It's turning into a tourist trap where city folks come to gobble up bargains and gawk at the natives. Can you blame us for wanting a spot of our own? A place where Rhineburgers can socialize without being bothered by these urban invaders?"

Caroline laughed. "Urban invaders? You make it sound like Rhineburg's under attack, Carl."

"In a way it is," the Professor muttered. He yanked open the door and ushered his friend into the lounge. "Mark my words, Cari. The Vikings thought their way of life would last forever, and look what happened to them."

Caroline rolled her eyes. "So you're still on *that* subject, are you? I thought after the faculty meeting you'd have given it up."

"Really? Then I guess you haven't heard the latest."

Caroline stopped dead in her tracks. "What latest? Out with

it, Carl. Just what are you planning now?"

"The downfall of the mighty," the white haired Atwater replied with a smile. "Come on, Cari. I'll fill you in on the news during dinner."

Like Moses parting the Red Sea, Carl elbowed his way across the crowded room roaring at the top of his lungs, "Out of my way, plebians! The king cometh!"

"Honestly, Carl," Caroline hissed as patrons of the Blue Cat scattered in all directions. "Act your age!"

Mumbling apologies left and right, she followed hard on his heels until at last they reached their table. Waiting for them were Martin and Nikki.

"I was beginning to think we'd have to start without you, mom." Martin Rhodes sprang to his feet and pulled out a chair for Caroline. A foot taller than she, he smiled down on his mother with unsuppressed mirth. "Bet you were on the phone to Krista or Kerry, right? And here I sit waiting, so hungry I could eat the menu."

Caroline cast a sympathetic glance in Nikki's direction. "You'd think food was a rare luxury. Is he always this bad?"

"Only when it comes to pizza," Nikki laughed. "Speaking of which, we ordered the specialty of the house. It has everything on it but the kitchen sink."

"Sounds appetizing," Caroline commented. She raised an eyebrow in Carl's direction. "I don't suppose it's low calorie."

"Good grief, woman! This is a party, not a wake." Carl motioned to the bartender and ordered a round of pint honey beers. "We're celebrating tonight, aren't we, Martin?"

"We sure are. This is an auspicious day in the history of Bruck University, a day to be remembered."

"Auspicious in what way?" Caroline demanded to know.

"Didn't the Professor tell you, mom? Why... Wait a minute while I get these." Martin reached for the tray the waiter had just brought. He passed a stein of foamy beer to each of them. "A toast!" he said, a crooked smile splitting the rugged features of his face. "To Andrew Littlewort's rune stone. May its discovery benefit us all!"

"Amen to that." Nikki's head bobbed in agreement.

Caroline refrained from joining the toast, and Carl noticed. He smiled soulfully at his assistant.

"Your mother's upset with us, Marty. She thinks we're hatching some terrible plot against President Hurst."

"And aren't you?" Caroline retorted. "I saw that look on your face when you ran off to the faculty meeting. You were grinning like the Cheshire Cat, which means you're up to no good."

"Now, mom. It's not all that bad. It's more like a harmless prank than..."

"Pranks have a way of backfiring, Martin," Caroline snapped. "Can you afford that?"

"Martin won't be involved, Cari. As I've told these two, you've already done most of the work for me."

"What?" Caroline stared open-mouthed at the Professor.

"When you warned Branch of the possibility of treasure hunters digging up his precious flower beds, you set the stage for some mighty fine fireworks," Carl said with a chuckle. "The head gardener came charging into our meeting, bellowing at the top of his lungs that the rune stone had to be destroyed before outsiders invaded the university. He was really off the wall, Cari, calling Littlewort a fool and accusing President Hurst of dereliction of duty. No one disputed his opinion of Andrew, but his views on the President were another matter altogether."

"I'm sure Hurst didn't take kindly to the verbal abuse."

"No, he didn't, Cari. The Emperor had just denied Andrew's request for a limited dig on Bruck Green, but after Branch's outburst, he changed his mind. Unfortunately, Hurst was stuck between a rock and a hard place. It's common knowledge he can't abide Professor Littlewort. But stand still for a public bashing from someone as low on the totem pole as Charlie Branch? No way! Garrison was forced to support his fellow faculty member over the school gardener."

"I can't believe it," Caroline mumbled weakly. "Hoisted on my own petard."

Nikki patted her mother-in-law's hand. "Don't take it so hard, mom. The dig won't take place until after the Festival of Knights. By that time the Field Museum folks will have proven the stone is fake." "But by then Professor Littlewort will have taken his story to the press," remarked Martin. He leaned back in his chair, visualizing the scenario. "We'll have reporters swarming over the campus, and Bruck Green will be awash with rock hounds eagerly investigating every stone in sight."

"The Emperor will be hard pressed to explain his gullibility once the truth is known," Nikki added. "He'll put a muzzle on Andrew Littlewort, revoke permission for the dig, and pray the Board of Regents doesn't blame him for the whole mess."

"Which they probably will," concluded Carl. "And if so, they just might ask Hurst for his resignation."

Caroline studied her dinner companions in complete amazement. Their foolishness both baffled and angered her. Apparently only she understood how difficult it was to topple the powerful. And Garrison Hurst, despite what the others thought, was a very powerful man indeed.

"You three are daydreaming. The one most likely to get hurt by this hoax is Professor Littlewort. I'm not especially fond of the man, but he sure doesn't deserve to go down this way."

"Andrew will be all right," Carl assured her. "He's tenured. He'd have to kill somebody before he could be fired."

Caroline bit back a reply as the waiter arrived with their pizza. The aroma of garlic and onions had a potent effect on her salivary glands and within minutes she was devouring her portion with gusto equaling her son's. By the time they'd finished dinner the conversation had progressed to a less controversial subject.

"How's the new job going, Nikki?"

"I hadn't thought I'd like it, Professor, but Emma Reiser is a fantastic person to work for. She's not only Rhineburg's postmistress but also the town counselor. It's amazing how many people drop by the post office just to seek her advice."

"So you're not too disappointed about working outside your field?"

Nikki shrugged. "Outside of the Social Service Department at St. Anne's, there aren't many jobs in Rhineburg requiring a bachelor's degree in psychology. And to tell the truth, I'm learning a lot just watching Mrs. Reiser in action. She's sympathetic but not meddling, knowing just when to interject a comment or question into the conversation. People really seem to trust her opinions."

"Sounds like she could be the Postal Service Employee of the Year," Martin joked. "A woman who delivers mail and advice at the same time."

"Behave yourself!" Nikki gave her husband an affectionate punch on the arm. "Mrs. Reiser is one of those people you just naturally confide in. She always has the kettle on in the back room, and folks pop in whenever they please for tea and conversation."

"And what do you do while your boss is loafing away the hours with the customers?" Martin teased.

Nikki replied with a saucy toss of her curly black hair. "I sell stamps and weigh packages and sort the mail, Mr. Smartypants!"

Caroline glanced at her son in amusement. It was the second time that day she'd heard a young man referred to in that way. Fortunately, Martin reacted quite differently than Branch's helper. He simply leaned over and gave Nikki a kiss on the forehead.

As he did so, a commotion broke out in the lounge. At a table in the far corner sat two men, one much younger than the other, the second more drunk than the first. The two were demanding drinks from a harried looking waiter who was clearly refusing to serve them. As Caroline and the others turned to watch, Shiloh hurried out from behind the bar and made his way towards them.

"Carl, isn't that Charlie Branch over there?"

Atwater nodded, a frown creasing his face.

"The other fellow is Sid Burke," Martin noted. "He's a real piece of work, mom. Obnoxious as hell, and sneaky to boot."

"Sid is in my History of Warfare class," the Professor explained. "He's an intelligent kid, but lazy. I'm pretty sure he cheats on tests. Unfortunately, I can never catch him at it."

"I wonder why he's here with Branch," Caroline mused. "They didn't seem particularly friendly when I saw them together earlier today." She told them about Burke's obscene gesture aimed at the head gardener. "Branch called Sid his helper, but the boy didn't seem to be doing much work."

Martin and the Professor exchanged amused looks.

"Probably pressed into service," Martin stated. "I'll bet he got into trouble and raking the Green was his punishment, compliments of the Archangels."

"But why would they be here together?" asked Nikki. "Branch doesn't normally hang out with the students. And Sid doesn't sound like the type who'd buddy up to the school gardener."

Branch had started to rise from his seat. He grabbed Shiloh's arm to steady himself, then collapsed in a heap over the table.

"The man is totally sloshed," Carl growled. "And I've never known him to drink." He pushed his chair back from the table. "Come on, Marty. It looks like Shiloh could use some assistance."

Caroline and Nikki watched as the two men helped ease Branch to the floor. Charlie was dead to the world. He lay without moving while Carl spoke first to Burke, then to Shiloh, and finally to Martin. Martin nodded twice, then walked back towards the women.

"The Professor is hopping mad," he told them gravely. "He blames Shiloh for over serving the two of them."

"Burke seems sober enough," Nikki noted.

"He's OK," Martin agreed. "But Branch is a goner. He drove himself here, and now the Professor is insisting we drive him home."

"I don't think we have any choice in the matter," Caroline replied testily. "It's probably our fault he got drunk in the first place."

She ignored the looks Martin and Nikki exchanged, but she knew they'd gotten the message. In Caroline's mind, Branch was the first victim of their foolish little prank. She stood up from the table.

"I'll wait outside while you men get Charlie on his feet."

A few minutes later Carl and Martin half carried, half dragged a very tipsy Branch out the door of the Blue Cat Lounge.

"Good lord, he's heavy!" exclaimed Atwater. "Get a hold of his arm, Carl. He keeps grabbing my face."

Caroline peeled Branch's hand off the Professor's nose. The gardener suddenly lifted his head and gave her a glowing smile.

"Kind of yous ta help a fella out," he mumbled. "Would ya like ta shtroll my pash a gold?"

Caroline shook her head. "No thanks, Charlie. Maybe some other time."

The gardener blinked twice before his head lolled forward and he passed out.

"Watch out!" Nikki cried. Branch had pitched to the left and was sliding to the ground, taking the Professor with him.

"Damn it, Sid! Give us a hand!"

Burke had followed them out of the roadhouse. He now stood leaning against the wall, a smirk on his face as he watched the two men struggle with his erstwhile companion. He straightened up slowly, took a lazy step forward, and grabbed Branch by the belt.

"Sorry, Mr. Rhodes. I thought you and the Professor were managing pretty well by yourselves."

Martin's only response was a growl.

"We'll put him in my Jeep," Carl said tersely. "You follow in his car, Burke, and then I'll drop you back at the university."

After much pushing and pulling they finally crammed the comatose Branch into the back seat of Carl's vehicle. Atwater told Martin and Nikki to go home, insisting that he and Burke could handle the situation. Martin put up an argument, but in the end the couple reluctantly agreed to go. Caroline was not as amenable to the Professor's plan. She pulled her Jeep in line behind Branch's car and followed the others out of the lot.

Five minutes later the three car procession pulled off the highway and headed up a gravel road stretching into the forest. Darkness surrounded them for half a mile before their headlights picked up the outline of a house set off in a clearing to the left.

Carl swung off the road and pulled up facing the front of the

building. He left the car's headlights on and climbed out.

"Open up, will you?" The Professor tossed a set of keys to Caroline. "Burke and I will bring him in."

Caroline nodded and walked up the tidy path leading to the two-storied house. The front door was illuminated by the Jeep's headlamps, and she had no trouble fitting the key in the lock. Once inside, she found a long hallway with entrances to a living room on the right and a den on the left. Halfway down the hall was a staircase extending to the second floor. Beyond the staircase stood a closed door presumably leading to the kitchen.

She flipped on the lights in the hallway and living room, then took the stairs to the second floor.

"Up here," she called to the men when they entered the house. She watched as Carl and Sid maneuvered Branch through the doorway and up the narrow flight of stairs.

"Bedroom's on the left."

Carl was perspiring freely as he and young Burke dragged their drunken companion past Caroline and into the tiny bedroom. They dropped Branch on the bed before collapsing themselves on a low wooden bench set beneath the room's one window. Caroline started undressing the sleeping gardener and after a moment's rest the Professor rose and joined her.

"Leave him," he muttered. "He can sleep with his shoes on."

But Caroline continued to unlace Branch's boots.

"Why ruin this beautiful quilt?" she replied. "These boots are caked with mud, grass, and straw."

Carl was more concerned with his jacket than with Branch's quilt. He sniffed the suede material and wrinkled his nose in distaste.

"I'll have to have this cleaned," he grumbled. "It reeks of alcohol."

Caroline threw a blanket over Branch. A corner of it brushed his cheek, and the slumbering man stirred.

"Pash of gold," he murmured before falling back asleep.

"I doubt Mr. Branch will be tending his gardens tomorrow. He's going to have one humdinger of a headache."

"Serves him right, Cari. What the hell does he think he's doing guzzling whiskey like that? Charlie Branch is no drinker. I've known the man for years and he hardly ever touches the stuff."

Caroline shrugged. "There's a first time for everything. Perhaps Mr. Burke can explain his odd behavior."

But Sid Burke had left the room. When Caroline and the Professor went downstairs they found him bent over the desk in Branch's den examining something.

"What are you doing in here, Burke?"

Sid spun around. As he turned, his hand brushed a pile of papers on the desk.

"Sorry, Professor. I got bored hanging around upstairs." He moved towards the doorway. "Can we leave now?"

Atwater grunted and motioned the boy to go ahead of him. When Burke was out of earshot, Carl turned to Caroline.

"Are you sure it's all right to leave Branch alone like this? He won't wake up and go staggering around the house, will he?"

"I doubt it. I've had a lot of experience with drunks in the ER. They usually don't awaken until they're sober. Considering his condition, I think Branch will sleep through the night."

Carl glanced up the staircase. "He's a good man, Cari. I wouldn't want to see him hurt himself."

"If it'll make you feel better, I'll stick around and look in on him in a few minutes. Go ahead and take Burke back to the dormitory. And on the way, try to find out what led up to this fiasco."

Carl nodded his gratitude. "I'll call you in the morning."

Caroline watched at the window as the Professor pulled out of the driveway and onto the graveled road. The house was quiet except for the noisy snoring of its owner. Branch didn't sound in distress, yet Caroline headed back up the stairs to check on him. Just as she thought, the gardener was dead to the world.

"Sleep tight," she murmured. She smoothed the blanket, opened the window a crack, then drew the shade and descended once more to the hall. A lamp still glowed in the den and she went in to shut it off.

"I wonder what Burke was doing in here."

Her eyes were drawn to the desk. A stack of seed and nursery catalogues piled left of center had toppled and now lay scattered across the wooden surface. Doubtful they held anything of interest to Burke, Caroline brushed them aside, exposing as she did so a scarred leather scrapbook. Curious, she sat down to examine it.

A faded clipping from a Springfield newspaper was pasted to the first page. Dated August 18, 1980, it gave a brief but concise account of a bank robbery in the state's capital. Next to it was taped a report from another Illinois town similarly victimized in early 1981.

Caroline leafed through the scrapbook. The first half of it contained old newspaper clippings from towns east of Rhineburg. Some of the articles originated in Indiana and Michigan while others were from states as far away as Pennsylvania. A common thread ran through all the stories. Apparently someone was plundering small town branch banks and getting away scot-free. The final entry in the scrapbook was from a Wisconsin paper dated October 28, 1989. It told of yet another robbery, this one resulting in a loss of five thousand dollars. But the reporter predicted the thief would soon be caught. With the installation of higher resolution cameras and, in some instances, the placement of armed guards, communities across the mid-west were acting to protect their banks. The response apparently paid off because the album contained no further tales of the man's exploits. Instead, the last pages were filled with snapshots of several young men. Posed individually and in groups, each of them bore an uncanny resemblance to Bruck U.'s head gardener.

Caroline leaned back in her chair and studied the multitude of framed photographs decorating the paneled walls of the den. Directly across from the desk hung a faded picture of a woman in her mid-thirties sitting on a rickety wooden porch swing. The woman was surrounded by five little boys whom Caroline recognized as miniatures of the youths in the album.

The adjoining walls were covered with family portraits taken over a span of years. One showed a smiling Branch decked out in formal wear and gazing fondly at his bride, a younger version of the woman on the swing. Another displayed the two of them sitting in the kitchen, an infant playing happily in the foreground.

Caroline's eyes wandered from photo to photo. There in the corner was Branch teaching his sons to fish. Below that, the five boys were captured on a tractor set in a sea of corn. Near the center of one wall a shot revealed Branch and another man standing beside a sleek black motorcycle. The two were shaking hands and grinning.

Caroline sighed. There was no sign of a wife about the house now. She'd seen no cosmetics in the upstairs bedrooms, no bottles of perfume or jars of face cream. The living room was equally devoid of a woman's touch. It had a musty, unlived-in quality about it that was accentuated by the unpolished surfaces of the tables and the general shabbiness of the furniture.

"I'll bet she's dead," she reasoned aloud. Divorced men usually didn't keep photos of their wives prominently displayed in their homes. This den had to be Branch's version of a shrine, a sacred place dedicated to a happier time in his life.

A grandfather clock in the living room began to chime the hour. Caroline glanced at her watch and was surprised to see it was already ten p.m. She'd stayed with Branch longer than she'd planned. After one last look around the picture gallery, she flipped off the lights in the den and walked into the hallway. At the foot of the stairs she stopped and gazed upward. The sound of snoring wafted down from the room above. Reassured the gardener was still asleep, Caroline slipped out of the house, locking the front door behind her.

CHAPTER 5

"I didn't expect to see you again tonight. Come on in."

Professor Atwater threw open the door and ushered Caroline into his tidy bungalow on Faculty Row. The house was dark except for the living room where the soft glow from an antique hanging lamp illuminated a trestle table set near the front windows. An assortment of swords, lances, and battle-axes covered the table's surface.

"Preparing for the next battle with President Hurst?" Caroline joked as she walked over to examine the weapons.

Carl wrinkled his nose. "Very funny, Cari. These are all for the Festival. The knights will be using them."

"You're going to let the kids duel with these swords?"

"Why not?" answered Carl, reacting with typical nonchalance to the surprise in Caroline's voice. "All the hand-to-hand combat is choreographed, and these particular arms are fashioned of hardened aluminum. Not at all like the real thing." He handed her a sword. "See how dull the edge is? You'd really have to whack somebody to draw blood with this."

Caroline ran her thumb along the blade. The edges were thick and blunt to the touch. The weapon's tip was round and dull.

"I suppose you know what you're doing," she replied rather dubiously. She placed the sword back on the table and dug deep in her pocket. "Here," she said, handing Carl a set of keys, "I locked Branch's front door when I left. Will you give these back to him

tomorrow?"

"Sure," replied the Professor. "I'll check up on him in the morning. You know, Cari, ever since his wife died Charlie's led a solitary existence. It seems to satisfy him, but I don't think it's a healthy lifestyle. He could drop dead tomorrow, and nobody would even notice."

"I figured he lived alone. There wasn't a hint of feminism in that house." Caroline told Carl about the wall of photographs. "His wife was a beautiful woman. What happened to her?"

Carl shrugged. "I'm not really sure. I saw Mrs. Branch at various university functions back when their boys were attending Bruck. She seemed the picture of health up until the time Rudy, the youngest son, graduated. Shortly after that she went into a decline. The word around town was that Julie had cancer, but when she died Alexsa Stromberg told me it was heart trouble."

"They were a close couple?"

"No doubt about it. From what I've heard, they spent every available moment together. But now that we're discussing it," Carl added, "I remember Rudy telling me his parents' relationship changed for the worst during those last few months of Julie's life. Of course, a disease like cancer can put quite a strain on people."

"That's true," Caroline agreed. "But it's been my experience that the stronger the relationship between a couple, the better they cope when one or the other faces a life threatening disease. Their mutual love seems to work in their favor."

"Everybody's different, Cari. Maybe the Branches just couldn't accept the inevitability of death." Carl headed towards the kitchen. He clapped his hands twice, and the light in the room flashed on. "How about a piece of pie? I've got lemon meringue in the frig.

"Caroline declined, deciding on a cup of tea instead. She

busied herself at the stove while Atwater cut himself an ample slice of the gooey dessert.

"Did you know Branch was a crime buff?   He has a scrapbook full of stories about bank robbers."

"Charlie probably wishes he could catch himself a crook," Carl joked. "A big reward would let him retire in comfort."

Caroline smiled. "What are his sons doing now?"

"They all have jobs out of town. The last time I saw them was at their mother's funeral five years ago."

"So how long has Branch been tending the flowers at Bruck?"

"Must be eight or nine years now." Carl eased his belt a notch and settled down on an oversized kitchen chair. He took a bite of pie before continuing. "Charlie's dad was head gardener for ages. When he died Charlie took over the job. Before that he'd worked as a driver for a cross country freight hauling company."

"That job must have paid better than the one at Bruck," Caroline commented as she carried her tea to the table.

"Kept him away from home too much. Branch was a family man."

"You sure know a lot about him. Are you two friends?"

Carl shook his head. "I taught three of his boys, so I got to know a bit about Charlie from comments they made. And naturally I attended Julie's funeral." He scraped his plate clean and pushed it aside. "As unofficial town historian, I try to keep tabs on current events in Rhineburg. When I got home tonight I checked my records on the Branch family. Charlie's little binge had me worried, and I wondered if it had something to do with today's date."

"Like an anniversary of some kind?"

"Exactly. But I didn't find anything to link this situation with the past. Frankly, this entire episode has me stumped."

"I think I can explain it," Caroline replied. "I'll bet Branch is upset over the possibility of treasure hunters digging up the campus."

Carl's bushy white eyebrows shot up. "But why? The Emperor will back off his promise to Professor Littlewort as soon as the rune stone's been proven a fake."

"Branch doesn't know that. All he heard was that the President is sanctioning a dig on his territory. The news was bound to upset him. It was apparent to me this afternoon that those gardens are his pride and joy. He was genuinely distressed over the idea of strangers tearing them up."

Carl stood up and began pacing the room. The floorboards quivered beneath his three-hundred-pound frame, and Caroline had to suck in her stomach each time he pushed past her. After a few minutes of silent cogitation, he thudded to a halt.

"I hate to see the fun spoiled," he said as he plopped down on his chair. "Still, I'd better explain things to Charlie. If he's that disturbed over this nonsense..."

"Oh, he's disturbed all right. As drunk as he was tonight, Branch's mind was still on his beloved flowers. He calls Bruck's daffodil beds his 'paths of gold'. His speech was slurred, but I could swear he mumbled that phrase before passing out up in the bedroom."

"So?"

"Carl, obviously you don't understand the passion that burns in the heart of a born gardener. We're a breed unto ourselves, a group of people so fixated on flowers that the highlight of the winter holidays is the arrival of the first seed catalogue in the mail. We tend to go a little nuts when somebody threatens to destroy our handiwork."

Carl held up one hand. "You've convinced me, Cari. I forgot you had something in common with Charlie."

"I was addicted to gardening when I lived in Chicago. For that very reason I should have known better than to get Branch so riled up this afternoon. I'm partially to blame for his drinking spree."

"It's more my fault," the Professor admitted. "I'll make a point of speaking to Charlie in the morning.

With that point settled, they moved on to a new but related subject.

"So why was Mr. Burke at the Blue Cat Lounge tonight?"

"Phff!" Carl snorted in disgust. "That Sid is a worthless lout. He claims he and Branch are friends, but we both know that's a lie. Burke was working off a punishment when you saw him on the Green today. Seems he was caught running a little con game on the freshmen. He printed up tickets to the Festival of Knights and was selling them to the more naïve students."

"But there's no admission fee for students."

"Right," replied the Professor. "We only charge visitors, and even then it's a nominal fee. But Sid figured rightly that some of the freshmen wouldn't know this."

"I'm surprised that his only punishment was raking the lawn."

"He's serving a three week sentence. Apparently he couldn't get around the Archangels as easily as he did President Hurst."

Caroline marveled once more at the Bruck brothers' disciplinary methods. The identical triplets ran a tight Security Department with Michael commanding the day shift, Rafael handling p.m.s, and Gabriel manning the office at night. At times the three descendents of Bruck U.'s founder joined forces to supervise an event such as the Festival. Since few students dared tangle with the blond giants, these occasions were marked by a decided lack of rowdiness. It was the ability of the Archangels to enforce such tranquility that endeared them to the conservative inhabitants of Rhineburg.

"I'm glad the Bruck boys nailed Mr. Burke, but tell me one thing. Why didn't Garrison Hurst just expel the little rat? Larceny doesn't seem to fit in with the university image Hurst promotes."

"Ever hear of Morgan Burke? The guy who's always yapping to the papers about how soft the courts are on criminals? Well, he's our local state representative and Sid is his son."

It was Caroline's turn to raise her eyebrows. "I get the picture. Hurst wouldn't dare enrage a state rep by tossing his kid out of college. Fundraising efforts could take an unexplainable nosedive."

"You're absolutely correct." Atwater rose from the table and wandered over to the refrigerator. "A nasty thought has entered my mind, and I'd like to run it by you," he said as he removed two bottles of beer from the bottom shelf. He handed one to Caroline, ignoring the teacup in her hand. "Burke is in my History of Warfare class. We discussed the Vikings and their raiding techniques earlier in the year. Sid is also studying literature under Professor Littlewort."

"Are you insinuating he's behind this rune stone hoax?"

"The possibility has occurred to me." Carl flipped the cap off his beer and took a long pull on the dark amber liquid. "Sid is lazy and conniving, but he's also pretty bright. He could mastermind a stunt like this if he wanted to embarrass a teacher he disliked."

"If Sid's as smart as you say, Andrew must drive him crazy."

"Exactly. Burke's due to graduate in June. He's attended past Festivals, and he knows the Maypole is always raised on that hilly section of the Green."

"And he had ample opportunity to bury the rock while assigned to groundskeeping chores." Caroline shook her head. "Sid could be our culprit, Carl, but how are you going to prove it? If he did it alone, there's no one to rat on him. He's perfectly safe unless he starts bragging about it."

"Burke's too clever for that." Carl pounded his fist on the table. "I've got a gut feeling about this, Cari. That young ruffian probably overheard your conversation with Branch this afternoon. Because he's angry at having to waste his time working for the gardener, he purposely played on Charlie's fears. I'll bet he feigned sympathy for the man, then suggested they share a few drinks together."

"Shiloh denied over serving them, didn't he? I wonder if Sid passed his own drinks on to Branch. He didn't strike me as being even slightly drunk while our gardener was certainly intoxicated."

"I wouldn't put it past him to do something like that."

"And remember that Burke wasn't driving tonight. I doubt he walked all the way to the Blue Cat so he must have gone there with Branch. You know, Carl, if we're right about this scenario, Sid Burke is one helluva nasty guy. Imagine baiting a man like Charlie just for the fun of it."

"Like I said before, I wouldn't put it past him. Sid's been in and out of trouble since the day he arrived at Bruck."

Caroline toyed with her unopened bottle of beer. "In fairness, we should consider all the possibilities before reaching a conclusion. Plenty of other people had access to the Green this week. Almost anyone could have buried the rune stone. And as for Sid's presence at the lounge, maybe he went there with his buddies and stumbled on Branch by accident."

"Burke doesn't have buddies," Carl answered sourly. "He's a loner with a mean streak. Students steer clear of him because he's trouble from the word go."

"Perhaps you're letting your personal feelings get in the way of your good judgment, Carl. After all, the young man must have at least one redeeming quality."

"Sure he does," the Professor exclaimed. "He's graduating this year!"

Caroline laughed as she pushed her chair back from the table. "It's almost midnight, my friend, and we're nowhere near to solving this little puzzle. I'm going home and crawl into my nice warm bed. I suggest you do the same." She rose to her feet and started towards the living room. "Once you explain things to Branch he'll quit worrying about intruders ripping out his daffodils."

"I'll also have a word with him about young Mr. Burke, although I seriously doubt Charlie will ever go out drinking with him again." Carl accompanied Caroline to the door. "Are you working tomorrow?"

"I'm on the evening shift in ER, so I intend to sleep away the morning. Not even an earthquake is going to rouse me before noon."

With a smile and a wave, Caroline headed for her car. She drove back to the dorm happily contemplating a rendezvous with her pillow. Little did she guess how short her slumber would actually be. By eight the next morning she'd be entrenched behind the main counter of Rhineburg's post office, up to her ears in mail and murder.

CHAPTER 6

Caroline bolted upright on her mattress. Sunlight streamed through the east window of the bedroom, and for a moment she imagined it was the brightness that had jolted her awake. Then the telephone rang, the sound loud and insistent in the quiet apartment, and she realized it was the same clamoring noise she'd heard in her dreams.

She glanced at the clock and groaned. 7:30 a.m. The only person who'd call this early in the day was her boss in the staffing office. Some nurse had probably reported in sick, and Corrine was searching for a replacement.

"There go my plans for a morning in bed," Caroline grumbled as she snatched the phone from its cradle. She tried to hide her annoyance with a stream of bright chatter.

"Hi there, Corrine. What's up, who's sick, and where do you want me to work today? Remember, I'm scheduled for..."

"Oh, mom! Thank God you finally answered!"

Caroline threw her legs over the side of the bed and sat up straight. She gripped the receiver with both hands and tried to control her voice as she answered, "What's wrong, Nikki? Has something happened to you and Martin?"

"No," Nikki sobbed. "We're OK. It's Emma Reiser. She fell down the stairs at the post office and she's dead!"

With a sigh of relief, Caroline fell back against the pillows and mentally thanked the Lord. It was just over a year now since Ed's death. Another tragedy in the family would have been hard to bear.

"Are you there, mom?"

"Yes, Nikki." She pulled her thoughts together and continued more sympathetically. "I'm sorry about Mrs. Reiser, dear. How did it happen?"

"I don't know! I arrived at work a few minutes ago, and the door was still locked. Emma always opens the post office at seven on the dot, but I figured maybe she overslept this one time. I let myself in with my key and called out to her. There was no answer. I started towards the back room, and that's when I saw her. She's lying at the foot of the staircase, mom, and..."

Caroline interrupted with a question.

"You mean this all happened just now? Have you called the paramedics, Nikki?"

"Yes," Nikki sniffled. "Then I..."

"Emma may not be dead." Caroline's nursing instincts had taken over and she began to issue instructions to the stunned girl on the other end of the line. "She may only be in a coma from the fall, Nikki. Feel for a pulse, then..."

"I did that already. There was none, and Emma's face is so blue!"

Caroline sighed. It was probably hopeless, still she told Nikki to administer CPR until the paramedics arrived.

"Then stay at the post office, Nikki. I'll be there as soon as possible."

It took Caroline less than five minutes to pull on jeans and a sweatshirt, apply some basic makeup, and comb her short graying hair. She grabbed her car keys off the dresser and ran out of the apartment. Another five minutes and she had traversed the underground passage from the nursing dorm to the ground floor of St.

Anne's Hospital. She took the corridor past the cafeteria, cut across the courtyard, and doubled back to ER. The department was empty of patients when she pushed open the double doors off the hallway.

"Hi, Caroline." Jane Gardner waved from behind the desk. "You're off to an early start today."

Caroline had first met Jane when the latter was nurse-manager of the Psychiatric Ward. Since then, Jane had been promoted to a supervisory position.

"Are you covering the day shift?"

Jane nodded. "I'm hoping it will be an uneventful eight hours."

"As any supervisor would," Caroline agreed. "I just got a call from my daughter-in-law. She works at the post office. When she arrived there this morning she found Emma Reiser lying on the floor. Nikki thinks she's dead."

"The paramedics radioed in. She's a triple zero," Jane replied, referring to an ER term for a patient exhibiting no life signs and beyond hope of resusitation. "Paul told them to stop CPR. He pronounced her in the field."

"I'd hoped Nikki was wrong." Caroline shook her head. "Poor thing. She was really upset over finding Emma's body."

"I don't blame her. It's hard when you're not used to it." Dr. Paul Wakely walked out of the radio room. He tossed a sheet of paper on the desk in front of Caroline. "Looks like she took quite a tumble. I was told there's a nasty wound to the skull."

Caroline grimaced as she scanned the report of the conversation between Paul and the paramedics.

"It'll be a coroner's case, right?"

"You bet," Paul said with a nod. "Emma was wearing a nightgown with a long rip in the hem. Probably caught her foot in it when she started down the stairs. Just another accident, but even so, the police will have to investigate."

"An unnatural death," Jane mused. "Old man Gordan won't be pleased."

Paul winked at Caroline. "Our poor coroner still hasn't recovered from all the activity around here last December. The paperwork alone was enough to throw him for a loop."

"Yet the voters keep electing him, don't they? He must be a real man of the people, Paul."

Dr. Wakely wrinkled his nose in disgust. He would have debated the subject, but Caroline was in a hurry. She waved good-bye and headed for the door leading to the parking garage.

Her Jeep was parked on the second level and Caroline descended at a prudent speed, then accelerated once on Circle Road. She cruised past the university before turning onto the highway leading to Rhineburg. Traffic was at a minimum there. She made good time and reached the Wilhelm exit just as an ambulance passed by going in the opposite direction. Its lights and siren were off, so Caroline guessed it was probably carrying the body of Emma Reiser.

Accustomed to sudden death from her years in the ER, Caroline's thoughts lingered only briefly on the post-mistress before the changing landscape captured her attention. Carl was right. Rhineburg was becoming a tourist trap. Cutesy shops featuring porcelain pigs, wooden birdhouses, and other non-essential items had sprung up all along Wilhelm Road. Several splendid old Victorians now sported signs advertising antiques while others had been converted into bed-and-breakfasts. All had been repainted in five-color schemes that entitled them to be designated 'painted ladies'.

Who could blame the enterprising souls of Rhineburg? They were coping the best they could with a flagging rural economy. God knew the old wooden houses required a massive amount of upkeep. Beautiful as they were, they were money pits, gobbling up incomes faster than they were earned. The homeowners may have sacrificed their privacy, but at least they weren't going bankrupt like so many of their counterparts across the countryside.

Caroline slid the Jeep into a parking space alongside the town square. The post office, a chunky two-story building constructed of pink rhyolite stone from the quarry outside of Rhineburg, squatted on the corner of Wilhelm and Kaiser across from the little park. Its thick walls blushed rosy red in the slanting sunlight, giving it an unsuitably cheerful appearance considering it was now a house of death.

Not surprisingly, a small crowd had gathered on the sidewalk. Caroline nodded to the few people she recognized and hurried into the building. She spotted Nikki behind the main counter surrounded by three policemen and the mayor of Rhineburg.

"Mom!" Nikki waved to her nervously. "I told them you were coming to help."

Caroline wasn't exactly sure what kind of help was expected from her, but she could see Nikki was a wreck. The girl's eyes were red rimmed and puffy from tears. She was clutching a box of tissues and a small wastebasket near her chair overflowed with the residue of grief.

"How are you doing, hon?" Caroline asked, slipping an arm around her daughter-in-law's shoulders.

"I'll be OK," Nikki responded. "It was just such a shock seeing Mrs. Reiser that way. I still can't believe she's dead."

"Emma was practically an institution around here." Jake Moeller, Rhineburg's square jawed Chief of Police, frowned down at the well-polished tips of his regulation black leather shoes. "People are really gonna miss her."

"But she will not be forgotten," Teddy Schoen pronounced solemnly. "From now on, this facility will be known as the Emma Reiser Post Office, dedicated to the memory of our longest serving post-mistress." The ever-politically-correct mayor pursed his lips and stared at the ceiling with furrowed brow. "Of course the Council will have to vote on it, but I'm sure everyone will agree Emma deserves a fitting memorial."

Moeller's frown deepened as he pretended to examine the wanted posters hanging on the wall next to the desk. Caroline noted the set of his mouth. She guessed the Chief was no more enamored by the pompous politician than she was.

"You have a more immediate problem to deal with," she reminded Hiz Honor with a ruthlessness bred of dislike. "The postal authorities need to be notified so they can send someone to take Emma's place. Until then, you'll have to close up shop here."

Schoen's salt and pepper eyebrows shot up in surprise. "Close the P.O.? Why should we do that when young Mrs. Rhodes can handle the job?" He turned to Nikki and flashed his signature smile. "You do know how to operate all this, don't you?" he asked, gesturing to the array of postal equipment lining the counter.

"I've only been here a few weeks," Nikki replied tentatively. "I suppose I could manage, but..."

"No buts about it, dear," the mayor boomed. "I have the utmost confidence in your ability to carry on in Emma's stead. In fact, I hereby appoint you temporary post-mistress of Rhineburg. I'll see about making it a permanent position when I talk to the boys in Washington." He smiled benignly. "After all, why should they appoint some outsider to the job when we've already got you?"

Nikki opened her mouth to object, but Schoen silenced her with an upraised hand.

"No need to thank me, young lady. Only doing my job." He turned to Moeller and jerked his head in the direction of the door. "Let's go, Chief. Now that this little business is wrapped up, these ladies need to get on with their work. The last thing they want," he added with a chuckle, "is a couple of men underfoot."

Moeller rolled his eyes as Schoen made his way to the door.

"If I were you," he said quietly, "I'd hang up the 'Closed' sign and give your daughter-in-law a cup of something strong. She looks like she could use it." Raising a finger to his cap, he winked at Caroline before motioning to the other officers. Together, they followed the Mayor out of the building.

Caroline locked the door and leaned against it, exasperation showing in every line of her face.

"It amazes me how that man has remained mayor for so many years. What does he do anyway? Hand out hundred dollar bills at the polling places?"

Nikki stood up and wandered over to the counter.

"He may sound like a fool, but Teddy Schoen's a pretty astute politician," the girl replied distractedly. She gathered up a stack of papers and moved them from one side of the counter to the other. "These change of address forms should be placed in a rack. They're only in the way here, but Mrs. Reiser insists on..."

Nikki suddenly broke into tears. Caroline put an arm around her and guided her to the back room. Moeller's recommendation had been wise. They could both do with a cup of something strong, but Caroline figured at this time in the morning, it had better be tea.

She busied herself preparing it while Nikki got her emotions back under control. By the time she carried the steaming mugs of Earl Grey to the table, the young woman had recovered enough to smile her thanks.

"It doesn't bother you any more, does it?" Nikki said as she thickened the tea with honey. "Seeing people die, I mean."

Caroline considered her answer. How could she explain the change that occurred within a person after witnessing death on a regular basis? It wasn't that you stopped caring about people; you just learned to accept death as the inevitable result of living.

"Shortly after graduating from nursing school, I cared for a patient who was slowly dying of cancer. Most of the time morphine didn't even control his pain, yet he always cracked a joke when I entered his room. I discovered that using humor was his way of staying in control of the situation.

"Over the weeks I grew quite fond of this patient and his family. One evening, only minutes after his wife had left for home, he suffered a cardiac arrest. He had never signed a DNR, a 'Do Not Resuscitate' order, so I called a code. Nikki, we worked on him for forty-five minutes -- a long time for any resuscitation attempt -- but it was a useless effort. When I finally left his room, I just stood in the hallway and cried. Losing him was like losing a friend. I couldn't believe we'd failed him."

"How did you handle it?" Nikki asked quietly.

"After work three of the older nurses sat me down and related their own first experiences with death. Nobody ever forgets the first time, Nikki, and all of them had felt as devastated as I did that night. But because they were nurses, they learned over time to control their feelings."

"You can't just bottle up emotions!" Nikki protested. "Once you harden your heart..."

Caroline shook her head. "I'm not talking about becoming hard, Nikki. I'm saying that if you want to retain your effectiveness, you can't allow yourself to be overwhelmed by sorrow. It's different when you're faced with the death of a family member or a loved one. Look at me," Caroline said with a sad smile. "I almost lost my mind when Martin's father died. But in my business, one has to think about facing the next patient. What kind of nurse would I be if I wore my emotions on my sleeve? Should I cry over the patient I just lost in Room Two while I'm caring for the person in Room Three?"

"Of course not," Nikki muttered.

"Of course not," Caroline repeated. "It would only decrease my effectiveness as a nurse. I need to be thinking of that second patient, and that second patient alone, when I'm dealing with him."

"I didn't mean to imply you don't care about Mrs. Reiser. It's just that you seem to take it all in stride while I'm sitting here like a kid who's lost a parent."

"You admired Emma Reiser, Nikki. And you've never witnessed sudden death before." Caroline leaned over the table and placed her hand over Nikki's. "Believe me, dear. There are worse things in life than dying. Loneliness and despair rank much higher on the list of human tragedies than death."

"I suppose you're right."

"I know I'm right. Don't mourn the dead, Nikki. They're at peace. Reserve your sympathy for the loved ones left behind."

"Mrs. Reiser didn't leave anyone behind. Her husband died years ago, and she had no children."

"No brothers or sisters?"

Nikki shrugged. "None that she ever spoke of. Of course, I'd only known her a few weeks. Maybe Chief Moeller would know if there's any family."

"We should call him," Caroline said, rising to her feet. "If there are relatives, they'll want to come by and pack up Emma's belongings."

"Will you do that while I clean up yesterday's paperwork and check the out-going mail? Ben will be here soon to pick up the bags."

Caroline nodded approvingly as Nikki walked briskly out of the room. She believed in the therapeutic value of work and hoped these routine duties would take her daughter-in-law's mind off Emma.

As for herself, Caroline was experiencing an overpowering desire for a cigarette. Smoking, which she'd given up several years earlier, had always comforted her in times of stress. Her non-smoking friends who labeled it a 'crutch' and a 'vice' simply had no idea how soothing a deep drag on a cigarette could be.

Still, she was not about to get hooked on the habit again. Casting all thoughts of cigarettes out of her mind, she puttered about cleaning up the tea things as she considered why her conversation with Nikki left her feeling so emotionally drained.

She'd told the girl the truth; death wasn't the curse most imagined it to be. In fact, when it came swiftly and silently, like it had to Emma Reiser, it was something of a blessing.

Still, having to defend herself to her daughter-in-law was a bit unnerving. Caroline had never before thought of herself as hardhearted. Now she wondered if her approach to life could be viewed as harsh and uncaring. She didn't think her colleagues would so consider it, but what about those outside her profession? What about her family?

"But I know exactly who I am," she muttered as she rinsed out the mugs in the little sink at the back of the room. "And I'm certainly not an insensitive person."

"Of course you're not. Whatever gave you such an idea?"

Caroline spun around and came face to face with a puzzled looking Professor Atwater.

"Carl! What are you doing here?"

"I heard about Emma's accident and stopped by to see if there was anything I could do to help. Nikki let me in." The Professor eased his enormous frame onto a less than sturdy chair. Its legs creaked ominously, but Atwater seemed not to notice as he concentrated on his friend. "So what's all this about you being insensitive?"

"Oh, nothing," Caroline replied shamefacedly. She dearly wished Carl hadn't overheard that testy remark. "Nikki was upset over finding Emma's body. I didn't react as she thought I should, and I don't think she entirely understood my explanation."

Carl stroked his beard. "You can't expect these young pups to think like you and I, Cari. They're a little short on life experience." When she didn't answer, the Professor wisely changed the subject. "So what needs to be done around here? I can sort mail, or sell stamps if you want."

"You'd better ask Nikki about that. I was just about to call Chief Moeller to see if Mrs. Reiser's family was coming by. They'll need to take clothes to the undertaker."

"Emma didn't have family in these parts. She was a widow, and I believe her only kin is a brother in New York."

"Hmm. Perhaps we'll have to do it then." Caroline picked up the phone and began to dial. "I wonder if she'll be buried here in Rhineburg?"

"I expect so. Her husband's lying in the town cemetery."

Someone picked up at the police station, and Caroline asked for Jake Moeller. She waited less than a minute before he answered.

"How's young Mrs. Rhodes doing?" The Chief's voice was filled with concern, and Caroline's liking for the man instantly grew.

"She's better now. Thanks for asking." Caroline told him why she was calling. "Professor Atwater is here, and he says Emma has a brother living out of town. Would you like us to pick out some clothes for the funeral?"

"I hadn't thought of clothes," the Chief conceded. "It certainly would help, if you have the time. I contacted the brother -- got his name from Emma's lawyer -- but he's laid up with a broken hip. Says he's too old and crippled to make a trip to Rhineburg and the lawyer should handle the funeral arrangements. Says he'll pray for her soul from his sickbed."

"Well, it shouldn't take the coroner's office long to clear the body. Perhaps Mrs. Reiser's lawyer knows her wishes concerning burial or cremation."

"According to Tom Crippen, he hasn't seen Emma since she made out her will three years ago. Why don't you go through her desk? Maybe she wrote something down, some instructions as to what she wanted done."

"Is it all right -- I mean, legally -- for me to go through her things?"

"This isn't Chicago, Mrs. Rhodes," the Chief chuckled. "We're a little looser with formalities here in Rhineburg." When Caroline didn't reply, he added hastily, "Looks to me like this was an accident, pure and simple. Emma caught her foot in the hem of her nightgown and tripped down those stairs, or else she had a heart attack and then fell. Whatever, there's no reason to treat the post office like a crime scene. You just take a look around and see if you can come up with anything that would help us out. And if you wouldn't mind packing up her things, I'll see to it they get sent on to her brother."

"If you say so, Chief Moeller." Caroline hung up and turned to Carl. "Emma left no burial plans with her lawyer, and her brother's too ill to coordinate a funeral."

"I take it the ball was thrown back into our court?"

"It definitely was. The Chief wants us to bundle up Emma's belongings. While we're at it, we're to search for some formal indication of her wishes. Maybe we'll get lucky," she added as she headed for the staircase. "Maybe Emma was one of those organized souls who makes lists to deal with any evenuality."

"Like what to do when the cat spits up a hairball."

Caroline laughed. "Hopefully the woman was a little more practical than that. Still, you've caught my drift. Let's go see what we can find in her bedroom."

The two friends climbed the creaky wooden staircase leading to the second floor. A narrow corridor ran the width of the building with doorways on either side of the stairs and what appeared to be a suite of rooms directly opposite the landing. Caroline crossed the carpeted hall and opened the door to Emma Reiser's private domain.

"Oh, my goodness!" she exclaimed as she flipped on the light switch. What lay before her was not the apartment of a small town post-mistress, but the interior of an nineteenth century mansion illuminated by a massive crystal chandelier.

CHAPTER 7

Caroline and the Professor were totally unprepared for the splendor that greeted them in Emma's drawing room. Everywhere they looked they saw objects that defied the notion that Reiser had been an ordinary middle class working woman.

Across from the door stood a rosewood sofa with carved cabriole legs and claw-and-ball feet. It was upholstered in a deep burgundy brocade and topped with a lacy cresting rail of carved grapevines and acorns. Two matching chairs were arranged opposite the sofa on either side of a mahogany tilt-top table. A Queen Anne highboy with carved fan and finials filled the far corner while an English parquetry breakfast table of rosewood, walnut, and coromandel occupied the near one. Heavy tapestries in rich strands of color overlaid ordinary shades on the only two windows in the room. They effectively blocked both outside light and the curiosity of passersby.

"Look at this," Carl exclaimed as he ran his hand over a marble topped chiffonier perched against one ivory painted wall. An engraved and enamelled glass vase was the sole decoration gracing the mahogany cupboard. "I'll bet this piece cost a fortune."

Caroline's attention had been drawn to a knee-hole writing desk flanking the doorway. She fingered the carved shell ornamentation topping each set of side drawers and shook her head in amazement.

"I'm no expert on antique furnishings, Carl, but I'll bet this room is worth a king's ransom. Just look at the size, design, and colors of this rug." She knelt down and turned back the edge of a Persian carpet covering the central part of the floor. "It's hand tied, not woven on a machine. Figuratively speaking, this is priceless."

"I didn't know postal employees were paid all that well, Cari. Especially ones who worked in backwater towns like Rhineburg."

Caroline stood up and walked over to an ebonized door at the far end of the room.

"You can be sure Emma didn't acquire all this on a government paycheck. She either inherited money or... Wow! Come look in here, Carl!"

Behind the door was a bedroom rivaling the drawing room in elegance. An ornate rosewood bed in the rococo revival style stood against one wall, its ivory silk sheets rumpled beneath a turned back comforter of wine and rose satin. A matching armoire with a curved pediment of pierced scrollwork hugged the opposite wall next to a window draped in burgundy damask. A mirrored chest of drawers and a marble-topped wash stand flanked a second window. A pearl-backed hand mirror with matching comb and brush lay on the wash stand alongside antique scent bottles and a flowered porcelain pitcher and basin. Reflected in the mirror, a jewelry case carved of ebony and inlaid with ivory rested atop the chest of drawers.

On an angle to the armoire was another door leading to a walk-in cedar closet. The closet was bare except for a dozen or so rather plain dresses, two cotton and two flannel nightgowns, a good wool coat, and four pairs of sensible walking shoes.

"She sure didn't spend money on clothes," Caroline remarked as she fingered the modest material of a two-piece suit draped by a dry cleaner's plastic bag. "This must have been her Sunday-go-to-meeting outfit. It doesn't look as worn as the others."

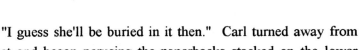

"I guess she'll be buried in it then." Carl turned away from the closet and began perusing the paperbacks stacked on the lower shelf of the wash stand. "Can't say I admire Emma's taste in literature. These all appear to be romance novels."

Caroline walked over to his side and glanced at the books. "Does all this seem as weird to you as it does to me?"

"Definitely," the Professor replied darkly. "I knew Emma a good many years, but nothing she said or did ever hinted at this kind of lifestyle. She was a plain talking woman who wore her hair in a bun and eschewed lipstick. She always came to civic events, attended church on a regular basis, and donated to any worthy cause that came up. This opulence just doesn't fit the Emma Resier who sold stamps at the Rhineburg P.O."

"I wonder what Nikki will say when she sees this apartment."

"It might change her opinion of the postmistress."

"Undoubtedly! What do you say we go investigate across the hall? Maybe we'll discover another treasure or two."

"First I want to look through Emma's desk. It's possible she left some final instructions in one of the drawers."

"Good grief," Caroline muttered in embarrassment. "I almost forgot the real purpose of our visit. I'll look around in here."

But she had no luck in the bedroom. The chest of drawers contained only the usual sweaters, stockings, and underwear while the armoire was totally bare except for a collection of dust bunnies.

"I hope you're doing better than I," she said as she reentered the drawing room. "There's nothing of a personal nature in there."

"Nothing here either." There was a puzzled look in Carl's eyes as he gazed about. "This is more like a museum than a home."

"I have a feeling Emma was role playing in this suite, Carl. There's no trace of a post-mistress here, no family pictures, no letters, not even a telephone on the desk. But there is a shelf-load of romance novels in the bedroom and all of them are set in Victorian times."

Carl pulled on his beard, an indication he was concentrating.

"You may have hit the nail on the head, Cari. And if Emma was pursuing a fantasy in here, her real life probably existed across the hall. Let's go have a look at those two rooms."

The first door led to a large but simple bathroom. They checked out the medicine cabinet there, but it held nothing of interest. When they moved on to the second door, they found it locked.

"Now what?" Caroline asked disgustedly. "Unless Nikki has a key, which I sorely doubt, we're not getting into this room."

"Jake entrusted us with a task, Cari. I intend to finish it."

With that said, Carl lifted a foot and kicked the door open.

"Good lord, Carl! I don't think Chief Moeller intended we tear the place down. Are you OK?"

Carl grimaced as he rubbed his right leg. "Sometimes I forget I'm no longer a kid."

Caroline smiled sympathetically. "Come on, Mr. Macho. Let's see what Miz Emma kept hidden away in here."

The room turned out to be an office. Cabinets lined one wall behind a desk bearing a computer linked to a fax machine and printer. Three telephones stood next to the computer, each one attached to an answering machine. On the opposite wall four sixteen-inch black and white TV sets rested on a metal shelf. A second shelf below the first contained a stack of *Daily Racing Forms*.

Carl was the first to recover his voice, but what he said was unprintable.

CHAPTER 8

Jake Moeller scratched his head in bewilderment.

"It looks like Emma Reiser was quite the professional bookie. Beats me how I never once caught wind of her operation."

"Rhineburgers are pretty good at keeping secrets," pointed out Carl. "Especially when those secrets benefit them financially."

"And Emma didn't flaunt her winnings," added Caroline. "She invested her money in antiques rather than banking it."

"A smart move on her part," the Chief conceded. He'd already seen Emma's personal suite, and while he himself knew next to nothing about old furnishings, his wife ran a profitable antique store out of their aging Queen Anne over on Adams Street. He'd called her twenty minutes after arriving and told her to hot foot it right over to the post office. "I don't know if it's real or if it's junk," he'd said on the phone. "But if illegal gambling paid for Emma's belongings, I'm going to confiscate every single piece of it."

"We have tough anti-racketeering laws in this country," Jake later explained. "I'm sure you've heard of RICO, the Racketeer Influenced and Corrupt Organizations Act. It allows law enforcement agencies to impound assets representing the proceeds of racketeering."

"I've read about the FBI impounding cars and boats belonging to drug dealers," replied Caroline dubiously. "But I didn't know a small town police chief could employ a federal law like RICO."

"I'll want to check out the finer points of the law before I do anything," Moeller replied. "But gambling is considered a racket, so I have the right to prevent her heirs from profiting off Emma's illegal activities. Besides that," he continued mulishly, "if I auction off all this stuff, we might be able to afford to buy another black-and-white."

Caroline guessed the Chief could buy an entire fleet of cars with the proceeds of such a sale, but she kept her thoughts to herself. Better to let Mrs. Moelller break the good news after she'd appraised Emma's furniture.

"You're going to need proof of a crime before you impound anything," she reminded the policeman. She ran her hand over the computer in Emma's second floor office. "I'll bet there's a ton of incriminating information stored in here. The problem is, you can't get at it unless you know Emma's password."

"One of my deputies is a computer geek. If anybody can solve this problem, it's him." Moeller turned and walked out of the office. "I'm going to place a seal on this entire upper floor. You take any clothes you want for the undertaker, Mrs. Rhodes. But please don't touch Emma's jewelry or anything else that might rightfully belong to the town of Rhineburg."

Caroline nodded and went off to collect the suit she'd seen hanging in Emma closet. She wasted precious little time choosing burial clothes as she was anxious to get downstairs and see how her daughter-in-law was taking the news of her boss' unusual sideline. The girl had been quite fond of Mrs. Reiser. It was possible she'd excuse Emma's transgressions out of a misguided sense of loyalty.

As it turned out, Caroline needn't have worried. Nikki was hopping mad, and from the top of the stairs she could hear the girl carrying on an animated conversation with Carl and the Chief.

"I can't believe I was such a fool!" Nikki sputtered as she placed a set of mugs on the table in the back room. "I thought Mrs. Reiser was just being neighborly when she offered someone a cup of tea. Now I discover she was actually taking bets back here." She plunked down a pot of coffee and steamed off to the pantry for sugar. "She must have figured me for a regular idiot," she called over her shoulder. "Someone who'd be too dumb to catch on to her scheme." She dumped half a box of sugar cubes into a bowl and slammed the dish down next to the coffeepot. "How long did she think I'd fall for that line about folks needing a sympathetic ear? Why, if you'd counted the people lined up at her door you'd have thought half the town of Rhineburg required the services of a psychiatrist."

Caroline slid into a chair beside the Professor and counted her blessings. Better for Nikki to be angry with Emma than to defend her. It was embarrassing to admit she'd been taken in by the woman, but with this outburst, Nikki had begun the process of disassociating herself from the postmistress.

"It would be helpful if you could recall the names of some of Emma's customers," said the Chief. "Those people were as guilty of breaking the law as Mrs. Reiser."

Nikki hesitated, and Caroline could guess why. Martin's wife needed the job at the post office, but would the mayor recommend her for the position if he heard she turned informer on her customers?

"Well..."

"Chief Moeller," Caroline interrupted. "Nikki's only worked here a few weeks. It could cause irreparable harm if she mistakenly identified someone as one of Emma's clients. Don't you think Mrs. Reiser kept records on the people who placed bets with her? Maybe they're locked away in those cabinets in her office. Or maybe they're on computer disks. Either way, your deputy is bound to find them."

Moeller started to object, but the rat-a-tat of knuckles tapping on glass distracted him. He frowned as Nikki hurried off to the front door. When she returned, it was with a slightly built woman with hair the color of pumpkin pie who marched over to the burly policeman and poked him in the chest with one crimson-tipped finger.

"This had better be good, Jake. I was that close" -- she spread her thumb and forefinger a quarter inch apart -- "to selling a complete set of Windsor china when you called and insisted I come over here. Ten more minutes and I could have persuaded that tourist it was exactly what she was looking for." She peeled off her jacket and tossed it on a chair, then turned and flashed a brilliant smile. "I adore making a difficult sale. It's like winning a battle over a worthy opponent. You never know if you've done your best until the cash is actually in your hands." She wiggled her manicured fingers at Carl. "How are you, Professor Atwater? Still drumming history into the heads of ungrateful youngsters at Bruck?"

Carl murmured a reply, but Mrs. Moeller ignored him, concentrating instead on the other two females in the room.

"You're Caroline Rhodes, the nurse who captured the Mad Bomber last winter. I saw your picture in the paper, dear. I must say you look better in real life than in those photographs. Oh, Nikki! You've made fresh coffee! If you could manage to find another mug, dear. And perhaps a donut or some cookies. I missed breakfast again," she confided to Carl. "And now I'm as hungry as a horse!"

Caroline suppressed a grin as she watched the little fireball whiz about the room, searching first for a teaspoon, then for a napkin, all the time carrying on her hectic monologue.

"Now tell me why you dragged me over here, Jake. Everyone's a-buzz over poor Mrs. Reiser, and because I'm the wife of the police chief, they expect me to know the gory details of the accident. Which I don't, of course, since you refused to answer even one little question when you called at the store. By the way," she said as she turned back to Caroline, "we haven't been properly introduced yet, have we? I'm Madeline Moeller, Jake's wife. My friends call me Maddy. Jake just calls me Mad."

Madeline's laughter was so beguiling that Caroline responded immediately with a broad smile of her own. She marveled over how the sober Chief of Police had somehow managed to attract this bubbly woman whose very being personified pure energy in motion.

"Mad Moeller's Antiques and Collectibles," Maddy continued. "That's the name of my shop, Caroline. Stop by some day and I'll give you a 20% discount on anything in the place."

Chief Moeller placed a restraining hand on his wife's arm.

"You've just got to cut down on the caffeine, honey."

"I don't drink that much coffee and you know it, Jake."

"Hush up, Mad. I need you to listen quietly for a moment."

"I always listen to you. You're the one who doesn't…"

"Maddy!" the Chief broke in. "Please go upstairs and appraise Emma's furniture. It's very important I know exactly what it's worth."

Maddy snapped her fingers. "No problem, Jake. If it's older than fifty years, I can put a price on it."

"I'm no expert," Caroline interjected. "But I'd say some of the furnishings were early nineteenth century, if not older."

Maddy stopped her fluttering and turned to stare at Caroline. "Are we talking American or European?" she asked gravely.

"Some of both, I think. The furniture and tapestries look like the real McCoy, and the Persian rug in the drawing room is absolutely magnificent. I'd give my eye teeth to own it."

Maddy walked over to the staircase and studied the second floor landing in total disbelief.

"If what you say is true…I mean, how in the world…" She shook her head and started over. "I'd better get to work. There's a calculator in my coat pocket, Jake. Would you get it for me?"

Moeller retrieved the needed item and followed his wife upstairs. When they were safely out of hearing range, Carl turned to the others and growled, "How in the world does he put up with that woman? She's a whirling dervish, completely out of control."

Caroline smiled over her coffee cup. "I like her, Carl. She's smart, funny, and full of life."

Carl frowned but held his peace. "While there's a pause in the action, I think I'll call the funeral parlor and inquire about dropping off those clothes." He rose to his feet and started towards the front of the P.O. "Call me when the Mad-woman returns."

Caroline grimaced at the pun. She looked over at Nikki, expecting to see a similar reaction, but her daughter-in-law apparently hadn't heard the Professor. She was leaning against the back door, her brows furrowed in concentration as she gazed at the floorboards.

"What's up, Nikki? You haven't said a word in ages."

"Hmm? Oh! Sorry, mom." Nikki straightened up and ran a hand through her closely cropped jet black hair. "I was thinking about something odd that happened earlier this morning. Nothing as important as Mrs. Reiser's death, but disconcerting all the same."

"Something here at the post office?"

Nikki nodded. "Ben arrived for the mail while you and the Professor were upstairs. He hadn't heard about Mrs. Reiser's death, and of course he was pretty shocked when I told him. We talked a little about Emma, then Ben offered to tag the letter bags while I loaded up the packages that came in yesterday.

"Now before I go on, I have to explain how Mrs. Reiser ran this place. She never trusted the computer system the postal service installed, so she kept a duplicate record of each and every transaction in a ledger book that sat out on the main desk. Whenever she bagged packages, she first checked them against the information in her ledger. That was her way of making sure mail didn't get lost before it left the station, and when I started working here, she taught me to follow the practice."

Caroline wasn't sure where all this was leading to, but she listened patiently as Nikki continued with her story.

"When I checked the ledger this morning, it listed five packages that were brought to this station yesterday. One of them was mailed by Professor Littlewort late in the afternoon. I'd already left for home so I never saw the box, but the record states it contained a rune stone."

"So he's already sent it off to the museum. You know, Nikki, that rock is going to cause so much trouble that I wish it would just up and disappear."

"Funny you should say that," Nikki replied miserably, "because I can't find that package anywhere in this post office. It's like the rune stone has just evaporated into thin air."

CHAPTER 9

"What will the mayor say?" Nikki moaned. "My first day as temporary postmistress and already I've misplaced a package!"

Caroline was taken aback. "That's impossible, Nikki. This building isn't big enough to lose a package in."

"Oh yeah? I've searched every nook and cranny, and let me tell you something, mom. That rune stone is not in this post office."

"How about the other mailbags? Maybe it got mixed up with the letters."

Nikki shook her head. "Ben and I went through them all. We checked the returned mail bin, the cabinet where we keep paper supplies, the shelves under the main counter, and even the garbage can out back. The only things we found were a moldy old book of twenty-nine cent stamps and a mouse trap with some mummified cheese stuck to it. Needless to say, I threw both objects in the trash."

"Well, the only other thing I can think of is that Emma took the package upstairs."

"Why in the world would she do that?"

Caroline shrugged. "God only knows, Nikki. You have to admit, the woman was a rather strange bird. Maybe she decided the stone would be safer in her apartment than down here. Or maybe she wanted to unwrap and examine it."

"Emma wouldn't tamper with the mail," Nikki said in a shocked voice. "That would have been against the law."

"Oh, sure. I forgot that Mrs. Reiser was elected Citizen of the Year by Gamblers Anonymous. She would have never…"

"Alright already! You've made your point. Let's have a look upstairs."

The two of them explained the situation to Chief Moeller. With his blessing they searched every room on the second floor but came up empty handed.

"I'll have to report this to the regional office," Nikki muttered as they headed back downstairs. "Worse than that, I'll have to call Andrew Littlewort."

"You could ask Carl to do it."

"No," the girl replied with a shake of her head. "I'm in charge now, at least until a replacement arrives, so I have to be the one to break the bad news to the Professor."

Caroline admired her daughter-in-law's resolve. It would be no picnic explaining the loss of the rune stone to an irate Professor Littlewort. The man was not known for his generous nature. He'd probably chew her up and spit her out in forty different directions.

"What's going on?" Carl Atwater entered the back room as Nikki left to make her calls.

"It's a long story," Caroline said. "How about I give you the condensed version?"

"Fire away." Carl lowered himself onto a chair and listened with growing interest as Caroline explained the situation.

"Maybe Andrew wised up and returned for the box."

"I doubt it, Carl. By the time he arrived at the post office, Nikki had already left for home. It was late in the afternoon and he would have had very little time to change his mind."

"Damn it!" Carl exclaimed. "If I ever get my hands on the person who buried that stone…"

"It's unbelievable. Simply unbelievable!"

Maddy and Jake were descending the staircase, Maddy triumphantly waving a notebook in the air and Jake looking for all the world like a punch drunk fighter down for the count.

"You were right, my dear," Maddy announced as she hugged Caroline. "Just look at these figures."

Caroline gazed in awe at the scribbled numbers strung across three pages of the notebook. She'd guessed the furnishings were valuable, but Maddy's estimate astounded her.

"Are you sure?" she asked, unable to hide the doubt in her voice.

Maddy picked up a sugar cube and popped it into her mouth.

"I told you I know my stuff. I may be off by a few thousand this way or that, but on the whole, these are pretty accurate numbers." She gulped down a mouthful of cold coffee from one of the mugs on the table, then grimaced in displeasure. "Whew! That's bad. Didn't Emma keep some champagne around this place? We sure could use a bottle to celebrate our good fortune."

"I think your husband needs something stronger than champagne," Caroline noted.

The Chief had collapsed on a chair and was staring off into space, slack jawed and blurry eyed. Maddy walked over and patted him on the back.

"He's just stunned, poor man. It'll wear off in time. The thing to do now is set a guard on the property. It'll have to be watched day and night until everything's properly crated and ready to be shipped."

"Shipped where?"

"Why, to Sotheby's, Professor," Maddy replied with a hint of surprise in her voice. "If you want top dollar, that's the place to go."

"Let me see those figures." Atwater slipped the notebook out of Caroline's hand and flipped through the pages. When he looked up again at the two women, his expression resembled Jake's.

"Another one bites the dust," Maddy snickered as the Professor's eyes continued to glaze over. She placed her hands on his shoulders and gently pushed him down onto a chair next to her husband. "Why don't you warm up the coffee, Caroline? Our two warriors could use a stimulant to get their blood flowing again."

Caroline was in full agreement with the antique dealer. She put the pot back on the stove and began rinsing out the coffee mugs.

"What I don't understand," she mused, "is how Emma accumulated enough money to buy all that stuff. Even with the gambling..."

"That's the part that really grates on me."

Caroline turned with a start and stared at Chief Moeller. He'd snapped out of his trance and was suddenly angry as hell.

"Do you know how many years she had to be operating a book to earn that kind of money?" The Chief stood up and pounded his fist on the table. "Not ten. Not fifteen. Not even twenty." He glared at the others, daring them to contradict him. "Emma Reiser ran the Rhineburg post office for nigh onto forty years. She probably started handling bets the day she arrived in town." He took a deep breath to steady himself. "That woman had me hoodwinked from day one. She probably thought I was the dumbest cop she'd ever met."

Caroline and Maddy exchanged glances. Both women realized it wasn't the money Emma had made that bothered the Chief. It was the embarrassment of having been deceived by someone he'd trusted that stuck in his craw. That and the ridicule he'd face once the story hit the newspapers. There'd be many a joke made at his expense, many a detractor ready to question his ability when it became known that a gambling den had operated unopposed less than half a block away from the police station.

"Oh, Jake!" Maddy moved to his side, but he angrily waved her off. He was in no mood for sympathy, especially from his wife. Confused as to how to help, Maddy drew back and held her tongue. Caroline took an opposite tack.

"Chief Moeller, perhaps you can stop pouting for a moment and listen to what I've got to say. Emma Reiser tricked a whole lot of people in this town. Folks took her for what she appeared to be, a slightly dowdy but nonetheless upstanding member of the community who attended church on Sundays and pedaled stamps the rest of the week. Only her betting customers knew the truth behind that innocent façade, and they weren't telling."

"You got that right," the Chief grumbled.

"For all we know," Caroline continued, "Emma's illegal activities may have extended well beyond gambling."

Moeller swung around to face her. "What do you mean by that?"

"I mean she could have made some of her money stealing from the post office or its patrons. Professor Littlewort brought a box here yesterday for shipment to Chicago. Strangely enough, it's nowhere to be found today. Perhaps it wasn't the first package to go missing from this place."

"I know you're trying to smooth my ruffled feathers, Mrs. Rhodes," Moeller remarked sarcastically. "But I'd hardly consider a rock worth stealing."

"Why not?" Carl countered. "Andrew Littlewort believes he found an archaeological treasure on the grounds of Bruck University. Andrew's not a cautious man, Jake. He's always talked too much for his own good. I'll bet he told quite a story when he posted that box."

Caroline studied the Chief's face as Carl continued to talk. Moeller had calmed down but his skepticism was evident as he listened to the Professor.

"There are unscrupulous collectors everywhere," Atwater was reminding his friend. "One of them might have paid handsomely for what Andrew Littlewort considered the find of the century."

"And you believe Emma could have unloaded that rock."

"She was well acquainted with the antiquities market," insisted Caroline. "She must have known collectors in fields other than her own."

"I guess it's possible," the Chief conceded. He turned to Carl. "This stone was really that important?"

"Personally, I doubt it. But Andrew believes it's valuable, and he can be quite persuasive when he thinks he's right. I could see him trying to convince Emma Reiser of the stone's worth."

Moeller removed his glasses and rubbed the bridge of his nose with a callused forefinger.

"Frankly, Professor, I think you and Mrs. Rhodes are barking up the wrong trail when it comes to that missing package. But I'll tell you what I'll do. If young Mrs. Rhodes doesn't find the box by this evening, I'll stop by the university and have a talk with Professor Littlewort. Right now I've got to get started on this gambling thing."

"Chief Moeller?" Nikki stuck her head around the doorway. "Mr. Gordon from the coroner's office is on the phone. If you pick up the extension, I'll transfer the call back here."

Moeller nodded his thanks and walked over to the wall phone. A second later it buzzed.

"Hi, Jerry. You got a report for me on Emma Reiser?"

The others watched with mounting curiosity as the Chief's normally solemn features grew even more sober.

"And you're sure the stairs couldn't have caused such a wound?"

Oh-oh, thought Caroline uneasily. The coroner was taking his time explaining the pathologist's report to Jake. It seemed like an eternity passed before the big policeman put down the phone.

"Looks like we'll have to start a search for that rock sooner than I expected," he said as he turned towards the others. "Emma Reiser didn't die of a heart attack or a fall down the stairs. She was hit on the head with a blunt object. Something round, smooth, and heavy. Something that left grains of dirt and rock embedded in her skull. Something, I suspect, very much like Professor Littlewort's rune stone."

CHAPTER 10

Caroline accompanied Nikki to the police station where she made a formal statement concerning the discovery of Emma Reiser's body. The post office was now officially a crime scene closed to both the temporary postmistress and the public. No one was getting in without the express permission of Jake Moeller, not even the Mayor of Rhineburg, Teddy Schoen.

"I'm sure the Chief didn't intend to include me in that order, son," Teddy insisted upon his arrival at the P.O. "Why, I have to inform the Town Council as to what's going on here."

Billy Wetzel was only six months on the force and in many ways still wet behind the ears. Nevertheless, he understood his duty and, in this case, enjoyed doing it.

"Sorry, Mr. Mayor. The Chief says nobody, and I mean nobody, goes in or out of this building without his OK."

"Well, why don't you go check with Chief Moeller while I..."

Schoen reached for the door handle, but the young officer blocked his way. With an apologetic shrug Billy unfolded his arms and shifted his right hand downward until it came to rest on the gun butt protruding from his holster. He countered the move with a lazy grin that didn't quite disguise the contempt in his eyes.

But Teddy refused to be bested by a man like Billy. He'd seen that same triumphal gleam in the eyes of worthier opponents, and to a man, none had survived to become his equal. Billy wouldn't survive either.

Turning to the small crowd that had gathered on the sidewalk, the mayor threw back his head and laughed long and hard.

"Looks like I've been put in my place, huh, folks?" His sheepish grin invited empathy, and he immediately received it from most of the onloookers. Sensing victory in the offing, Schoen flung his arm around Billy and clapped him on the shoulder. "This young fellow says he has orders, and like any other good citizen of Rhineburg, I must respect them. But as your mayor it's my duty to see to it that you, the public, are not overly inconvenienced by the closure of this post office. For that reason I will now go and confer with Chief Moeller."

He stepped away from Billy, managing in the process to shove the officer up against the doorjamb. Billy winced as the hard stone cut between his shoulder blades, but the crowd didn't notice. Their eyes were glued on Teddy Schoen as he strode purposely towards the police station.

Caroline observed the entire incident from across the street. She and Nikki were seated on a bench in the town square waiting for Carl Atwater. The Professor was inside the police station attempting to calm a furious Andrew Littlewort who had arrived just moments after Nikki finished her deposition.

"Despite his smooth words, Mayor Schoen looks a bit angry."

"He can't be as ticked off as Professor Littlewort," Nikki retorted. "I thought he was going to scratch my eyes out when he stormed into the Chief's office."

"You're not to blame for the loss of his precious rune stone, Nikki. That's the fault of our murderer." Caroline suddenly laughed. "He did cause a stir, though, when he came bursting into the station."

Nikki giggled. "He looked so weird flapping his arms in the

air and shouting at the top of his lungs. I thought the Chief was going to arrest him for disturbing the peace!"

"Andrew certainly is a strange man," Caroline agreed. "I hear his temper tantrums are something to behold."

"Oh yeah. I swear, mom, one of these days that man is going to explode and end up with a stroke."

"Speaking of popping a blood vessel, just take a look at Carl."

Professor Atwater had emerged from the police station and was making his way across the street. His face was beet red and he was dripping with perspiration.

"I take it your peacekeeping mission failed," Caroline said as the Professor sank down on the end on the bench.

"Miserably," Carl growled. He yanked out his pipe and tamped a wad of tobacco into the bowl with a ferocity that matched his scowl. "Andrew is a complete idiot! He actually dismissed Emma Reiser's death as 'trivial' compared to the loss of his damned rock."

Caroline's eyebrows shot up. "I'd call that a rather warped point of view."

"Cold-blooded is more like it," murmured Nikki.

"And he became downright apoplectic when informed that his rune stone most likely was the murder weapon."

"Good grief! The more I learn about Andrew Littlewort, the less I like him."

"You're not the only one who feels that way, Cari. When Jake started questioning him about his visit to the P.O. yesterday, Andrew totally clammed up. He refused to answer any questions without his lawyer present."

"Now that's odd," Caroline remarked. "Why would Andrew be so skittish about answering a few simple questions?'

"I really don't know," Carl answered with a shrug. "But Jake's ready to give him the third degree. He wants to know what Andrew said to Emma and if she seemed overly interested in the contents of his package."

"Chief Moeller appears to be on the right trail. If the rune stone really was used to kill Emma, then either she or the murderer opened that box."

"It sure didn't unwrap itself," agreed the Professor. "Which leads me to think we were right when we hypothesized the existence of some kind of collector."

"And the willingness of Emma to both steal from her customers and sell what she stole."

"Do you think the killer came from around here, Professor?" Nikki asked.

"Not necessarily. The highway runs right past town. Anyone in the state could drive here within a matter of hours."

"I wonder if the asking price was too high," mused Caroline.

"You mean it was easier to steal the stone from Emma than pay for it."

Caroline stood up and stretched. "Greed has always been a motive for murder. But let me remind you, if it happened according to our theory, there's little chance either the stone or the killer will ever be found. I propose we leave this puzzle to the police and return to Bruck where we're really needed."

"Needed for what?"

"The Festival of Knights, Nikki. It begins tomorrow and there's still a lot to do."

"Since I'm temporarily out of a job, I guess I could help."

"You'll have to," Caroline replied. "What with all the excitement today, I totally forgot about the roses for the Maypole. I promised to deliver them to the decorations committee by noon, but it's past two o'clock already. I have to be at work at three."

"Don't worry about it. I'll see that the students get them."

"I have a couple of late classes to teach, so I'm going to head back too," Carl announced. "There'll be a general dress rehearsal for the knights and their ladies tomorrow morning, Caroline. Why don't you drop by the Green and watch the fun?"

"I just may do that." Caroline glanced at her watch. "Oh dear! Look at the time. We really have to get going, Nikki."

With a wave to the Professor, Caroline hurried off to her car, her daughter-in-law following close behind.

CHAPTER 11

Calm enveloped the Emergency Room that evening. Outside of Tommy McGruff's appendicitis and Bertha Meyer's heart attack, little occurred to tax the p.m. shift's medical skills. By nine o'clock the room was empty except for an embarrassed Bruck student who'd hammered his hand instead of a nail while erecting a stall for the Festival.

Caroline had just finished splinting the boy's broken finger when a familiar voice hailed her from the triage area. Suppressing a groan, she discharged her patient before turning to greet the visitor.

"Back in town so soon, Mr. Evans?"

FBI Special Agent Tom Evans dismissed the question with a bored shrug. "What can I say, Mrs. Rhodes? If you Rhineburgers persist in breaking federal laws, I'll be forced to set up a permanent office in your town."

"You'd resign from the force before you did that."

"You're probably right. Hell would be a cozier place to live than Rhineburg."

Caroline shook her head in mock dismay. "Haven't changed a bit, have you? You're still the same charming person I grew to know and hate last December."

Evans grunted noncommittally as he strolled past Caroline and entered the ER's main room. He'd lost interest in their war of words and was now busy sizing up the area. His eyes raked the empty cubicles right and left of the desk before coming to rest on the open door leading to the Cast Room. Caroline stifled a grin as the agent's bulldog head twitched forward on its massive neck, and Evans peered intently into the darkened area. She wanted to assure him that no hardened criminals lurked behind the shelves of hand splints and knee immobilizers, but she contained herself and said instead:

"Your last adventure out here in the boonies proved rather nerve wracking, didn't it?"

Evans transferred his gaze from the Cast Room to the ceiling. He seemed to be counting the tiles as he contemplated his answer.

"It wouldn't have been," he finally said, "if you'd come to me with your suspicions instead of tackling the murderer alone. And all that rigamarole afterwards." He shook his head ruefully. "You must have friends in high places, Mrs. Rhodes. I hadn't even finished my report before I was being pressured to re-evaluate the evidence. Seems like everyone wanted a certain person's name cleared."

"Am I supposed to feel sorry for you?" Caroline retorted. "If I remember correctly, I'd been pegged as the prime suspect in the case. You were more interested in proving I was crazy than I listening to anything I had to say."

"And if I remember correctly, you removed evidence from a crime scene. If we'd had that diary earlier, we'd have caught our man before he almost did you in."

Caroline rolled her eyes. "I doubt you dropped by to discuss old times," she said tartly. "Let's cut the small talk and get down to business. You want to question me about Emma Reiser, right?"

"Reiser was a federal employee killed on federal property. The Postal Service will be involved, but the FBI, in the person of yours truly, is in charge of the investigation." Evans glanced over at the desk where another nurse was busily shuffling paperwork while pretending not to eavesdrop. "Is there some place we could speak privately? Just for a few moments?"

Caroline neither liked nor trusted Tom Evans, but the man did have a job to do. And after all, who was she to obstruct justice?

"I'll be in the break room if you need me," she called over her shoulder. "This way, Mr. Evans."

Evans followed her to the back of the ER where a doorway led onto a narrow corridor skirting the rear of the department. Half way down the corridor was a small room crammed with lockers and cast off furniture. Caroline waved the agent in and closed the door.

"Make yourself at home. It's not exactly the Taj Mahal, but it'll do for cold dinners and short breaks."

Evans' tough boy image slipped a bit as he examined his crowded surroundings. The battered tweed couch leaning against the south wall of the room sagged precipitously to the left, its missing legs replaced by out-of-date medical books wedged between sand filled coffee cans. Scratched and dented metal lockers lined the adjacent wall below a shelf piled high with hospital scrubs and patient gowns. Across from the lockers stood a miniature refrigerator and an open-faced cabinet stocked with coffee, tea, sugar, and paper goods. The center of the room was occupied by four mismatched chairs and a scarred wooden table on which lay the remains of a pepperoni pizza and an empty two liter pop bottle. The only modern accouterment in the room was a shiny glass coffee maker, and that, according to the penciled sign taped to the wall, wasn't working.

"Jeez! And I thought my boss was cheap! Is St. Anne's so poor it can't afford anything better than this junk?"

"The money goes where the public will see it," Caroline replied with as little sarcasm as possible. She pulled out a chair, sat down, and motioned Evans to do the same. "Haven't you noticed all

the changes made to the front lobby? Looks more like a hotel now than a hospital."

"One of Paine's last ventures, wasn't it?" Evans asked, referring to the former Administrator. "How's the new guy in charge? Or shouldn't I ask?"

Caroline shrugged. "All hospital administrators are poured from the same mold nowadays. They're businessmen, and they see their job as making and saving money." She made a sweeping gesture that included everything in the room. "Why pay for new furniture that the paying customers will never see and use? Spend your money instead on whatever you think will impress the patients and their visitors."

"You're one cynical lady, aren't you?"

"You get that way after twenty years in this business. Tell me your job hasn't affected you!"

Evans rubbed his jaw with the backside of one hand. "Oh, I admit I'm cynical. Why else would I have questioned your story last winter?"

Their eyes locked for a moment, and Caroline suddenly felt ashamed. Tom Evans might not be the most congenial of men, but he'd made a career of solving tough cases through hard work and persistence. She, on the other hand, had unmasked a killer only by accidentally stumbling on the truth. So what right had she to criticize the man? None at all that she could see.

"If our roles had been reversed, I might have come to the same conclusion you did, Mr. Evans."

"And I might have been just as angry about it as you were, Mrs. Rhodes. But that's all water under the bridge. I've got a new case here in Rhineburg that I'd like to wrap up quickly. Will you answer a few questions for me?"

"Of course. Although I don't think there's much I can tell you about the murder."

The federal agent permitted himself the barest of smiles as he pulled a battered notebook from an inside pocket of his jacket.

"Then tell me what you know about Andrew Littlewort."

"Littlewort?" Caroline repeated in surprise. "What's he got to do with Emma's death besides taking that bogus stone to the P.O.?"

Evans sighed. "Here we go again with you asking the questions instead of answering them. Please, Mrs. Rhodes. Just tell me about yesterday morning and the discovery of this so-called rune stone."

"Don't talk down to me in that patronizing tone of voice," Caroline snapped. "You caught me off guard asking about Professor Littlewort. I thought you'd want to know about the antique collector."

Evans stared for a moment before asking in exasperation, "What antique collector?"

Caroline explained her and Carl's theory about an unknown person who'd killed Emma after coming to Rhineburg to purchase the rune stone. Evans didn't seem enthralled with the theory and said as much.

"It's too far-fetched, if you ask me. Most crimes occur for much simpler reasons. I think this murder was committed on the spur of the moment. It was totally unpremeditated, and our killer probably regretted it immediately."

"It sounds like you have a pretty good idea of who did it."

Evans nodded. "That's why I want to hear your account of yesterday's happenings. Be as accurate as you can with the details."

Caroline related the previous day's events with a heavy heart. She'd already guessed who Evans suspected of the murder, and she couldn't help but worry about the fallout from his arrest.

"And did Professor Littlewort exhibit any signs of anger when Professor Atwater suggested the stone was a fake?"

"He was upset, but..."

"The students who were present at the dig have testified that the Professor was more than just upset, Mrs. Rhodes. They say he shouted at Carl Atwater before storming off with the stone. They also say the Professor's well known for his temper tantrums."

"So I've heard," Caroline replied miserably. "But you have to understand how eccentric Andrew Littlewort is. He thrives on controversies like this one about Leif Erikson."

"Given to obsessions, would you say?"

"That term can be defined in several ways, Mr. Evans. I'm not sure I'm qualified to analyze Andrew Littlewort's personality."

Evans scribbled something in his notebook.

"You saw the Professor today in the police station, right?"

"Andrew arrived shortly before Nikki and I left."

"He was pretty angry with your daughter-in-law, wasn't he?"

Caroline nodded.

"Was that anger real or faked do you think?"

"I haven't even considered the possibility that it was faked. Professor Littlewort seemed genuinely upset both with Nikki and Chief Moeller."

"Why Moeller? Had the Chief accused him of something?"

Caroline shook her head. She knew Evans was drawing her into a trap, but she could see no way out of it.

"He wanted his rune stone back, and he thought Jake should be doing more to find it."

"Well, I agree with him on that point. Moeller doesn't seem to be putting much effort into the search for the murder weapon. In fact, I may have to call in more of my own men just to find it."

The hackles rose on the back of Caroline's neck. Where did
Evans come off criticizing a man like Jake Moeller? Being an
outsider, Evans had no idea how easily one could lose a rock in
Rhineburg. Toss it in the forest, or better yet in the quarry, and it
would never be seen again.

"You're trying to pin this murder on Andrew Littlewort, aren't
you?"

"He had a pretty strong motive," Evans answered mildly.
"And plenty of opportunity. I believe that sometime yesterday
Littlewort began to realize he'd been tricked. He regretted his
decision to send the rune stone to Chicago, and he went back to the
post office to retrieve it. It was late at night, and when he couldn't
wake Mrs. Reiser who was asleep up on the second floor, he broke
into the building through the cellar door. He found his package in the
mail room, but in the process he woke up the postmistress. She
discovered him holding the stone, and they argued over the break-in
and Littlewort's plan to abscond with a piece of U.S. mail."

"Without the stone..."

"Emma may have done other things for a living, but primarily
she was a U.S. Postal Service employee. According to everyone I
talked to today, she was very proud of her work. She never would
have allowed Professor Littlewort to leave with that package."

"And you think the argument turned ugly, and Andrew hit
Emma with the rock."

It was Evans' turn to nod. "Professor Littlewort has been
answering questions all afternoon. He's going to crack before long
and tell us the truth. Until then, I plan to gather as much testimony as
to his actions and state of mind as I possibly can. This may not have
been premeditated murder, but it was still pretty cold-blooded.
Andrew Littlewort knew the Field Museum would label his find a

hoax, and he couldn't stand to have folks laugh at him. He killed Emma Reiser to save his own reputation."

Evans had a credible theory, and Caroline couldn't fault him. Carl had told her Littlewort possessed a short fuse. He'd fought with practically every faculty member, so it wasn't difficult to envision him taking on the postmistress of Rhineburg.

"You'll probably be called on to testify in court," Evans said. "I hope that's the only way you involve yourself in this case."

"Involve myself?" Caroline asked with a frown. "Would you care to elaborate on that statement, Agent Evans?"

"Don't bother trying to pin this crime on some imaginary antique collector. You were lucky once, but in this business you need more than luck to catch a killer." Chair legs scraped the floor as Evans pushed back from the table and stood up. He suddenly laughed. "You know, that police chief of yours is a real riot. He actually thought he could confiscate everything in Mrs. Reiser's apartment under the RICO act." He shook his head. "He didn't know the law can only be employed by federal agencies like the FBI or the IRS, and you can only attach the assets of a living person. Once they're dead, you can't touch them. Moeller's not a bright cop, is he?"

Caroline felt compelled to come to Jake's defense.

"We don't see a lot of high profile crime around here, Mr. Evans. I think the Chief can be excused for misunderstanding a statute he's never before been called on to use."

Evans grunted. "Think what you want, Mrs. Rhodes, but professional lawmen ought to know the law." He started to leave the room, then turned back in the doorway. "I'll want a written statement from you, so stop by the police station tomorrow."

Caroline nodded her assent and watched as Evans headed down the corridor leading back to the ER. When she was sure he was out of hearing range, she reached for the wall phone and punched in a group of numbers.

"Hello?"

"Carl, it's Caroline. Can you drop what you're doing and come over to St. Anne's? I think the university has a problem. A *big* problem!"

CHAPTER 12

Caroline drove to the police station early the next morning. It took less than fifteen minutes to repeat her statement to Annie Holtzbrinck, the silver-haired dispatcher who also served as secretary to Jake Moeller. Annie typed up a draft of the account and after a minor change in wording Caroline signed it, shook hands with the Chief, and exited the station as inconspicuously as possible. Tongues would be wagging soon enough and she had no desire to add fuel to the fire by drawing attention to her own status as a witness. She was relieved, therefore, to find the sidewalk empty of Rhineburgers when she made her way over to the post office. Nikki was waiting for her at the back door and she quickly slipped inside.

"I'm glad I thought to call you before leaving the station," Caroline said as she shed her jacket. "I dreaded running into someone on the street and having to explain why I'd been in the Chief's office."

"Well, mom, I hate to burst your bubble, but I doubt your visit will stay a secret for long. The town grapevine has gone into high gear, and I expect the P.O. will be inundated with curious customers this morning."

"I can't believe Tom Evans allowed you to open this place already. Why, it was only yesterday that Emma was murdered."

"Apparently Evans and his crew know how to work quickly. I was pretty surprised when he called me last night and said he'd taken the seal off the building. But then he told me the postal authorities had requested the ground floor be reopened for business as soon as possible."

"I wish you'd had a little more time, Nikki."

Knowing exactly what her mother-in-law meant, Nikki gave Caroline an appreciative hug.

"Don't worry about me, mom. I'm over the shaky stage now. Mrs. Reiser's death certainly came as a shock, but now all I want to do is help find her killer. It's true Emma deceived me right along with everyone else in this town. Still, I learned a lot from her. She was kind to me, and she didn't deserve to die that way."

Their conversation was interrupted by a loud "you-who!" that echoed through the post office. Nikki rolled her eyes in mock exasperation.

"The doors haven't been unlocked five minutes and already the masses are descending on us! Come on up front with me. You can listen in on the gossip while I sell stamps."

Caroline reluctantly trailed after Martin's wife. She'd hoped for a cozy chat with Nikki, a mother-daughter bonding session meant to put her own mind at ease. But the girl seemed to be handling the murder fairly well today. Perhaps she'd misjudged Nikki's resilience.

"Good morning, dear. I hope those new commemoratives are finally here."

Mrs. Bertha Meyer, the baker's wife, resembled one of those sugary delicacies displayed in her husband's shop. A diminutive woman in height, she was amply proportioned in every other way with a face as round and plump as a bismarck punctuated by twin dots of licorice for eyes. Her head was capped by a crown of short fluffy hair the color of vanilla buttercream frosting. Below a set of double chins, her figure rolled downward in ever broadening stages with an imposing bosom topping a torso aptly described as butterball in shape. All this magnificence was firmly encased in a starched white apron peppered with splotches of strawberry jam beneath a fine dusting of powdered sugar.

Standing in the doorway with the morning sun bouncing off her shoulders, Mrs. Meyer resembled nothing less than a shimmering three-tiered wedding cake festooned with red roses and baby's breath. Caroline was so captivated by the little woman that she couldn't help but break into a grin.

"They haven't come in yet," she heard Nikki say. "I told you that last night when you called me at home."

The baker's wife had the decency to blush. "I thought perhaps today..."

Nikki shook her head. "Ben hasn't arrived yet today. If he brings them along with the other things I ordered, I'll put the first page aside and call you at the bakery."

Bertha heaved a mighty sigh, then broke into a fit of coughing as powdered sugar erupted from the bib of her apron.

"Oh, dear!" she cried. She swatted at the fine particles until they dispersed in the air. "I almost forgot my other reason for coming by." She waddled over to the counter and handed Nikki a brown paper sack. "I made these especially for you."

Nikki opened the bag and lifted out a fat chocolate donut. She smiled down at her benefactress. "My favorite breakfast food! Thank you, Mrs. Meyer."

"I knew you'd have lots of people coming in today," Bertha whispered conspiratorially. "It's always nice to be able to offer them a donut to go with their tea."

Caroline caught on long before Nikki and said, "I'll bet you could go for a cup of tea right about now, Mrs. Meyer. I know how early in the morning you and your husband start baking."

"That would be lovely, Mrs. Rhodes. I must say, I am a bit tired today. What with all the excitement yesterday, I hardly slept a wink all night. A little refreshment would perk me up nicely." Bertha unlatched the gate in the counter. "But don't you bother yourself over me. I know where the tea things are, so I'll start the water boiling and put the donuts out while you help Nikki with the customers. We'll be ready for company in no time flat!"

With a smile and a nod of her head, Bertha vanished into the back room.

"Customers? What customers?" Nikki asked with a frown.

"Those, I expect." Caroline pointed out the front window. From both ends of the square a half dozen women were rapidly converging on the post office. "Looks like a regular Rhineburg delegation."

The words were barely out of her mouth when the door flew open and Eleanor Naumann stepped over the threshold. Tall and angular, the woman clutched an oblong package to her flat breast with long bony fingers while hard on her heels came the rest of the group.

"Good morning!" the horse-faced Eleanor trilled. She thrust the package at Nikki with a nervous smile. "Been meaning to send this book to my sister in Baltimore for weeks now and just never got around to it. Today I said to myself, 'Eleanor, get your act together before it's too late!' I guess I was thinking of poor Emma. One tends to put things off and then, poof! The unexpected happens."

Eleanor's speech was well received by her companions. None of them believed that business about the book, still all applauded the tragic eloquence of her words with a respectful moment of silence. This was finally broken by a silver haired woman in sun glasses who treated Naumann to a pat on the shoulder before stating, "I know exactly what you mean, Ellie. I was going to wait until Saturday to buy my stamps, but really, there's no time like the present for getting chores done. God only knows what tomorrow will bring!"

Not to be outdone, the other ladies broke into a chorus of explanations as to their own reasons for visiting the post office. The common thread uniting them all seemed to be a sudden distrust of the immediate future.

The temporary postmistress tuned out the chitchat as she tallied the postage on Eleanor's book and sorted out stamps for the rest of her customers. Watching from the sidelines, Caroline was not so inclined to ignore the conversation. She listened first with amusement and then with growing interest as the women expounded on Emma's personality and habits. The group seemed indisposed to leave the post office, an oddity Caroline understood only after Mrs. Meyer emerged from the back room, thumped her fist on the service bell, and announced loudly,

"There's tea and donuts in the back room, ladies. Why don't you all come in and sit a spell?"

"Don't mind if we do," Eleanor replied for her friends. Chattering happily, the six of them filed past an astonished Nikki and headed for the rear of the building.

"Won't you join us?" Sarah Sonnenschein, Rhineburg's elderly head librarian, issued her invitation to Caroline in a whisper. "We've really come to see you, you know."

Nikki continued to stand there slack-mouthed, but Caroline rose to the occasion with a smile and a murmured thank you. She followed Ms. Sonnenschein into the back room where Mrs. Meyer was playing hostess.

"Pull up a chair, Mrs. Rhodes," the baker's wife commanded as she handed Caroline a cup of tea. She pointed to a tiny woman dressed in black who sat at the head of the table. "Agatha here saw some peculiar goings on the night of the murder. We figured you better hear her story first hand since it might help you track down Emma's killer."

Caroline nearly choked on her tea. She lowered her cup and looked Bertha straight in the eye.

"Mrs. Meyer, I am not, and I repeat *not*, involved in this investigation. I came here yesterday only because my daughter-in-law discovered Emma's body. The poor girl was naturally upset, and I did what I could to help her."

"Oh, poo!"

Agatha Hagendorf, proprietor of the Rhineburg Boarding House and Home for Gentle Women situated across the street from the post office's side entrance, registered total disdain for Caroline's statement with a toss of her blue rinsed curls.

"Of course you have no *official* role in the case, but we all know that FBI agent will get nowhere without your help. Look how he botched that business with the bomber. If it hadn't been for you..."

"We really do admire your work," interrupted Ms. Sonnenschein in a subdued voice.

"And you must realize, Mrs. Rhodes, that man is not one of us! He doesn't know the people of our town the way you do."

With vigorous nods and murmurs of approval, the others signaled their endorsement of Eleanor Naumann's viewpoint. Caroline felt her resolve crumbling under the weight of the group's flattery.

"I do feel like I'm a part of this town now," she conceded.

"I should hope so, Mrs. Rhodes," purred Bertha Meyer. "After all, you're a highly valued member of our community. Why, look at the work you do at the hospital. My John might have bled to death if you hadn't been on duty the day I brought him to ER."

"It was a very small cut, Mrs. Meyer. It only required a couple of stitches."

Bertha waved off the objection. "If you hadn't insisted he get a tetanus shot, John's hand might have become infected. I ask you now, what's a baker to do if he can't use his hands? No, Mrs. Rhodes, you mustn't underestimate your contributions to Rhineburg. Beside being an excellent nurse, you have a way of sniffing out the truth in puzzling situations."

"None of us have your talent for detecting," added Eleanor. "Or your experience."

The only thing Caroline detected at the moment was a full load of Rhineburg blarney being shoveled in her direction. Under other circumstances, it would have annoyed her to know that the ladies had staged this conversation, but she had to admit she was intrigued by Emma's murder. She was equally curious as to why the women were employing such devious tactics.

"And that nice Professor Atwater could help out again like he did last winter."

'That nice Professor Atwater' was currently in Caroline's doghouse. When she'd called him from the ER the night before, he'd dismissed her concerns in a rather cavalier manner. She'd been downright annoyed with her friend by the time they'd hung up, and remembering that now, she reacted without further hesitation.

"One does have a duty to the truth, ladies. If I can help point the FBI in the right direction, then I have no choice but to become involved. Now, Mrs. Hagendorf, why don't you tell me about your experience the night of the murder."

The woman in black, as Caroline had come to think of her, waited until she had everyone's undivided attention before launching into her story.

"It was quite late, well after midnight I'd say, and I was just about to close the drapes in my bedroom when this racket erupted across the street."

"You're sure of the time?" Caroline interrupted.

Agatha nodded. "I'd been viewing the stars through a telescope just as my husband Harold -- God rest his soul -- did every night for fifty-two years before his premature departure from this earth. After fixing each constellation in the sky, I rolled up Harold's star charts and made my preparations for bed. I turned down the blankets before stepping to the window to close the drapes. There was no light on at the time, and my eyes were adjusted to the dark when I peered down at the street."

"Just tell Mrs. Rhodes what you saw, Agatha," Eleanor Naumann commanded impatiently.

But Mrs. Hagendorf was not to be hurried. She took a bite of her donut, then a sip of tea before sighing, "I certainly will miss poor Emma. We shared many a fine conversation at this table."

"So did we all," Bertha Meyer muttered through clenched teeth. "Do get on with it, Agatha. I have to get back to the bakery."

Mrs. Hagendorf sniffed noisily as if to remind the other women just who was running this show. She did, however, condescend to continue.

"As I was saying, a racket erupted across the street. At first I thought it was a raccoon rummaging around in the garbage cans, but then I saw someone come stumbling out from behind the post office. There's a lamppost a few feet down the block, and the figure stumbled off in that direction. I didn't get a good look at the man, but the way he moved, I thought he must have been drinking. He was not at all steady on his feet."

"Could you describe the man?" Caroline asked.

"The first one was rather tall and broad in the shoulders," Agatha replied. "A robust, out-doorsy looking fellow. The other man appeared much shorter."

"Wait a minute! There were two men down in the street?"

"I wouldn't have mentioned the second one if he hadn't been there, now would I? Of course I didn't see them at the same time so I can't be exactly sure how tall either of them was. And then one ran up the street while the other went down the other way."

Caroline was now totally confused. She glanced at the faces of the other women in the room, but none of them seemed to share her problem.

"I'm afraid I'm not quite following you, Mrs. Hagendorf. You say one ran up the street..."

Agatha's head bobbed up and down. "Yes, dear. The two took off in opposite directions at different times. Looking down from the angle of my bedroom, it was difficult to compare their heights."

"I see," murmured Caroline, although she really didn't see at all. "Please go on."

"Well, as I thought he was nothing more than a common drunk, I didn't pay much attention to the first fellow. I closed the drapes, got into bed, and was just about to fall asleep when the noise started up all over again. Déjà vu, I thought, and I jumped up ready to haul open the window and give that drunk a piece of my mind. I was angry alright, but when I looked out I saw a different fellow, a skinny runt of a man whose arms flapped like chicken wings as he pranced down the street. I looked over at the post office, but there were no lights on in the building. I figured Emma had been lucky enough to sleep through the uproar." Agatha shook her head, her eyes suddenly bright with tears. "Now I wonder if she didn't hear all the ruckus because she'd already gone to her eternal rest."

There was dead silence in the room as the group contemplated Agatha's words. The little woman shook her head again, then looked up at Caroline.

"One of those men probably killed Emma," she said sadly. "Maybe you can figure out who it was."

"That's a matter for the police, don't you think?"

Eight heads swung round to face the doorway. Eight mouths fell open and then quickly shut again as Professor Carl Atwater entered the room, his eyes blazing with anger.

"What do you women think you're doing?" he roared. He pointed at Caroline. "She nearly got herself killed the last time she tried to solve a murder. Don't you think you should leave the detecting to those who are trained to do it?"

Caroline rose from her chair. "Now, Carl..."

"Don't 'Carl' me!" growled the Professor.

"I think we'd better be going," muttered Mrs. Meyer as she gathered up the last two donuts and whisked them back into the bag.

"I agree," chirped Mrs. Hagendorf. "I have quite a few chores to do."

"Not so fast," snarled Carl. He placed a hand on the elderly woman's arm as she tried to edge past him. "Your chores will have to wait, Agatha. You're coming with me to the police station where you'll repeat your story to Chief Moeller and FBI Agent Evans."

"Oh, no!" cried Agatha. "I really don't want to get involved!"

"You have no choice in the matter," Carl told her grimly. He shot a look at Caroline before dragging Agatha out the back door. "Stay put 'til I get back. I want to talk to you."

Caroline bit back an angry reply. Just who did Carl think he was ordering her about that way? She had half a mind to follow him, but the other ladies were now closing ranks around her.

"He has quite a temper, doesn't he?" whispered Sarah Sonnenschein.

"Typical man, if you ask me," replied Mrs. Naumann.

"I think we should go over to the boarding house and wait for Agatha to return," suggested a third woman whom Caroline had not been introduced to.

"Good thinking, Myrtle," said Mrs. Meyer. "I really must get back to the bakery, but Agatha will need some cheering up when she's done at the station. I'm sure she'll appreciate your being there."

No more was said on the subject of Caroline's involvement in the case until the entire crew had filed out the front door of the post office. Then Bertha Meyer turned back and with a thumbs-up gesture called out to Caroline,

"Don't worry about Professor Atwater, dear. We have every faith in your ability to handle this investigation on your own."

A crooked smile tugged at Caroline's lips. The baker's wife had opened a can of worms at this morning's tea party, and she now expected Caroline to clean up the mess. But how could she? Agatha Hagendorf was very nearly an eye witness to the murder of Emma Reiser. Her explosive testimony would undoubtedly prove to be the cornerstone of the prosecution's case against Professor Andrew Littlewort.

'They'll probably arrest him today,' Caroline thought.

And why not? He was the only man she knew of who not only fit Agatha's description of the high stepping, arm flapping stranger but also had a motive for killing Emma.

"What a pity," she mused aloud. "Especially since there's no way Andrew could have committed the crime."

CHAPTER 13

Professor Atwater's mood was subdued when he returned to the post office an hour later. With little more than a cursory nod to Nikki, he passed through the gate in the front desk and trudged towards the back room where Caroline was sorting a stack of outgoing mail.

"Evans means to arrest Andrew Littlewort," he said as he slid into a chair next to the table where his friend was working. "He's bringing him in for questioning right now."

"I figured he would," Caroline replied without looking up from the job at hand. "Given Agatha's testimony, he probably thinks he has a good case against the professor."

"They haven't found the murder weapon yet."

"Well, that's one thing in Littlewort's favor."

Caroline separated three letters from the pile and placed them to one side of the table. She continued to group the mail by zip code, her lips tightly compressed as she worked. Carl sat there quietly watching her. He couldn't miss the obvious signs of her displeasure and he ducked his head, concentrating his own anger on an open bag of rubber bands lying on the table. He fiddled with the bands until the silence in the room had dragged on for an uncomfortable length of time. Then he abruptly swept them aside and slapped the tabletop with both hands.

"See here, Caroline," he began.

Caroline raised one hand and fixed the Professor with a steely-eyed look that stopped him in his tracks.

"Don't use that tone of voice with me, Carl Atwater. You and I are friends, but you are not my father, my guardian, or my boss. You have no right to tell me what I can or can't do, and you especially have no right to embarrass me in public."

Carl's jaw went slack. "Embarrass you in public? Cari! I was only trying to prevent you from getting mixed up in another murder! Don't you remember what almost happened the last time you tangled with a killer?"

"I could hardly forget an experience like that," Caroline answered impatiently. "And how can you forget that it was you who involved me in that case in the first place?"

Carl opened his mouth to reply, then promptly shut it again.

"Exactly!" Caroline slapped the remaining letters on the table and pulled up a chair next to the Professor. "Listen to me, Carl. I don't know who killed Emma Reiser, but I'm pretty sure it wasn't Andrew Littlewort. Andrew is under suspicion because of you! And partly because of me," she added in a less intense tone of voice. "You could have stopped this rune stone nonsense at the start if you hadn't been so intent on embarrassing Garrison Hurst. And I should never have used Charlie Branch the way I did. I thought Hurst would be swayed by Charlie's objections and forbid the dig, but it didn't work out that way."

Carl stroked his beard to cover his discomfort.

"I'll admit my dislike of the Emperor may have clouded my judgment, but I believe Andrew would have mailed that stone to the Field Museum regardless of opposition from Hurst. If he later changed his mind and came back to the post office..."

"We know he returned here, Carl. Agatha clearly saw him."

"What she saw was a figure running away from the post office. There's no proof it was Andrew."

"Trust me on this," Caroline replied. "Agatha didn't tell us everything she knows, but she isn't lying about seeing Littlewort."

The Professor shook his head. "I don't want to think of Andrew as a killer, but maybe he did it, Cari."

"Good grief! Not you too, Carl." Caroline stood up and went back to sorting the mail. "It seems like every man I know has lost his senses in the past two days."

"And what's that supposed to mean?"

"It means none of you are seeing the obvious. Look, Carl. I feel partially responsible for what's happened here. Mrs. Meyer and the other ladies have asked me to look into this matter, and I intend to do just that. I'd appreciate your help, but if you're not willing..."

"Hello, Professor. Hi, Mrs. Rhodes."

Caroline and Carl turned simultaneously towards the doorway. Michael Bruck was standing there, a ledger in one hand and a six pack of cola in the other.

"I didn't mean to break into your conversation," he said with a smile, "but I'm here on official business. Jake Moeller asked me to take a look at Emma's computer programs." The head of security for Bruck University walked over to the table and glanced down at the mail. "I see Nikki's training you as her new assistant."

"Hardly," Caroline replied with a grin. She was genuinely fond of this blond giant who'd proved so helpful during last winter's troubles. The young man had a good head on his shoulders and a sympathetic manner to match. "But I thought the Chief was assigning a deputy to that job."

"Billy's too busy searching for the murder weapon, so I'm going to help out on the gambling end of the case."

"There's quite a setup upstairs."

"So I heard, Professor. By the way, shouldn't you be over at the college? Everything's just about set for the dress rehearsal."

Carl frowned and glanced down at his watch. "I didn't think it was this late already," he said as he got to his feet. "Will I see you at the practice, Cari?"

Caroline hesitated. "I'm not sure I'll make it. I need to stop in at the hospital and a couple of other places first."

Carl frowned again but he didn't push the matter. "Then I'll see you later tonight. Remember, the banquet starts at six o'clock."

"Don't worry. I'll meet you and Martin and Nikki by the Maypole around five-thirty."

Carl headed for the front door as Michael started upstairs. When she was sure both men were out of hearing range, Caroline picked up the phone and dialed the number for Mad Moeller's Antiques and Collectibles. The Chief's wife answered on the third ring.

"Madeline Moeller speaking. May I help you?"

"Maddy? It's Caroline Rhodes. I was wondering..."

"Oh, Caroline! Thank goodness you called. I've been so upset this morning, and I wanted to talk to you but I didn't know your phone number. Are you at home?"

"I'm at the post office, Maddy. I was wondering..."

"Stay right there! I'm on my way over."

Caroline pulled the receiver away from her ear as Madeline slammed down the telephone.

"Who was that?" Nikki had entered the room and was staring quizzically at her mother-in-law.

"Maddy Moeller," Caroline answered with a laugh. "It really is difficult to get a word in edgewise with that woman."

"You're telling me! She's a bit on the excitable side, but I hear she's an excellent saleswoman."

"She seemed to know her business when she was here yesterday. I was hoping to pump her for a little information."

"About what?" Nikki walked over to the tiny refrigerator next to the sink and took out a pitcher of iced tea. "I made this fresh today. Would you like a glass?"

Caroline nodded. "Carl says FBI Agent Evans is building a case against Andrew Littlewort. It looks like he'll be charged with the murder of Emma Reiser."

Nikki let out a low whistle. "Littlewort's a nut case, but I never thought he was crazy enough to kill someone."

"I don't think he did." Caroline accepted the glass Nikki proffered and walked over to the staircase where she stood staring at the steps while sipping the icy brew. "How tall was Emma?"

"How tall? I'd say about five foot nine or ten. She was a large woman, but due to her height she never appeared overweight."

"And how tall is Professor Littlewort?"

Nikki frowned. "About the same as me, five foot five inches."

"That's what I thought," said Caroline. She turned to her daughter-in-law and pointed to the stairs. "You found five foot nine Emma lying dead of a head injury at the bottom of this staircase. Assuming five foot five Andrew hit her with that rock, he'd have had to stand up on the second step to generate enough downward momentum to fracture her skull. You know what, Nikki? That scenario just doesn't make sense to me.

"The only other way he could have killed her was to swing the rock upward from the side and catch her at the base of the skull. I'm going to stop by the hospital later and see what I can find out about the autopsy."

"Hello, Nikki? Caroline? Are you back there?"

"Sounds like Madeline," said Nikki as she put down her drink and walked over to the doorway leading to the main room of the post office. "We're back here, Mrs. Moeller. Come join us."

CHAPTER 14

Ben arrived with the day's mail just as Madeline Moeller walked in the door of the Rhineburg post office. After the usual genial greetings, Ben and Nikki busied themselves at the front desk while Caroline and Maddy went off to the back room to discuss Emma's murder.

"Jake is fit to be tied," Maddy announced in a querulous voice. "This Evans character is behaving like he's God's gift to law enforcement while Jake is just some hillbilly sheriff with a mushroom for a brain. I tell you, Cari, it's maddening to be treated that way."

Caroline could easily commiserate with the Chief. "I know how Jake feels. I had my own problems with Mr. Evans last winter."

"So I heard. And that's why I immediately thought of you when Jake came home last night all upset over this RICO business."

"You thought of me? Whatever for?"

"Well, you outwitted Evans once before. I thought maybe you'd like to do it again."

Caroline raised one eyebrow and stared at the Chief's wife.

"Maddy, I'm not sure where you're heading with all this, but I must tell you I know about the mix-up with the RICO regulations. Evans came to see me at work last night and he referred to it in passing."

"I'm sure he did," Maddy retorted. "He's probably been laughing himself sick ever since Jake made the mistake of mentioning it to him. But I assure you, Cari, Jake made an honest mistake. No policeman can possibly keep track of every little nuance in the law."

Caroline considered the distinction between dead and alive to be more than a nuance, but she refrained from saying so. Instead, she tried to calm her fiery visitor with soothing words.

"Maddy, you don't need to defend your husband to me or anyone else in this town. I've heard a lot of good things about Jake from people whose opinions I respect. It's true he's under a bit of pressure right now, but he'll survive."

"You don't understand, Caroline. My Jake is a proud man. Being made a fool of first by Emma and then by this FBI jerk is really tearing him up. I tell you, it's shaken his self-confidence."

The two women stared at each other in silence for a moment before Caroline got up from the table and went over to the refrigerator. She took out the iced tea and poured them each a glass.

"Let's cut to the chase, Maddy," she said as she handed the antique dealer her drink. "You said you want to outwit Tom Evans. How do you intend to do it? Where do I fit in to the plan?"

Madeline pushed her tea aside and looked Caroline straight in the eye.

"Jake is all I have, Caroline. He means the world to me, and I won't let him be destroyed by the gossip that's bound to spring up over this murder. People will say he should have known what Emma was up to long ago. They'll make fun of him and laugh behind his back over this stupid RICO business." She paused and took a deep breath before continuing. "I want Jake to catch Emma's killer before Tom Evans does. I want people to respect him again, and I want him to respect himself. It's as simple as that, Caroline."

Caroline nodded. Having once loved a man herself, she understood the pain the other woman was experiencing.

"Tell me something, Maddy. Have you heard that Evans is planning to charge Professor Andrew Littlewort with Emma's murder?"

"Really? When did that happen?"

Caroline filled Madeline in on the morning's events. The Chief's wife listened intently, interrupting only once or twice with questions. When Caroline explained why she thought Evans was arresting the wrong man, Maddy perked up considerably.

"Your reasoning makes perfect sense to me, and I'm sure it will to Jake also. I propose we join forces, Caroline. I'll pass on every bit of information I can worm out of my husband, and you use it the best way you can. If you need any other kind of help ... "

"Let's settle one point before we go any further," Caroline insisted. "I have my own reasons for getting involved in this case. None of them have to do with pursuing a vendetta against Tom Evans. True, I don't like the man, but I won't obstruct justice by withholding information if he asks for it."

"I have no problem with that," Maddy said with a shrug. "We'll just make sure Jake hears everything first."

"That's fine with me," Caroline agreed. "So what do you say we get down to work? I have lots of questions that need answering."

Maddy pulled out a notebook and a pen. "Shoot, boss."

"First of all, how did the killer get into the post office?"

"I can answer that one." Nikki walked into the room with a mail sack over her shoulder. She tossed the bag on a shelf and pulled a chair up to the table. "I take it you two are unofficially working on this case."

"We're just sharing some ideas," Madeline murmured.

"Don't worry about me blowing the whistle on you," Nikki said as she sat down. "I want to help catch this killer too."

Madeline looked over at Caroline with raised eyebrows.

"Nikki has her own special interest in this matter," Caroline told her. She turned to her daughter-in-law. "If we discover anything of value, we take it to Chief Moeller. He's the action man this time. We only work on ideas. So tell me how the killer got in."

Nikki pointed to a small door set back under the staircase. "That leads down to the basement. There's an outside entrance below ground level on the alley side of the building. You reach it by a flight of stairs."

"I take it the door is usually locked."

"The outside one was, but the lock was pretty old and rusty. Not much of a deterrent for criminals."

"This upstairs door was open?"

"Unlocked but not open."

"Anybody could have known about that entrance," Caroline mused. "What about footprints, Maddy? Did Jake find any?"

"Oh sure. The ground back there was soft from all the rain so there were plenty of impressions. The problem was, there were too many impressions. Jake said it looked like an army marched past that back door."

"Nothing they could use?"

"Jake didn't think so, but then Evans arrived with his team and they took over both inside and out. Jake and his men have been spending their time searching for that rune stone."

"So they haven't found the weapon yet?"

Maddy shook her head. "I talked to Jake before I came over here, and they were still looking."

"If Evans pulled Professor Littlewort in for questioning, he probably got a search warrant for his house. I'm sure they'll hunt for the stone over there."

"And if they find it?"

"Then we have a problem, Nikki." Caroline stood up and began to pace the room. "Andrew just doesn't have the personality of a cold-blooded killer, and be assured this was a cold-blooded killing."

"My husband says the Professor has a terrible temper. He didn't seem at all concerned about Emma's death until Jake started questioning him. Then he flew into a rage and demanded a lawyer."

"Which is a point in his favor, strange as it may seem. Think about it, ladies. If Andrew had killed Emma, wouldn't he try to cover it with a show of concern rather than a display of anger? The man is a typical coward. He intimidates people with his raving and ranting, but that's as far as it ever goes. When he's done reaming you out, he simply turns around and walks away."

"You know, mom, you're right. I use to watch him in class. He always picked on people who wouldn't, or couldn't, stand up to him. Maybe they lacked self-confidence, or it just wasn't in their nature to fight back."

"Blessed are the meek," Maddy murmured.

"Emma was anything but meek," Caroline responded. She walked over to the back door and opened it. "I want to have a look at the alley. Agatha says she saw two men back there the night of the murder, but according to the Chief there were enough footprints to account for several people."

Madeline and Nikki followed her outside, Nikki pointing the way to the basement entrance. The alley was a typical clay and gravel affair bordered by a wide dirt strip on both sides. Weeds grew on the opposite side of the alley, but the strip near the post office was clean of debris.

"Emma always planted annuals back here," Nikki told the others. "She was waiting for Memorial Day to put them in."

"So we're in luck," Caroline commented as she stooped to examine the churned up dirt. The ground had dried to a hardened mass since the night of the murder. Overlapping ridges and gullies could be seen on both sides of the entranceway, and there was dried mud on the steps leading down to the basement. While the signs clearly indicated the presence of more than one person, no single footprint was distinguishable from the rest.

They were about to go back inside when something caught Caroline's eye. She bent down to get a closer look.

"What do you think this is?" she asked the others.

Maddy shrugged her shoulders. "All I see are some dried up grass clippings imbedded in the dirt."

"And a couple pieces of yellow straw," Nikki added.

Caroline stood up and looked Nikki straight in the eye.

"Think, girl. Where did those clippings come from? Where have you seen fresh straw recently laid?"

Nikki's hand flew to her mouth. "Oh my gosh! Bruck Green!"

Caroline nodded. "Branch mowed the Green right before the students put up the Festival tents. He was there supervising when they scattered straw over the jousting field." She turned to Maddy. "Get Jake to come over and see this. Then urge him to interrogate Charlie."

"But why?"

"Charlie was opposed to Andrew sending his rock to Chicago. He was afraid people would invade the campus looking for more rune stones. The night of Emma's murder Charlie got drunk at the Blue Cat Lounge. Carl and I ended up taking him home, and when we put him to bed I peeled off his boots. Maddy, they were caked with grass clippings and straw."

"It looks," said Maddy, "like we have another suspect!"

CHAPTER 15

Caroline swung off the highway and took the road leading to the university campus. She hadn't waited for Jake to arrive at the post office, preferring instead to seek out Carl and fill him in on the news. Now as she turned onto Circle Road she wondered if she'd done the right thing. Pointing a finger at Charlie might help Andrew Littlewort, but it certainly bode ill for the gardener. Besides that, it increased Caroline's feelings of guilt.

If Charlie Branch had killed Emma while in a drunken stupor, it was at least partially her fault. She was the one who'd told him about the rune stone and egged him into confronting President Hurst at the faculty meeting. She was also the one who'd assured Carl that Charlie was so intoxicated he'd sleep straight through the night.

That part of it still puzzled her. Carl had said he'd never seen Branch take a drink, yet Caroline's experience told her only true alcoholics recovered from a binge so quickly. Maybe Branch drank only at home. She'd seen no evidence of it in the living room or den. Still, she hadn't investigated Charlie's kitchen.

'I slipped up,' she thought in disgust. 'Some ER nurse I am.'

Contemplating the mess she'd created, Caroline took no notice of the activities on Bruck Green as she pulled into the driveway of St. Anne's Hospital. She turned into the parking garage, nosed the Jeep up the narrow ramp, and drove to the second level where she parked and locked the car. Minutes later she was crossing the driveway headed for the Emergency Room entrance.

"Hi, Cari. How's it going?"

Jane Gardner was just walking out when Caroline passed through the first set of automatic doors labeled 'ER'. The two women stopped to chat in the enclosed passage between the inner and outer entrances.

"I'm glad I ran into you," said Caroline. "I need some information, and you're just the person who can give it to me."

"If it's about that mix-up with the paychecks..."

"No, no, nothing like that. I need to see a copy of the autopsy report on Emma Reiser, and I need it today if possible."

"Wow! You don't ask for much, do you?" Jane replied with a grin. "I'd love to help you out on this one, Caroline, but I'm just leaving for the day. I have a class over at the university in twenty minutes, and I can't miss it."

"I understand. Do you know if Paul Wakely's on duty today?"

"Yeah." Jane thumbed over her shoulder. "He's sewing up a kid on Cart One. Look, Caroline, I have to run. Are you going to the Festival banquet tonight?"

"Wouldn't miss it for the world."

"Great. I'll see you on the Green then."

Jane headed out the door with a backward wave of her hand while Caroline stood in the entranceway considering her next move. Paul was probably too busy to see her, but he seemed the best bet as a source of information. It didn't seem likely the morgue attendant would let her in to view Emma's body if, in fact, the corpse was still there and not already at the funeral parlor.

"Why didn't I think of the undertaker?" Caroline muttered. "He'd be able to tell me exactly where the injury was."

Probably because you've been worrying about too many other things, she told herself.

"Are you going to stand there all day?"

Caroline came out of her reverie with a start. She spun around and found Paul Wakely standing in the inner doorway grinning from ear to ear.

"Gathering wool out here?" he joked.

"At the moment I feel like my brain is made of the stuff." Caroline shook her head as she walked towards the doctor. "I get so preoccupied at times that I forget where I am."

"Bad sign, Mrs. Rhodes. Sounds like you're suffering from detection overload. I prescribe a nice vacation away from solving murder cases."

"And who says I'm doing any detecting, Dr. Wakely?"

Paul just laughed as he stepped back and let Caroline pass by him. The two friends walked through the triage area and into the main room where a couple of nurses were attending to half a dozen patients on carts.

"Busy day," Caroline noted. She sank down on a chair behind the desk and waved to one of her co-workers who was bandaging a cut on the head of a five-year-old. "Have you got a minute to talk, Paul?"

"Sure." Paul jerked his head in the direction of the six filled cubicles. "All those folks are waiting for test results and per usual, the lab is short of help. Until I get some answers there's little more I can do for them. So tell me about Emma's murder. I hear Agatha Hagendorf had quite a tale to tell you."

Caroline rolled her eyes in disbelief. "I'll never understand how news travels so quickly in this town. I only met Mrs. Hagendorf a few hours ago and already you've got the scoop on the story."

"Credit the Rhineburg grapevine. It's a marvelous instrument of communication in this town."

"So how do you manage to tap in to it when you're stuck in the ER all day?"

"Very easily. Every time another patient comes in I simply ask, 'So what's new?'. It's amazing how eager people are to tell me the latest gossip."

"Hmm. Well, I hope you're as eager to open up to me."

"About what?"

"I need a copy of the autopsy report on Emma Reiser."

"What for?"

"So I can find out the exact location of Emma's head injury."

Paul rocked back in his chair and ran the fingers of one hand through his short sandy hair. "Why are you getting mixed up in this, Caroline? You were almost killed last winter when you investigated the bombing here at St. Anne's."

"Now you're beginning to sound like Carl Atwater. The Professor's not too happy with what I'm doing either, but I have good reasons for getting involved, Paul. Trust me on this one."

Paul stared at her for a moment before replying, "Just be careful, OK? We can't afford to lose a good nurse in this place."

"Can you get me the report?"

Paul shook his head. "I don't have the authority for that. But since I pronounced her when she came in, I can tell you what killed her. Emma died of massive trauma to the brain from a blow to the roof of the cranium. She had a depressed skull fracture involving both parietal bones. I saw no other injuries to the rest of her body."

"Was the fracture closer to the frontal bone or the occipital?"

"The frontal," Paul answered instantly. "I'd say it was just posterior to the coronal suture and bisected the sagittal suture."

"In other words, top and center."

Paul nodded. "It was a nasty injury with some extrusion of brain matter. I don't blame the paramedics for their initial assessment of the trauma as fall related. The torn gown and the fact she was found at the foot of the staircase indicated to them that Emma took a tumble. Since they were taught that skull fractures are common complications in elderly folks who have fallen, they automatically assumed that was the case with Mrs. Reiser. As soon as I saw it, though, I knew that wound was caused by something other than a wooden stair. The shape of the wound and the amount of bone depression just weren't right for the scenario described by the EMTs."

"How much force would it take to create that kind of fracture?" Caroline asked.

"I'm not an expert," Paul responded, "but I'd guess whoever did it was no weakling. Emma's skull was pretty well bashed in."

Caroline wrinkled her nose. "Her death couldn't have been unintentional. You don't hit someone that hard without meaning to."

Paul nodded a second time. "I'd say that pretty well sums it up. If I were trying to analyze our murderer, I'd credit the guy with a vicious personality."

"Labs results on Mr. Miller." One of the nurses on duty walked over to where they were sitting and handed Paul a computer printout. "His potassium level is really low. Do you want me to hang a 'K' rider?"

Caroline slipped away from the desk as Paul and the nurse conferred on their patient. She'd gotten the information she needed to confirm her belief in Andrew Littlewort's innocence. Now all she had to do was convince Tom Evans he was pursuing the wrong man.

Knowing the FBI agent, that wouldn't be an easy thing to do.

CHAPTER 16

After a quick lunch in the hospital cafeteria, Caroline left St. Anne's and went in search of Carl Atwater. She found him on Bruck Green supervising a mock sword fight between two earnest young men.

"Use your shield, Arnold. This has got to look real."

"It looks real enough to me," Caroline said as she drew level with the white-haired professor of history. "Unless you're waiting for a little blood to flow."

"It better not," growled Carl without taking his eyes off the boys. "I don't need any more casualties among this group. We've already lost one boy to a strained knee ligament, and another fellow was stepped on by his horse. Damned nag broke the kid's foot."

"Sounds like you have problems."

"I had to get replacements for both of them or we would have been short a couple of knights. It wasn't easy finding two more men who could ride well enough to control both a horse and a jousting pole. Thank goodness Charlie was willing to help out."

"Charlie Branch?" Caroline said in surprise. "He's going to substitute for one of the injured students?"

The Professor nodded. "He's filled in for riders in past years, so he more or less knows the routine. Sid Burke volunteered to replace the kid with the broken foot. One thing I'll say for Sid. He really knows how to handle a horse."

"I hate to break this to you, Carl, but you'd better look for another surrogate knight. I have a feeling Charlie's not going to be available tomorrow."

Carl looked at her sharply. "Why not?"

"He may be spending the day in the police station answering questions about Emma Reiser's murder."

The Professor's jaw went slack. He stared at Caroline for a moment, then turned abruptly and called out to the two boys on the field.

"That's enough for now. Go check out your costumes, and tell the others to do the same."

He turned back to Caroline and took her by the arm. "Let's take a walk. I'd rather the students didn't hear any of this."

They left the jousting field and strolled aimlessly about the Green, Caroline updating the Professor as they went. When they reached a row of benches stationed along the center path, Carl called for a halt and sank down wearily on one of the hard wooden seats.

"What a mess, Caroline." The Professor passed a chubby hand over the Santaesque features of his face. "It certainly would help if Agatha could identify the two men she saw in the alley."

"She could if she wanted to," Caroline replied. "Of that I'm convinced."

Carl's bushy white eyebrows shot up in surprise. "You think Agatha's holding out on us? But why?"

"I haven't quite figured that out yet. It's obvious, though, that this morning's little tea party was prearranged by Mrs. Meyer and her gang of silver-haired senior citizens. Bertha phoned Nikki at home last night. She supposedly called about some commemorative stamps she'd ordered, but the woman actually wanted to find out if Nikki and I would be in the post office today. When Nikki opened for business this morning, Bertha and her buddies were the first to show up. Bertha brought a bag of donuts, and before you could say 'pop goes the weasel', she and the other ladies were parked around the table in the back room."

"Then Mrs. Meyer was the ring leader of the group."

Caroline nodded. "She instructed Agatha as to what she should and should not say. Bertha and another woman, Eleanor Naumann, kept Agatha pretty well in line during the entire conversation."

"So they were setting you up."

"You've got it, Carl. First they buttered me up like I was an ear of corn at a Sunday picnic. They paid me every compliment under the sun until I agreed to help them. Then Mrs. Hagendorf described Professor Littlewort to a 'T' while claiming she couldn't really tell who he was. The other man she saw, the inebriated one, was obviously Charlie Branch. Agatha said he was tall, broad shouldered, and had an 'out-doorsy' appearance. Maybe there were a few other drunks in Rhineburg that night, but the only one I know of who had any reason at all to be near the post office was Charlie."

"They wanted you to take this story to the police," Carl said.

"I think so," agreed Caroline. "They must have thought they could keep Agatha in the clear if I was the one to rat on Andrew and Charlie. Like I said before, I'm not sure why they decided to use me, but I aim to find out. Later tonight I intend to pay a visit to the Rhineburg Boarding House and Home for Gentle Women."

"Mind if I come along?" asked the Professor.

"Not at all. But I thought you didn't approve of my investigating this murder."

Carl shifted his position on the bench. He looked out over the Green, his jaw set and his eyes suddenly less troubled.

"Now that you've told me all this, I don't see that I have any choice but to help." He pushed himself up off the bench and reached in his back pocket for his pipe. "I owe it to Andrew and Charlie. And to you."

Caroline smiled at her friend. "I knew I could count on you," she said as she hooked her arm in his and started off down the path. "We make a good team, Carl Atwater. If we put our heads together, we're bound to come up with a few answers."

"Let's just hope they're the right ones," grunted Carl. He suddenly stopped dead in his tracks. "Well, look over there now. If it isn't Congressman Morgan Burke with our dearly beloved President."

Caroline looked in the direction Carl was pointing. As usual, the sight of Garrison Hurst caused her stomach muscles to tighten in apprehension. A tall balding man in his early sixties, Hurst was as lean as Andrew Littlewort, but there the similarity ended. Where Littlewort was clumsy and awkward, Hurst carried himself like a king in his castle. His suits were expertly tailored to hide his spindly arms and scrawny chest, and he wore only the most expensive ties and leather shoes. If it hadn't been for the coldness in his hooded eyes, one might have been impressed with the man. As it was, those dark pools of granite behind horn-rimmed glasses were so off-putting that many people felt uneasy in his presence.

Apparently Morgan Burke was not so affected by the President. Younger than Hurst by a half dozen years, and taller by two or three inches, Burke was a well built man with a full head of salt and pepper hair. His clothes were equivalent to Garrison's in price and style, but unlike the President, Burke had no need to hide his physique. Here was a man who worked out on a daily basis. His shoulders were naturally broad, and his upper body was sculptured by exercise to match.

Burke's brow was furrowed and his full lips compressed as he listened intently to whatever the President was saying. Caroline imagined he'd be quite handsome with a smile replacing that frown.

"I see where Sid gets his good looks," she murmured. "Has the Congressman come for the Festival, or do you imagine he's here because of Emma's murder?"

"He usually attends any major activity here," Carl responded. "It's good for his image, and like I told you before, he's bound and determined his son will graduate from this school. He's smooth-talked Sid out of more than one jam since the boy arrived at Bruck."

"Oh dear, Carl. It looks like they've seen us, and they're coming our way."

Atwater groaned, but he held his ground as the two men approached.

"Good afternoon, Professor." Hurst nodded to Carl before turning to Caroline. "Mrs. Rhodes, I would like you to meet Congressman Morgan Burke."

Burke extended a hand to Caroline. "I'm pleased to meet you, Mrs. Rhodes. President Hurst has just been telling me how you saved the university from quite a bit of embarrassment last winter."

Caroline returned the Congressman's smile with one of her own. "It was unfortunate that the FBI felt it necessary to examine the school's student records," she replied. "Still, it's understandable in a case like that. The police are forced to suspect everyone."

"The Congressman and I were just discussing the problem of Emma Reiser's murder," Hurst purred. "I was hoping I could persuade you to lend your talents to the school one more time."

"In what way could I be of help, President Hurst?"

The President glanced at Morgan Burke, but the Congressman's face was set in a look of polite interest only.

"Congressman Burke thinks it would be better if we left this matter to the police," began Hurst. "I, on the other hand, feel the school has a responsibility to protect its faculty if at all possible. I have been told that Andrew Littlewort is being detained by the police on suspicion of murder. They apparently feel that unfortunate business with the rune stone gave Andrew some kind of motive for killing Emma Reiser. Of course that's a lot of nonsense, but we all know how stubborn the police can be once they've decided on a course of action."

"From what I've heard, they have a pretty good case against your professor," Burke said mildly. "I really think it's unnecessary to waste this lady's time, Garrison."

"Do you realize the kind of publicity we'll get if Littlewort is put on trial?" Hurst's voice soared from petulant to shrill as he objected to Burke's assessment of the situation. "Last winter was bad enough, Morgan, but if the parents start believing one of our teachers is a murderer, they'll pull their students right out of Bruck. This could harm us irreparably."

"You're getting worked up over nothing, Garrison. If the FBI make a quick arrest, this'll all blow over during the summer. When school starts in the fall, you'll find your classrooms full again." Burke turned to Caroline with a smile. "Don't you agree, Mrs. Rhodes?"

"Actually, Congressman..."

"President Hurst is correct when he says we'll lose students," interrupted Carl. He looked over at Hurst who stared back in shock and suspicion. "We agree on very little, Garrison, but this time I'm backing you. Neither Caroline nor I believe Andrew Littlewort is a murderer. Given a little time, and the cooperation of the university, we intend to prove Andrew's innocence."

Burke threw back his head and laughed.

"Get lucky once and you suddenly think you're smarter than the police. Well, who am I to stop you? Just keep me informed, Garrison. I hate to be caught unawares by the press."

Morgan nodded to Caroline and Carl, then strode off in the direction of Bruck Hall. Hurst watched him go with some annoyance.

"Burke's a typical politician." The President spat out the last word as if it had a filthy taste to it. "He doesn't understand what's going on here at Bruck. He just wants to profit from his association with us." He squared his shoulders. "Well, we'll have to proceed without his blessing. Let me know if I can be of any help to your investigation, Mrs. Rhodes." His eyes swiveled in Carl's direction and he nodded slightly. "Good day, Professor Atwater."

Carl chuckled as the President hurried off after Burke.

"If he thinks he has troubles now, just wait until he hears about Charlie Branch."

"You're right," agreed Caroline. "It's bad enough having one Bruck employee suspected of murder, but having two of them detained by the police is a downright nightmare."

"It couldn't get worse than that, could it?"

If Carl had been a betting man, he would have lost his shirt on that last statement.

CHAPTER 17

"Make a way for the Duke and Duchess of Rhineburg!"

"No, no, no! Not 'make a way'. It's just plain 'make way'." A frazzled looking woman in an olive drab sweater and beige slacks pounded her fist on one of the long wooden tables set up for the evening's feast. "How many times must we go over this before you people get it right?"

Caroline suppressed a smile as she meandered about the Green observing the students at practice. Most had their parts down pat while a few who were obviously new to this game looked about in confusion when asked to perform. On the whole, the rehearsal was going quite well. The week ahead promised to be interesting.

She was almost abreast of the fortune teller's tent when Caroline spied Morgan Burke over by the jousting field. The Congressman was deep in conversation with Charlie Branch, and while she couldn't make out their words, Caroline could tell the two men were arguing. The discussion ended abruptly with the arrival of Sid Burke. Morgan said something to his son who seemed at first to object, but then fell silent when the elder Burke turned on his heel and strode off towards Bruck Hall. Sid hesitated before jogging off after his father. Charlie also started to follow. He was brought up short by the voice of Jake Moeller calling to him from across the lawn.

The Chief was down on one knee gathering bits of straw from the jousting field. He motioned to Branch to join him.

"Milady seems troubled by what she sees."

Caroline spun around to find a young girl standing at her elbow. The child was perhaps ten years old, and she was dressed in the same medieval garb as the other performers at the faire, though on her the clothing seemed to be normal attire rather than a costume. The cross-laced maroon bodice covering her long sleeved collarless blouse was patched and faded from wear. It barely overlapped the waistband of a long coffee colored skirt that grazed the tips of scuffed black slippers. Greasy stains streaked the cotton a dark walnut where grubby fingers had rubbed the material, and the hemline was frayed and torn.

None of this seemed to bother the girl who gazed up at the older woman with a poise and bearing that belied her age. Through eyes the color of violets in spring, the child briefly studied Caroline before continuing the one sided conversation.

"Perhaps my grandmother could be of assistance."

Before Caroline could reply, the child took her by the hand and led her to the entrance of the fortune teller's tent.

"Wait in there." She pulled back the flap and pointed to the dimly lit interior where a table and two folding chairs filled most of the visible space. "I'll go get her."

The child ran off leaving Caroline with no choice but to enter the tent.

'Why am I doing this,' she wondered as she pulled out one of the chairs and sat down. Any moment now some college student would appear and go through the pretense of predicting her future with a phony crystal ball. Well, it was all part of the fun of a Renaissance Faire, and the kids did need someone to practice on before the big show started tonight. 'It might as well be me,' she mused with a sigh of resignation.

"The child says you are in need, and the little one is rarely wrong."

Caroline had expected her 'gypsy' to make a grand entrance at the front of the tent, but the grizzled old woman now walking towards her had emerged instead from behind one of the many curtains lining the inside walls. Wrapped in a black shawl, and supported by a cane the likes of which Caroline had never seen before, the woman stopped just short of the table and stared at her guest through narrowed eyes.

"Yes, I see that you are indeed worried. Something is very wrong, isn't it?"

Her speech was so guttural and heavily accented that at first Caroline had difficulty understanding her. Then she realized that part of the problem was due to the woman's coarse breathing. Caroline rose from her chair and crossed to the fortune teller's side.

"Let me help you," she said as she pulled out the other folding chair. "How long have you had this lung problem?"

The old lady waved Caroline off. "Too many years to count. Some days are worse than others. Today is one of them." She motioned Caroline back to her chair. "There are several methods for divining the future. You may choose tarot cards, runes, or..."

"Did you say runes? Like in rune stones?"

"The runes are pictographic symbols of certain forces in nature that affect our lives. Some early alphabets were comprised of runes, and at one time runes were carved into stone to tell stories or serve as memorials."

Caroline leaned forward, suddenly anxious to learn more about this woman.

"Wait a minute, please. I was under the impression that this...this fortune telling business was...well, just a fun kind of event run by the students. But you're not...I mean..."

The old woman smiled. "No, I am not a student at this school. My name is Maria Gregori, and I am Rom. To you, Rom means gypsy. To me, it means family. The Rom are my people, my family."

"And this is how you earn your living?"

"In the summer my grand-daughter and I go from fair to fair doing what we know how to do. The little one, Bricole, takes after me. We have what some call 'second sight'. I call it the 'gift'."

She's for real, Caroline thought. Or at least she thinks she's for real.

"I'd like you to tell me about one particular rune." Caroline pulled a scrap of paper and a pen from her pocket and started to draw. "I saw this carved on a stone the other day."

Maria looked at the drawing Caroline had made and shrugged her shoulders.

"That is Thurisaz, the rune associated with protection and luck, except that in your drawing it is reversed. If the rune was upright, it would indicate unexpected good luck. When it is reversed, it may mean your luck is running out. You must make no hasty decisions at this time because they are based on a weakness within yourself, and you will live to regret them. If you deceive yourself concerning your motives, you will create severe problems that you may not be able to rectify."

"You've got to be kidding. That one rune says all that?"

"I do not kid when it comes to explaining the runes," Maria said with a trace of annoyance in her voice. "Now I will see why you are so bothered, and what will come of it."

Maria withdrew a deck of cards from the pocket of her long black skirt. She shuffled the deck before placing the cards one at a time face up on the table. Each move in the deal brought a deeper scowl to her face until she could apparently stand it no longer. She gathered up the deck and thrust it back into her pocket.

"Something wrong?" Caroline inquired.

"Very much so. I do not know what is happening here, but there is something wicked in the air, something that threatens us all. We are surrounded by death and there is no way to stop it. No way at all."

Maria Gregori got to her feet. She swayed as she turned from the table, and Caroline jumped up to catch her. The old woman shook her off. She started towards the back of the tent, supporting herself with her cane, then suddenly stopped and looked back at Caroline.

"Go now, lady, and do not come back. I beg you, stay away from Bricole!"

CHAPTER 18

Caroline returned to the nursing dormitory to change into something more appropriate for the festival banquet. A slight breeze had sprung up, and the temperature, although still mild, was definitely falling. It was bound to get cooler as the evening wore on.

Her mind was occupied with thoughts of Maria Gregori as she slipped into a gray ribbed turtleneck sweater and navy corduroy slacks. The nurse in her wondered about Maria's lung disease. If the woman traveled as much as she said, she probably didn't see a doctor on a regular basis. That fact alone portended trouble for the old lady.

On a more personal note, Caroline wondered what she'd said or done to disturb Maria so badly. The woman had pushed her away when she'd tried to help, and her warning to stay away from Bricole was more a command than a request.

It had to have been the tarot cards that did it. Caroline knew next to nothing about tarot reading, but she'd once worked with a hospital secretary who firmly believed in the power of the cards to foretell the future. The little she'd gleaned from conversations with the woman led her to believe that certain cards, when placed next to each other, predicted death and destruction.

The deck must have fallen that way this afternoon. Perhaps in Maria's mind the coming disaster was linked to Caroline, maybe even caused by her. That would certainly account for the sudden change in the fortune teller's behavior towards her guest.

Caroline chose a fleece lined winter jacket from the closet. She slipped a pair of brown suede gloves into one pocket and a pale blue scarf into the other. Gathering up her keys, she locked the door of the apartment, and headed towards the stairs leading to the lobby of the dormitory.

Outside the building, the wind had died down to a whisper. The excited laughter of students at work on the Green floated towards her as Caroline made her way down the dormitory driveway and over to Circle Road. She was just about to cross the street when a jaunty little sports car pulled up to the curb next to her. Madeline Moeller leaned over from the driver's side and rolled down open window.

"Just the person I was looking for. Hop in, Caroline. I've got lots to tell you." Maddy swung back into traffic as Caroline buckled on her seatbelt. "I've been all around town today, and did people ever clam up when they saw me coming. I felt like the Black Plague descending on Europe."

Caroline chuckled. "You mean no one rolled out the red carpet for the police chief's wife?"

"Hardly. The only placed I scored was at the Dip-N-Do. There was a bevy of women in the beauty shop when I arrived, but by the time Dolores finished my cut, rinse, and set, I was the only one left to talk to. Since Dolores can't resist passing on the latest gossip, I let her yack away to her heart's content."

"I assume you inserted a few appropriate questions into the conversation."

Maddy looked properly shocked as she replied, "But of course! And, boy! Did I get results." She pulled into the university parking lot, and nosed the car into a slot between two pick-up trucks. "First of all, though, let me tell you about the rune stone. It still hasn't been found. The FBI searched Andrew Littlewort's place today.

Practically tore the house apart according to Jake. They also went up and down the alley behind the post office. They raked through every patch of weeds and emptied every garbage can without success."

"The FBI may never find that rock," said Caroline. "It could be in the bottom of the river by now. Or the killer might have thrown it away in the forest."

Maddy nodded agreement. "Jake says it'll take a miracle for that stone to show up."

"What about Charlie Branch? I saw your husband earlier this afternoon gathering samples of straw from the jousting field. He called out to Charlie, but I was distracted by the granddaughter of the fortune teller, and I didn't see what happened next."

"Jake pulled him in for questioning, but Charlie didn't admit to anything. Tom Evans was no help either. He claimed the straw and grass we found could have come from anywhere around here. With so many farms surrounding Rhineburg, he does have a point."

"Yes, but give me the name of one farmer who had a motive to kill Emma."

"Someone who couldn't pay off his betting debts?"

Caroline sighed. "There's always that possibility. Until Michael Bruck comes up with some answers from Emma's computer, I'm afraid we're stuck on that one."

"Maybe not," said Maddy. "Dolores had quite a bit to say about some people and their possible gambling habits. Come on. Let's go find the Nikki and the men. I'll tell you all about Dolores while we're walking."

Maddy locked up the car, and the two women headed towards Bruck Green. The grassy oval was a beehive of activity as students rushed about putting the final touches on the tables and booths. Fires glowed at the north end of the Green where several large grills had been set up. The smell of barbecued chicken and ribs filled the air, and Caroline's mouth watered in anticipation.

Maddy had just begun to describe her trip to the hairdresser when Caroline caught sight of Martin and Nikki in the distance.

"Hold that thought," she told the other woman. "I'd like Professor Atwater to hear this story also. Are you and Jake going to join us at our table?"

"We'd love to, Cari. You know, Jake is so embarrassed over all this business with Emma that he didn't even want to come tonight. He still thinks people will be laughing at him, but I told him it's better to stand up and face the crowd than hide away at home like he had something to be ashamed of." The tiny woman pushed a pumpkin colored curl away from her forehead in a dismissive gesture. "Who cares what the town thinks anyway? Jake's been a darned good Chief of Police for many a year, and one little incident shouldn't turn folks against him."

"Of course not, Maddy. Personally, I haven't heard anyone criticize your husband. I'm glad you talked him into coming tonight, and I think you should both try to relax and enjoy the evening."

"Hi, mom. Hello there, Mrs. Moeller." Martin Rhodes bounded up to the pair and gave his mother a hug. With his dark hair and rugged good looks, Caroline's tall lanky son was a handsome young man, especially when he was smiling like now. "Nikki picked out a table close to the dais so you'll get a good view of the Duke and Duchess. The knights will be seated to both sides of the platform along with their ladies. They'll be attended by squires and pages."

Caroline frowned. "Pages were little more than children, weren't they?"

"I know what you're thinking, mom, and you're right. A college student would look kind of silly playing the role of a page.

That's why we use local high school boys as squires and grade school kids as pages. They really enjoy getting in on the act, and it guarantees their parents will show up at the Festival."

"I should have known better," Caroline laughed. "Carl told me the first Festival of Knights was held in 1967. By now the coordinators must have everything down pat."

"No slip ups allowed," agreed Martin.

The three of them proceeded across the lawn still talking about the history of the evening's celebration. The Green was rapidly becoming more crowded as townsfolk and visitors alike arrived for the banquet. Many of the guests wandered about the grounds checking out the craft and exhibit booths while others were content to sit and visit with their neighbors at the long wooden tables set in rows across the grass.

Caroline noticed only a smattering of children among the banquet's attendees. She commented on this to Nikki when they met up at their table.

"I don't know how it started," her daughter-in-law replied, "but it seems to be a tradition that the Friday evening dinner is an adults only affair. You'll see plenty of children here Saturday and Sunday, and the school kids come with their teachers during the week. The only ones here tonight are the children of parents who couldn't find babysitters."

"And the fortune teller's granddaughter."

Caroline had spied the little girl crouched behind the trunk of an imposing old oak tree. The youngster had peeked around the tree, then quickly hidden herself when Caroline glanced her way.

"A cute little ragamuffin," Maddy remarked when the child skittered out from her hiding place and ran towards her grandmother's striped tent. "You met her this afternoon, didn't you, Cari?"

"She came up to me while I was watching Jake collect straw. She's a persistent little thing, and quite grave for a girl her age."

"She's had a tough childhood."

This latest came from Professor Atwater who had approached the group while they were all watching Bricole.

"Well, hello there, Mr. Chairman," said a surprised Mrs. Moeller. "Sneaking up behind our backs, are you?"

Carl's eyes twinkled as he replied, "No man my size can sneak up on anyone, Miss Madeline. Especially an observant woman like you."

Caroline jabbed the Professor in the ribs as Maddy turned away, her face screwed up in an expression of bewilderment.

"Behave yourself, will you?" Caroline hissed. "The woman is a wreck worrying about her husband, and she doesn't need you poking fun at her."

Carl rolled his eyes.

"That was a thought provoking comment you just made, Professor Atwater. Everyone sit down for a moment," Maddy commanded. "Something's come to me and I want to run it past you."

The four of them did as they were told and then waited while Maddy gathered her thoughts. After a moment, the Chief's wife pointed at Caroline and Carl.

"Yesterday morning at the post office you two tried to persuade Jake that Emma was killed by an antiquities collector."

"That's right," said the Professor. "We thought perhaps she'd contacted someone in hopes of selling the rune stone."

"It's a plausible argument," offered Martin. "After all, there has to be an explanation as to why the stone was unwrapped. Showing it to a potential buyer is as good a reason as any."

"There's a problem with your theory."

"What's that?" asked Carl.

"Do you really believe Emma Reiser would have discussed business with some man while dressed in nothing but a nightgown?"

Silence descended on the group as they stared at each other in consternation. Caroline was the first to react to Maddy's bombshell.

"You're right, of course. I don't know how we missed that."

"And another thing, Professor. When you said that about a big man sneaking up on someone, it suddenly flashed through my mind that it's not easy for anyone to sneak up on anyone else. I mean, people are naturally noisy, and they're especially noisy if they're stumbling around in the dark. Jake told me that according to Agatha Hagendorf, there were no lights on all night in the post office. But Emma was found at the foot of the stairs."

"Could the murderer have been waiting at the top of the landing?"

"It doesn't make sense, Nikki," said Caroline. "Paul Wakely examined Emma's body when she was brought in by the paramedics. He told me there were no visible injuries except for the skull fracture. If Emma was killed at the top of the landing, and then tumbled down the stairs, don't you think there would have been other fractures or lacerations to the skin?" Caroline shook her head. "If you look at all the possible scenarios involving a buyer, you can easily punch holes in each of them. Say Emma did contact some out-of-town collector. If the person arrived at the agreed upon hour, Emma would have been dressed and Agatha would have seen a light on in the post office."

"What if the buyer became greedy, skipped the arranged meeting, and then broke in after Emma had gone to bed?"

"I still see a problem with it, Martin. If she'd heard him moving about on the first floor, Emma would have never walked down those steps in the dark. There's a switch on the second floor landing.   Surely Emma would have turned on the lights before checking out the noise."

"You're still missing my point," argued Madeline. "If Emma was found lying with her head on the first step, and she didn't take a tumble from the landing, then how did the killer sneak up behind her on the staircase?"

"That's easy, Maddy. The answer is, Emma wasn't killed where she was found."

All eyes were now glued on Caroline as she explained.

"Tom Evans wants to pin this murder on Andrew Littlewort, but it won't work. Andrew is a short little fellow, and Emma Reiser was quite tall for a woman. According to Dr. Wakely, the blow was delivered to the crown of the head. That means Andrew would have had to be standing above Emma on the staircase in order to gather enough force to fracture her skull with the rune stone.

"He couldn't have hit her when she was standing on the landing because he wasn't tall enough to reach up and deliver that kind of blow. And we know she didn't fall down the stairs because there were no other injuries to her body. So we have to assume she descended the staircase on her own, and apparently she did so in the dark."

Caroline took a deep breath before continuing.

"Now those stairs are old and creaky. When Carl and I walked up to the second floor, we made enough noise to wake the dead. Still, Agent Evans is assuming that Andrew either went up to the landing and then followed Emma back down, or he crept around her, and climbed just high enough on the staircase to give her a good whack on the head. Evans must also be assuming Emma was totally deaf."

"There's no way she wouldn't have heard her killer."

Caroline nodded. "Exactly, Carl. And that's why I believe Emma was killed somewhere else in the post office. Paul told me it would take a powerful person to crush Emma's skull that way. I think whoever did it was bigger and stronger than Mrs. Reiser. I think that after he hit her with the rune stone, he picked up her body and placed it at the foot of the stairs. He laid her head on the bottom step to make it look like she'd fallen so we'd all believe it was an accident."

"And he did this all in the dark?"

"I don't see how, Martin. I think Agatha lied when she said she saw no light on in the post office."

"But why would she do that, mom?"

Caroline shrugged. "There's only one obvious answer to that question. Agatha Hagendorf is protecting someone."

CHAPTER 19

"My lords and my ladies! Make a way for the Duke and Duchess of Rhineburg!"

Caroline had to contain her laughter as she watched the poor woman who had worked so long and hard to teach the boy that line. If she'd been frazzled before, she was now ready to cry. Her head fell forward, and she buried her face in both hands before collapsing on a nearby bench.

"I can't believe he said it wrong again," Caroline said with a smile. "His instructor made him go over that line at least a dozen times during dress rehearsal today."

"Which just goes to prove, practice doesn't always make perfect."

All heads turned at the sound of a new voice in their midst.

"Jake! I'm so glad you're here." Maddy jumped up and rushed over to her husband. The way she gathered him in her arms reminded Caroline of a sad little puppy trying any trick to make its master smile. It was almost too pathetic to watch.

"Whoa there, woman. You're going to squeeze the life out of me." Jake disentangled himself from his wife with a sheepish grin. "She's not always so demonstrative," he said.

"Demonstrative is sometimes nice," Caroline replied with a smile. "Come sit down and watch the show with us. You're just in time for the knights' grand entrance."

Just as she said that, a lone trumpet sounded in the distance. A hush fell over the crowd as out from behind Bruck Hall came a string of horsemen preceded by a band of young men beating on drums. The knights were dressed in closely woven mail shirts and bright surcoats emblazoned with their heraldic arms. Their heads were bare and they bore no weapons as they guided their hooded and bedecked horses across the campus. Beside each knight walked a young squire bearing a banner in his master's colors. Behind them rode the knights' ladies.

The ladies wore pastel gowns with embroidered bodices and dropped waists under hooded cloaks of pale brown or gray. They rode sidesaddle on their horses, and they were followed by a group of peasant girls carrying baskets of spring flowers. The girls scattered blossoms before a horse drawn cart that trailed the main body of the procession by two or three yards. Aboard the cart on a cushioned seat sat the Duke and Duchess of Rhineburg.

"Look at that," exclaimed Caroline in delight. More than two dozen pages walked solemnly in line behind the Duke and Duchess. Playing wooden flutes and rattling tambourines, the children preceded twenty trumpeters and a company of armed foot soldiers that brought up the rear of the parade.

"I can't believe Carl is missing all this," she muttered to her daughter-in-law. "He said he had some business to attend to, but I didn't think he'd be gone this long."

Nikki's responded with a shrug. "He'll be here soon. Look, mom. They're lining up right in front of us."

Each squire led his knight to a designated spot next to the raised platform while the ladies positioned themselves in front of the dais. The banner bearers and the drummers stood off to one side with the pages gathered in front of them. When the jangle of spurs and the creaking of leather saddles subsided, the Duke's cart, which had halted some yards back, trundled forward to the sound of a trumpet fanfare.

"Lords and ladies of the realm!   All rise for His Lordship, Duke Richard of Rhineburg!"

The speaker bowed with a flourish, and extended his hand in the direction of the cart. Down stepped a heavyset man whose rotund little body was almost completely enveloped in a forest green ermine edged cloak. The hood of the cloak hid the man's features, but when he turned to accept the applause of the crowd, it slipped back to reveal a familiar face.

"Carl!"

The Duke's blue eyes twinkled as he winked at Caroline.

"Her Ladyship, Duchess Alexandra of Rhineburg."

Carl extended his hand to his silver haired 'wife' amid cheers from the knights and their ladies. Duchess Alexandra acknowledged the ovation with a smile before lifting the hem of her cobalt blue gown and stepping daintily to the ground. The applause continued as the royal couple ascended the stairs to the top of the platform. They were met there by two attendants dressed in the livery of the Duke's court. One of the young men accompanied the Duchess to the center of the dais where stood a pair of tall-backed thrones upholstered in dark red velvet. The other attendant handed Carl a scroll that he unrolled and began to read from.

"Let it be known to all here that, having acquitted himself well as both page and squire, Guy Freeborn of Rhineburg will, on the morrow, be awarded the rank of Knight of the Realm.

"On the occasion of his knighting, I hereby declare a week long tournament commencing with a banquet in honor of Guy Freeborn. While our candidate remains in solitude tonight preparing in body and spirit to assume his knightly duties, let us make merry at this opening celebration of the Festival of Knights.

"Lords and ladies of the realm, I welcome you to Bruck Green and invite you to partake of the hospitality of our court. May good fortune embrace you in all your endeavors. And now, kind visitors, let the feasting begin!"

CHAPTER 20

"I managed to surprise you, didn't I?"

Having finished his third helping of barbecued chicken and ribs, Duke Richard had abandoned the dais to mingle with his guests. He was now enjoying a cup of mulled cider with Caroline.

"You certainly did, Carl. I had no inkling of what you were up to."

The Professor stroked his luxuriant beard with one hand and reached for his pipe with the other. "I'm too old to ride a horse or fight in a mock battle, so the students graciously assigned me this role."

"I think they were lucky to get you, Carl. You make a great Duke of Rhineburg."

"I'll second that," said Jake Moeller as he and Madeline strolled over to the table where Carl and Caroline were sitting. "You fit the part perfectly. The same can be said for the lovely Alexandra."

"Who's playing the Duchess?" asked Caroline. "I don't believe I've ever seen her before."

"That's Judith Applegate, Garrison Hurst's secretary. The woman is an absolute jewel, Cari. She's not only pleasant, but also efficient, organized, and discreet. I sure wish she worked in my department instead of for the Emperor."

"Did you say she's discreet?" asked the Chief. "If that's so, maybe I'll try to lure her away for myself. We could use someone in the office who knows how to keep police matters confidential."

Carl grinned at the big policeman. "Has Annie been talking too much again?"

"Annie Holtzbrinck is the number one purveyor of gossip in this town," Jake responded as he sat down across from the Professor. "Say she takes a call about a domestic disturbance in the trailer park. First she tells me, and then she phones every one of her old cronies. Annie has friends all up and down the grapevine, and they're privy to every bit of news that hits the station."

"Why don't you just fire her?"

"He can't, Cari," replied Madeline smugly. "Annie's husband was Chief of Police before Jake, and she used to run the office for him. Harry died quite suddenly, and when my soft hearted husband took over, he promised Annie she could stay on as long as she liked."

"She is a good secretary," Jake said grudgingly. Then he added, "This business with Emma Reiser has her hopping mad. Harry was Chief for a long time, and apparently Emma bamboozled him too. Now Annie's determined to find out the names of Emma's customers. She wants to personally nail their hides to the barn door."

"Maybe her tendency to gossip will prove helpful this time," said Caroline. "She might hear something that you, as Chief of Police, would never be told."

Maddy bobbed her head up and down. "That's right, Jake. Maybe she can confirm what I heard at the Dip-N-Do this afternoon." She turned to Caroline. "We got sidetracked earlier when I started to tell you about this, and I didn't want to ruin Jake's dinner with talk of the murder."

"So what did Dolores tell you?"

"Well, Cari, it seems Mayor Schoen may have been one of Emma's best clients."

"Teddy a gambler? I don't believe it."

Madeline looked down her nose at Professor Atwater. "And why not, pray tell? The office of Mayor doesn't pay all that well, and you know most of their personal wealth was in Martha's name. Teddy didn't even inherit from his wife when she died."

Martha Schoen had been killed in last winter's explosion at St. Anne's Hospital. Due to the terms of a tontine established by her predecessors, Martha's money had passed to her nearest living blood relative, the wealthy Alexsa Stromberg Morgan.

"What exactly did Dolores say?" Jake inquired.

"Dolores told me the mayor's wife came into the shop every Friday for a wash and set. More often than not, she arrived upset over something Teddy had done, and most of her complaints had to do with money. Once she said the Mayor had lost a packet on the Super Bowl. Martha was furious because he'd gambled with funds she'd earmarked for a new roof on their house. Another time she found a bundle of cash stashed in the Mayor's sock drawer. When she asked him about it, he said he'd gotten lucky on a basketball game."

"That's all very interesting, Maddy, but you know if I go to Mayor Schoen with this story, he'll deny everything. I sure as heck can't question Martha, and Dolores' testimony is only hearsay."

"Then you should talk to Mrs. Meyer, the baker's wife. Bertha has her hair done at the Dip-N-Do also. Dolores told me that several times Bertha left very large tips. When Dolores tried to thank her, Mrs. Meyer blew it off saying she'd made a little extra that week, and she could afford to be generous. Then a couple of times Dolores overheard Bertha gabbing with the other customers about sporting events. She thought it was kind of funny because all these women seemed pretty knowledgeable about teams and statistics. That's not a trait you'd usually associate with the likes of our local librarian, Miss Sarah Sonnenschein, or the church secretary, Eleanor Naumann."

Caroline's eyebrows shot up. "But those are the very ladies who asked me to investigate Agatha's story about the night of the murder. I'll bet you anything Mrs. Hagendorf is withholding information. I think she saw someone else outside the post office that night. Someone besides Andrew Littlewort and..."

"Good evening, ladies. Chief Moeller." Morgan Burke emerged from the crowd and favored the foursome with a broad smile. "Congratulations on a nice performance, Professor Atwater. You look like a real English noble in that outfit of yours."

"Thank you, Congressman. The students worked very hard on the costumes this year."

"So I see. Hey there, wench!" Burke signaled to a young girl in a long flowing skirt and shirred bodice who was moving through the crowd with a tray of drinks. When she approached the table, he took the tray from her and passed it to Caroline.

"This should cover it." He drew a fifty-dollar bill out of his wallet and handed it to the astonished student before dismissing her with a wave of his hand. "Now come on, everyone. Drink up!"

Burke gestured to the tray and the foursome murmured their thanks as each took a cup of mulled cider.

"So tell me, Chief Moeller. How's the investigation going? Have you got the goods on that professor yet?"

Jake took a sip of the spicy cider. "I'm sorry, Congressman. There's not much I can tell you that you don't already know. My office is cooperating with the FBI and..."

"Oh, come on, Chief," interrupted Burke. "The press is already hounding my people with questions about Mrs. Reiser's murder. As Congressman of this district, I have to supply them with some answers, or end up in hot water myself."

"I understand your position, but certain aspects..."

"I'm not asking for confidential information, Chief. Just tell me if you have a good suspect, somebody who may be charged soon."

Jake relented. "We haven't found the murder weapon yet, Congressman. Without the weapon or an eyewitness, it'll be hard to charge anyone with the crime. Still, we have interviewed two men in connection with the case."

"Two men?" Burke looked uncomfortably surprised. "You're investigating someone other than Andrew Littlewort?"

"We brought in a man named Charlie Branch for questioning today. Charlie is head gardener here at Bruck."

"Really."

"Personally, I don't think Charlie had anything to do with Emma's murder, but he may have been at the post office that night."

"Hmm. Do you have any other leads?"

Jake shook his head. "Nothing so far."

Burke set down his cup. "Well, I wish you luck, Chief. If you ask me, that Littlewort fellow is your man. I've heard he has quite a temper." He turned to the women. "It's been a pleasure, ladies. I hope to see you all tomorrow. Nice meeting you again, Professor." He nodded to Carl before turning on his heel and disappearing into the crowd.

The Professor drained his cup and set it down on the tray. "Maybe I'm just prejudiced against politicians, Cari, but I don't trust Morgan Burke. The man's a little too slick for me."

"It's strange how Burke reacted when Jake mentioned Branch's name. He pretended not to know Charlie."

"Why should he know him, Cari?" asked Madeline. "Bigwigs like Burke don't hang around with university gardeners."

"Oh, really?" retorted Caroline. "Then how come I saw him carrying on a long conversation with Charlie just this afternoon?"

CHAPTER 21

"I may have an explanation for what you saw," Carl said after hearing Caroline's tale of the meeting between Branch and Burke that afternoon on Bruck Green. "If you recall, young Mr. Burke is working off a punishment meted out by the Archangels. He pulled three weeks duty as Charlie's helper."

"You think the Congressman was trying to smooth things over for his boy?"

"Yes, I do, Jake. It wouldn't be the first time Morgan ran interference for his son. Sid's always getting himself in trouble."

"Speak of the devil," exclaimed Caroline. "Here comes Sid now." She pointed him out to Maddy. "Good looking kid, isn't he?"

Dressed in tan knee breeches and a loose fitting red shirt with bloused sleeves and an open v-neck, Sid cut a dashing figure as he sauntered by.

"Makes your heart beat a little faster," Madeline replied. Feeling Jake's eyes boring into her back, she quickly added, "If you were a teenager, that is."

"Why don't we go take a look at some of the booths," her husband suggested. "It might take your mind off all the young lions roving the Green."

"Oh, Jake!" Maddy laughed. She winked at Caroline as she linked her arm in the Chief's and strolled off.

"They make quite a couple," Carl commented.

"They certainly do," agreed Caroline. "It's good to see them enjoying themselves. Maddy was very tense earlier tonight, and she said Jake didn't even want to come to the banquet."

"Why not?"

Caroline shrugged. "He's got it in his head that people are going to poke fun at him over this gambling business."

"He still thinks he should have caught on to Emma long before she died."

Caroline nodded. She pulled her coat closer around her.

"It's getting chilly. Why don't we walk around a bit?"

The Professor struggled to get up off the bench.

"Something tells me I shouldn't have kicked in the door to Emma's room. I think I pulled a muscle in my leg."

Caroline laughed. "That'll teach you to act your age."

The two of them wandered up the Green, stopping along the way to view a candle maker at work in one of the booths and a potter at her wheel in another. Caroline bought a ring and a beaded necklace from a man hawking hand made jewelry. Carl indulged in his favorite hobby -- eating -- at a stall featuring a dozen varieties of fudge.

"Don't you dare mention the word cholesterol," he warned Caroline as he wiped his mouth with a napkin. He handed her a piece of the gooey confection. "Here. Have your dessert."

Caroline couldn't resist the tempting morsel of fudge, and she downed it without complaint.

"Caught you!"

Caroline felt a tap on her shoulder. When she swung around, there were Martin and Nikki. Martin held up a small white box.

"I bought you a present, a pound of chocolate bark that I forbid you to share with anyone. Enjoy it in front of TV tomorrow."

"Why, thank you, Marty. But what makes you think I'll be home watching television tomorrow?"

"Did you forget there's an NBA play-off game in the afternoon? I was sure you'd tune in to it."

"Since Jordan retired and the team broke up, basketball hasn't been as much fun for me."

"Martin feels the same way," said Nikki as she eyed her husband mischievously. "He misses yelling at the referees and throwing pillows at the TV set."

Martin made a face at his wife. "You exaggerate, woman. I pride myself on my self-control. Dad was the one who went nuts over the Bulls, didn't he, mom?"

Caroline smiled. "Ed was a real fan. He never missed a game when he was home."

It was strange how easily she could speak of her dead husband. Six months ago that would have been impossible, but a lot had changed in six months. Mostly, she had changed.

"Look," exclaimed Nikki. "There's a portrait artist working over by the Maypole. Why don't we ask him to draw your picture, Professor? You can be immortalized as the Duke of Rhineburg."

Carl protested, but in the end he gave in. The four of them trooped over to where the artist had set up his easel in a canvas covered stall. Minutes later money exchanged hands, and the man set about preparing to sketch the Professor.

A small crowd gathered to watch. Some of the people knew Carl well, and they cheered when he tossed aside his cloak and struck a lordly pose in his red velvet doublet and knee breeches. With his chin held high, and one bushy white eyebrow arched in regal disdain for those standing on the sidelines, Carl fit the part of the aristocratic Duke Richard to perfection.

Caroline glanced at the people standing opposite her. While most seemed to be enjoying the Professor's performance, she noticed two who appeared completely detached from the merriment.

The first was Maria Gregori's granddaughter. The little girl's face was screwed up in a look of intense concentration as she stared not at Carl, but at the man who was sketching him. As Caroline watched, Bricole stepped away from the ring of people surrounding the Professor. She edged closer to the artist, rising up on tiptoe and craning her neck to get a better look at the emerging portrait. Her gaze flickered repeatedly between the picture and its creator, and her eyes took in every stroke of charcoal on paper.

Positioned a few feet to Bricole's left and directly across from Caroline was Alexsa Stromberg Morgan. The ninety-year-old matriarch of the wealthy Morgan clan looked profoundly sad as she stood there leaning on her cane, her attention riveted on the gypsy child. She seemed to follow every move the girl made, and Caroline wondered what it was about Bricole that merited the old woman's interest.

Caroline hadn't seen Alexsa since her granddaughter-in-law Elizabeth's funeral in January. Mrs. Morgan seemed older and more tired looking than she had last winter. That was probably due to the emotional aftermath of Elizabeth's tragic death. Caroline guessed the consequences of that event were far from resolved for either Alexsa or Elizabeth's husband, Jim Morgan.*

She wasn't sure Alexsa would speak to her. Their last meeting had ended on a cool note due to Caroline's discovery of a Morgan family secret. Still, Caroline felt she couldn't ignore Alexsa's presence on the Green. She had to make some attempt at cordial conversation.

*See *A DEADLY LITTLE CHRISTMAS*

"Good evening, Mrs. Morgan. Hello, Bill."

Caroline had circled the artist's stall and come up behind Alexsa. She hadn't noticed Bill Morgan standing there in the crowd, but Alexsa's son must have seen her. The graying owner of Stromberg and Morgan Auto Sales greeted her like a long lost friend.

"Long time no see, Mrs. Rhodes. How's that Jeep we sold you?"

"It's a wonderful car, Bill. I really enjoy driving it."

"That's great, really great. Now if it ever gives you any trouble, you just bring it in to the service center, and we'll whip it back into shape."

Caroline thought the man was being overly hearty, but when she looked at Alexsa, she figured she knew why. Up close, the elderly woman's face appeared gray and pinched. She'd lost considerable weight, and where she'd feigned a fragile condition last winter, she was now truly frail.

Without putting it into words, Bill communicated his fears for his mother. His eyes darted back and forth from Caroline to Alexsa as he cheerfully rambled on about nothing in particular. This forced bravado didn't fool Caroline one bit. She recognized a coping mechanism when she saw one, and Bill's way of coping was certainly not unusual. By acting as if everything was normal in his life, he was denying the fact that it wasn't.

When he finally began to wind down, Caroline broke in with a question for Alexsa.

"I noticed you watching little Bricole. Have you met her grandmother, Maria Gregori?"

Alexsa's eyes took on a far away look. It was as if she was seeing something in the distant past.

"We met many years ago in Europe."

The brevity of the statement coupled with the expression on Alexsa's face discouraged further discussion of the Gregori family. Caroline took the rebuke in stride, and was about to offer an innocuous comment on the evening's festivities when Alexsa suddenly said,

"I understand Agatha Hagendorf came to see you today."

Caroline marveled at Mrs. Morgan's continued ability to keep up with events in Rhineburg. While the old woman's physical health had deteriorated since January, her mental agility had not been curbed in the least.

"She was part of a delegation that tracked me down this morning. The purpose of their visit, so they said, was to enlist my aid in discovering the identities of two men Agatha claims she saw on the night of Emma Reiser's murder."

"I suppose she'd been spying on the post office through her telescope."

Caroline nodded. "It sounds like you've already heard Agatha's story."

"Only the bare bones of it. The friend who called me was unable to supply any details."

Carl had once said that Alexsa was privy to inside information on every family in town. Knowing what she did now, Caroline guessed Mrs. Morgan's primary source for information was Chief Moeller's loquacious secretary, Annie Holtzbrinck.

"Perhaps we could sit down," Alexsa said as she pointed to a bench a few feet away. "It's been a long evening, and I seem to tire easily these days."

She motioned Bill to stay put, and together with Caroline, she walked the short distance to a flagstoned pathway that cut diagonally across Bruck Green.

"That's better," she said as she sank down on one of the rough hewn wooden seats placed on either side of the trail. "You're probably wondering why I'm so interested in what Agatha had to say."

"That question did cross my mind," replied Caroline.

Alexsa rested both hands on the carved knob topping her walking stick and looked out over the Gree.

"I was told Charlie Branch was brought in for questioning by the police."

"That's right. Jake Moeller spoke with him this afternoon."

"I was a friend of his wife. Julie worked for me up at the house."

"Carl told me she died several years ago."

Alexsa nodded. "Before she passed away she asked me to keep an eye on Charlie and the boys. Of course I said yes, even though I didn't see how I could do anything for them. Her sons were grown men by the time their mother died, and Charlie isn't the sort to ask for help from anyone."

"It does sound like a strange request."

"It was typical of Julie. She worried too much about her family, especially during those last months."

"What did Julie die of?"

Alexsa hesitated before answering, "Heart trouble. Anyway, I feel I have an obligation to do what I can for Charlie. I'm sure he's not a murderer."

"Agatha described two men she saw outside the post office. The police think one of the men was Andrew Littlewort. The other was apparently a drunk who fit the description of Charlie Branch." Caroline told Alexsa about the incident at the Blue Cat Lounge. "Carl said Charlie never touched liquor, but it's been my experience that only confirmed alcoholics recover that quickly after getting drunk."

"Charlie's a secret drinker," Alexsa stated. "He started after Julie died, mostly out of regret, I think. He doesn't go to bars, though. He only indulges at home."

"How do you know all this?" Caroline asked the question out of curiosity, although she already had a pretty good idea of what the answer would be.

"There aren't that many places in town that sell booze. Word gets around."

"The Rhineburg grapevine at its busiest and best."

Alexsa nodded. "Charlie's not the only person in town with that particular vice, Caroline. Agatha might have seen someone else the night of the murder, and simply mistaken him for Charlie."

"It's possible," Caroline conceded. "But Charlie had a motive. He didn't want to see a dig here on the Green. He was furious over the idea of his flower beds being ruined." She pointed to the row of daffodils lining the walk. "Charlie called those his paths of gold. He seemed very concerned that they might be uprooted by rock hounds, and in his drunken state...well, who knows what he may have done?"

Alexsa stared down at the flowers next to the bench.

"Paths of gold," she murmured. "That might be enough to kill for." She struggled to her feet. "This evening has taken more out of me than I bargained for. I think I should be getting home."

Caroline rose from the bench and accompanied Alexsa back to the artist's booth. The old lady seemed unsteady on her feet, and she leaned heavily on her cane as they walked.

"This stick belonged to my late husband. It's probably one of the most useful things he left me when he died."

Caroline smiled. "It has an unusual handle. That's a cobra, isn't it?"

"A rather worn cobra," Alexsa responded. "It was carved in England, and given to my husband as a gift. He took it with him everywhere he went, but never had to use it for its true purpose."

Caroline looked puzzled, and Alexsa explained.

"It's a sword cane actually. The snake's head is attached to a blade."

"How interesting."

"Are you ready to leave, mother?" Bill Morgan came striding towards them, but stopped when Alexsa held up her hand.

"Just one minute, Bill." She turned to Caroline. "You said Sid Burke was in the roadhouse with Charlie."

Caroline nodded.

"Be careful of his father, Mrs. Rhodes. The man wields a lot of power in these parts, and he can be nasty when he wants to be."

"You mean he'll protect Sid regardless of anything the boy does."

"That, and other things. Morgan Burke is a conniver who clawed his way to the top. Today he wears the clothes of a Congressman, but he's looking to go farther. He'll do anything to get what he wants."

With that said, Alexsa turned and walked off, leaving Caroline alone in the gathering darkness to ponder the old woman's warning.

CHAPTER 22

By nine o'clock the crowd on Bruck Green had thinned considerably due to the weather. The temperature had reached a balmy seventy-five during the day, but a late evening breeze had chilled the air by twenty degrees and sent many folks scurrying for their cars. Caroline was glad she'd chosen a winter jacket rather than a windbreaker or sweatshirt as worn by the majority of the students. She might not look as fashionable as they, but she surely was a lot warmer.

She was just remarking on that fact to Carl when Madeline Moeller came hurrying towards them from across the Green.

"You-hoo!" Maddy yodeled while waving at them with both hands. "Carl! Cari! Wait up!"

"Good grief," Carl growled. "It's the Mad-woman again. I thought we'd managed to lose her for the evening."

"Behave yourself," Caroline retorted with a smile.

"You won't believe what I've heard," Maddy panted as she slid to a halt in front of them. She grasped Caroline's arm and gave it a squeeze. "I'm so excited, Cari, I can hardly breathe."

Carl grumbled something under his breath about the effects of oxygen deprivation to the brain. Caroline shot him a withering look before turning her full attention to Madeline.

"You certainly look excited, Maddy. Now what's going on?"

"It's Emma's code, Cari. Michael Bruck has broken it!"

"The computer code?" The Professor was suddenly interested in what Madeline had to say. "I knew Michael was good at that stuff, but even for him, that's fast."

"He said it wasn't all that difficult to do. Either Emma was sloppy, or she thought no one would ever see her records."

"There's a third choice," said Caroline. "Maybe Emma wanted someone to break the code."

"But why, Cari? That doesn't make any sense."

"Sure it does, Carl. Just think about it for awhile. Emma was no fool, so she had to realize there was some danger in running a book. What if one of her customers decided to wipe out a big debt by wiping out Mrs. Reiser? Emma had to make sure no one even considered doing such a thing. She probably told each new bettor that his name was encoded in her records, but it was encoded in such a way that any computer geek could figure it out. She may have hinted at the existence of multiple disks stashed away in safety deposit boxes. Or maybe she said her lawyer kept copies of all her accounts."

"You're saying Emma insured her life by making it easy for the law to catch up with her clients."

"Exactly, Maddy. I don't think Emma was the sloppy type, and I haven't heard anyone accuse her of arrogance. Emma ran a very business-like operation out of her second floor office. She didn't miss a trick, and I'll bet that included insuring her own survival."

"So you're discounting any of her clients as the murderer."

"I think it's highly unlikely that one of them killed Emma, and then left without destroying her records. But they can all be checked out if Michael deciphered their names."

Madeline looked over both shoulders, then quickly checked out the landscape behind Caroline and Carl. It appeared they were the only people left in the immediate area.

"I don't want anyone to overhear us," she said quietly. She lowered her voice even more as she continued. "When Michael tracked us down over by the cider booth, all he said was, 'I've done it'. I didn't know what he meant by that, but Jake got all excited, and he started slapping Michael on the back. Then Jake told me to wait for him by the booth while he and Michael discussed some police business. The two of them walked over to one of the benches along the center path, and when they'd made sure there was no one else around, they sat down and started talking." Maddy paused to take a deep breath. She performed a second visual check of their surroundings before finally continuing with her tale.

"By that time I'd remembered what Michael was up to. Of course I was curious to know what he'd found out, so I worked my way from tree to tree until I was close enough to hear what he was saying. He was being very careful not to mention any names, but I heard him tell Jake that the 'top man in town' had been placing bets with Emma for years." Madeline drew closer to the others and said in a meaningful way, "None of us need to be told who the 'top man in town' is, now do we?"

"Mayor Teddy Schoen," murmured Caroline.

"Exactly," agreed Madeline. "Now we know why the Mayor hotfooted it over to the post office so quickly the day Emma's body was discovered. He was scared stiff over what Jake might find there."

"It would also account for why he made such a scene the next day when he was blocked from entering the building."

"He came storming into the police station when he couldn't get into the P.O.," added Carl. "He demanded to see the official records of the investigation."

"Jake says Teddy's been an absolute pain in the neck. He visits the station at least three times a day to check up on the case."

"This corroborates what Dolores at the Dip-N-Do told you," said Caroline. "But I still don't see Teddy as a murderer."

"Well, I also heard Michael say something like 'the gardener was in on it'. He must have been talking about Charlie Branch."

"I could see Charlie as a gambler," remarked the Professor. "I always wondered how he could afford to pay the tuition at Bruck for five sons. It's not a cheap school, you know."

"Betting with a bookie is a risky way to subsidize your kids' education. What if he lost more than he won?"

Carl shrugged. "His position at the university can't pay all that well, Cari. He must have made money with Emma. Back when Julie was alive, the family never seemed to lack for anything. Julie drove a nice car, and Charlie tooled around on a swanky motorcycle."

Caroline recalled the photographs she'd seen in Charlie's den. One of them had featured Charlie and another man standing beside an expensive looking cycle. The picture had seemed quite ordinary at the time, but something about it bothered her now. She couldn't imagine what it was, but it would come to her eventually.

"What else did Michael say?" she asked Maddy.

"I couldn't catch what he said after that, but he handed Jake a piece of paper, and I could tell my husband was surprised by what was on it. I assumed it was a list of names because Jake started laughing, and then he said, 'What a bunch of petty criminals'. He told Michael to keep quiet about the list until he'd had a chance to check out the people on it."

"He's not going to turn it over to the FBI?"

"I don't think so, Professor. Jake really wants to crack this case on his own. I heard him tell Michael he was going to talk to Charlie in the morning. I backed off then because the two of them got up and started walking back to where I was supposed to be waiting."

"So Jake doesn't know you overheard this conversation."

Maddy shook her head. "He told me he and Michael had some business to attend to, and he'd meet me back at the house later tonight. We have to help Jake, Cari, but he mustn't know we're doing it. You understand, don't you?"

Caroline did understand. The Chief's pride had suffered one blow already. If he found out his wife was snooping around on his behalf, it would upset him even more.

"We'll just have to be careful not to appear too curious when we're around your husband. Don't ask too many questions when you're alone with him at home. Don't give Jake any reason to suspect the three of us are investigating this murder."

"I can do that," Maddy replied emphatically. "I know how to keep my mouth shut."

Carl rolled his eyes, but fortunately Maddy's attention was riveted on Caroline.

"So what do we do now? Should I try to get my hands on that list?"

Caroline shook her head. "Definitely not. Leave the list to Jake, OK? What you can do is get friendly with Annie Holtzbrinck. If Jake's secretary is the gossip he claims her to be, she'll be eager to tell you everything that's going on over at the police station. We need to know what Tom Evans is up to. Is he ready to charge Andrew Littlewort, or is he considering anyone else as a suspect?"

"Try to find out what evidence he has," added the Professor.

"I'll work on it tomorrow," Maddy promised.

"Good. As long as you're free for a while, how about driving into Rhineburg with me?" Caroline glanced up at the sky. It was a clear night, and the stars were shining. "I want to pay a call on Agatha Hagendorf."

"What are you up to now?"

"I'd like to check out Agatha's telescope, Carl. It would be interesting to see how powerful it really is."

A broad grin split Carl's face. "That's hard to tell unless you have something to look at. Maybe I should go stand across the street from Agatha's house."

"Why not? I'm sure Mrs. Hagendorf will be stargazing on a night as beautiful as this. Don't you agree, Madeline?"

But Maddy wasn't listening. She was staring over Carl's shoulder at a stand of trees a few feet away. By the look on her face, Caroline could tell the woman wasn't happy with what she saw.

"What's wrong, Maddy?"

"Someone was eavesdropping behind those trees. Look! There he goes!"

Caroline and the Professor turned in time to see a shadowy figure jog away across the Green. Despite the electric torches set at intervals in the lawn, it was too dark to make out who it was.

CHAPTER 23

"Good evening, Mrs. Hagendorf. I hope it's not too late for a little chat."

Agatha visibly paled when she saw Caroline and Maddy standing on her doorstep.

"I was just about to turn off the lights and go to bed."

"Then it's a good thing we arrived when we did." Caroline slipped by Agatha and entered the foyer of the old Victorian. "What a lovely place you have. You take in boarders, don't you?"

"Yes," whimpered Agatha as she pushed the door closed behind Maddy. "Five other ladies live here."

"Are they all at home tonight?"

Agatha glanced over at the staircase before answering nervously, "I...I imagine so. In fact, I know so. I know they're here, I mean. Here in the house." Her voice trailed off to a whisper when she caught sight of Maddy lusting over a mirrored hallstand in the foyer. Tearing her eyes away from the pert little antique dealer, she said to Caroline, "Why don't we go into the living room?"

"I'd much rather go upstairs," replied Caroline with a smile. "That way you could show us your telescope."

"My telescope?" Agatha squeaked. "But why do you want to see that?"

"It's a beautiful night outside. We thought you could show us the stars."

"The stars?"

A confused Agatha could do nothing more than repeat Caroline's words. She looked around anxiously for support, but there was no one in sight to rescue the agitated woman. Apparently Mrs. Hagendorf's boarders were all tucked away upstairs.

"I've always been interested in the stars," Caroline said glibly. "And Madeline dabbles in astrology. She knows everything about the constellations."

Madeline shot her a look that indicated she knew nothing at all about the subject, but Caroline just winked at her friend. She headed for the staircase and began climbing it.

"Your telescope is upstairs, I presume."

"Yes, Mrs. Rhodes, but..."

"Then upstairs we must go." Maddy took their hostess by the arm and gently propelled her up the steps. "You know, Agatha, your hallstand is an excellent example of Renaissance Revival craftsmanship. If you ever decide to sell it..."

Mrs. Hagendorf disengaged her arm from Maddy's grip, and gazed at the other woman in horror.

"I wouldn't think of parting with a single piece of furniture in this house. Why, Emma Reiser told me that hallstand alone is worth..."

Agatha's hand flew to her mouth. Her eyes widened in distress as she realized what she'd said.

"You were smart to ask for Emma's opinion," Maddy countered smoothly. "Mrs. Reiser was quite knowledgeable about antiques."

That sent Agatha into a paroxysm of nervous giggles. The elderly woman turned on her heel and fled up the staircase after Caroline.

Her guest was waiting on the second floor landing.

"Which way do we go?" she asked sweetly.

Agatha motioned towards a door midway down the hallway. Caroline gestured for her to lead the way, and Mrs. Hagendorf, totally upset now by the turn of events, meekly complied.

The room she led them to was situated at the front of the house. It featured two large windows that faced onto Kaiser Street and lent a clear view of the entire block. Directly across, and in a line with the windows, stood the Rhineburg Post Office.

A large cloth covered object was tucked away in one corner of the room. Caroline walked over to it and removed the covering.

"My goodness," remarked a surprised Caroline. "This is quite a telescope."

"Harold only bought the best." Agatha ran her hand over the smooth black tube that comprised the body of the instrument. "It's a eight inch compound reflector telescope on a German equatorial mount." She pointed to a shorter compact tube attached to the top of the telescope. "This is a finderscope."

Agatha visibly relaxed as she lectured them on the finer points of the telescope.

"The mirror inside is eight inches in diameter, so you can view even faint stars with this telescope. Harold always wanted a twenty inch telescope, but they cost way too much money. He had to be content with this."

"It sounds like your husband loved astronomy."

"Oh, yes. Harold read everything he could on the subject. He taught me how to use a starfinder chart to recognize the constellations and the locations of the planets."

Caroline leaned forward and looked up at the sky through the window.

"What stars can we see tonight?"

"The constellation Virgo should be visible," answered Agatha. She began to drag the telescope over while motioning to Madeline. "Open that, will you? Harold replaced the old windows with ones that swing to the side. So much easier for maneuvering the telescope." She pointed the scope towards the west and squinted through the finderscope. "Turn off the overhead light, Mrs. Rhodes. Now Spica is the brightest star in Virgo, so I'll look for it first. Mars should also be visible this month. Ah! There we are."

Agatha twisted a knob to focus the telescope. Then she stepped back and let Caroline take her place.

"What a beautiful sight," Caroline murmured. She slowly swung the scope around so it faced the post office. Then she lowered it until Carl came into view leaning against the lamppost.

The Professor had been watching the window. When he saw the telescope point in his direction, he waved his hand in the air, then straightened up and walked off down the street. He stopped and made an about face at the far corner before heading back towards the post office.

When Carl reached the alley behind the building, he turned into it and was momentarily lost from view. A few seconds later he emerged and began walking briskly towards Wilhelm Road.

Caroline backed away from the telescope, satisfied with what she'd seen. She motioned to Maddy who nodded in return.

"Let's go back downstairs," Madeline said to Agatha. Once again a look of confusion entered the older woman's eyes as Maddy gripped her arm and guided her out of the room. She glanced back at Caroline as they passed her near the doorway.

"I'll be right behind you," Caroline said. "Just let me close the window."

174

Agatha nodded mutely before allowing Maddy to usher her down the staircase. Caroline watched them go, then returned to the window and latched it shut. Apparently the Professor had gone off to his car because the street below her was now deserted.

"It sure wasn't this quiet on the night of the murder," she murmured to herself. That evening there'd been plenty of people roaming the street. All but one had been gamblers.

Caroline left the room and walked down the hall, knocking on doors as she went. A few minutes later she was headed downstairs preceded by five very frightened women.

"It's time to get a few things straight," she said as she motioned each woman to a chair in the living room. Madeline was already there with Agatha, and she came now and stood silently beside Caroline.

"First of all, there are a few of you here whose names I don't know, even though we shared a cup of tea at the post office this morning." She smiled at the silver haired lady she'd last seen wearing sunglasses. "Why don't we start with you?"

"I'm Marie Moser," the woman said nervously. "I'm a widow, and I've lived here since I sold my house seven years ago."

"Very good. You see, ladies? It's not all that hard to tell the truth." Caroline turned to the woman seated next to Mrs. Moser on the sofa. "And you?"

"Myrtle Jennings," came the reply. "I'm Marie's sister, and I moved in a year ago when Angela Cummings died, and her room came up for rent. I used to live in Ohio, and I'm single by choice."

"Welcome to Illinois, Miss Jennings."

Caroline pointed to a third woman huddled on the couch.

"I've seen you at the hospital, but we were never formally introduced."

"I'm Emily O'Hara, and I'm the medical librarian at St. Anne's. I also work part time in Accounts and Billing."

"How long have you boarded with Mrs. Hagendorf?" Caroline asked the rosy-cheeked little woman.

"Ever since Mr. O'Hara passed on four years ago. My children wanted me to move in with them, but I'm young yet, and I prefer my freedom."

Mrs. O'Hara was sixty-five if she was a day. Still, she was the youngest of the lot, and Caroline appreciated her desire to remain independent.

"Mrs. Naumann and Miss Sonnenschein I know, and it goes without saying that Mrs. Hagendorf indelibly impressed herself upon my memory." Caroline motioned to Madeline. "I'm sure you're all acquainted with Mrs. Moeller."

The six women nodded in unison.

"So now that the introductions have been made, let's get down to business." Caroline began to pace the floor while Maddy settled down on an overstuffed chair in the corner. Caroline averted her eyes from the group as she began to speak, but she sensed they were avidly watching her.

"This morning the six of you arrived at the Rhineburg P.O. with a most unusual story. Supposedly Mrs. Hagendorf saw two men outside the post office on the night of Emma Reiser's murder."

"But I did see two men," insisted Agatha. "I didn't make that up."

"Of course you didn't, dear." Ellie Naumann reached over and patted Agatha's hand. "Now don't let her ruffle your feathers. You know we're all behind you a hundred percent."

"You'd better not be," snarled Maddy, "or you'll be charged with obstruction of justice just like your friend, Mrs. Hagendorf."

Mrs. Naumann was tempted to reply, but thought better of it. She clamped her mouth shut and contented herself with a 'who-do-you-think-you're-talking-to?' look aimed at Madeline. Maddy bit her tongue and simply glared back, but Ellie's supporters refused to take the insult lying down. Three of Agatha's boarders broke into a babble of protest directed at the Chief's wife.

"May I continue?"

Caroline's raised voice penetrated the din. She stared the women into silence, and when she was sure even Maddy had calmed down, she continued to outline the events of the morning.

"With the assistance of Bertha Meyer, you attempted to lure me into acting as a mouthpiece for Mrs. Hagendorf. You wanted me to repeat your story to Chief Moeller, including those very accurate descriptions of Professor Andrew Littlewort and Charlie Branch."

The six ladies exchanged worried looks, but no one attempted a denial.

"Your little plan didn't work. Professor Atwater interrupted our tea party and dragged Agatha off to the police station where she was interrogated by Agent Tom Evans of the FBI. I know how hard that must have been for you, Agatha," Caroline said, her voice softening as she directed her words to the unhappy Mrs. Hagendorf. "Agent Evans questioned me last winter. He's not a very gentle man."

Tears welled up in Agatha's eyes when she replied, "I was afraid of him. He made me repeat myself three times."

"Which is hard to do when you're not telling the complete truth." Caroline stopped pacing and planted herself in front of Agatha. "Why did you do it, Mrs. Hagendorf? Were you protecting your friends?"

"Oh, dear," whispered Miss Sonnenschein.

"Be quiet," commanded Mrs. Naumann.

Caroline ignored them both as she spoke to Agatha.

"You own a powerful telescope, Mrs. Hagendorf, but you don't always use it to look at the stars. Sometimes you aim it at the alley behind the post office." She paused for effect, then continued to grind away at Agatha. "You saw people coming and going in that alley at all hours of the night, and you suspected they were visiting Emma Reiser. One day you got up the nerve to ask her about it."

Myrtle gasped when Agatha nodded. The others appeared equally shocked, but Caroline gave them no chance to speak.

"Emma was forced into telling you her secret. She paid for your silence by giving you tips on betting, and you began to make money on the deal. No one can blame you for wanting some extra cash, Agatha. A widow's life can be difficult, especially when you have a large house to keep up and very little income."

"Harold's pension didn't even cover the utility bills," Agatha sighed. "I only get a minimum payment from Social Security."

"So what you won on the horses helped a great deal."

"Oh, I never played the ponies, Mrs. Rhodes." Agatha wrinkled her nose at the very thought. "That's much too risky. I just threw a few dollars in the football and basketball pools, and I was lucky enough to win."

"You gambled on sports?"

Agatha's head bobbed up and down. "Harold was a great fan of the Bears and the Bulls. He taught me all about statistics and averages. Since he died, I've also kept up with baseball and hockey."

Flashbulbs popped in Caroline's brain. She thought of the box of fudge laying on the seat of her car, and she remembered why Martin had given it to her.

"The NBA play-offs start tomorrow. Did you put money on those games, Mrs. Hagendorf?"

Agatha realized she'd said too much. She looked about wildly, her eyes sliding over the faces of her friends in a futile search for support. When none of them spoke up, she slumped down in her chair and dropped her head in defeat.

"Tell me the truth, Agatha. Did you place a bet with Emma on the night she was murdered? Or were you simply on look-out duty for these other women?"

"How dare you!" thundered Mrs. Naumann. "You have no right to accuse the rest of us just because Agatha admitted to gambling."

"But Ellie..."

If looks could kill, Eleanor's would have sent Sarah Sonnenschein to an early grave.

"Keep still," she hissed at the librarian.

"We can't keep still." Emily O'Hara stood up and walked over to Agatha. She placed an arm around the other woman's shoulders and said, "I'm sorry, dear. I guess I was just too afraid to speak up earlier." Emily looked up at Caroline. "Are we all going to jail?"

"I doubt the Chief will press charges if you all agree to cooperate." Caroline glanced over at Madeline who nodded in agreement. "You'll have to go see him first thing in the morning, though. He won't be understanding if you put it off."

"How did you find out about us?" asked Mrs. Moser.

"Michael Bruck has been deciphering Mrs. Reiser's records for the police. Emma kept a list of the people who placed bets with her, and your names were on it." Caroline pulled up a chair and sat down facing Agatha. "Now let's go over your testimony again, and this time, don't leave anything out."

"We'll help you," Myrtle said kindly.

Agatha smiled weakly, but then she cleared her throat and plunged into her story.

"You were right about the play-offs, Mrs. Rhodes. We all intended to bet on them, but we never got the chance. The night Emma died, the six of us were gathered in this room discussing possible outcomes in the weekend games. By the time we finally decided on our picks, it was well after eleven o'clock."

"Almost eleven thirty," grumbled Mrs. Naumann who had decided to go along with the crowd rather than face the music alone. "We argued so much about the scores that we lost track of time."

"*Some* people argued about the scores." Agatha corrected the other woman without bothering to look at her.

"The time didn't matter, though," Emily reminded them. "We couldn't have gone to the post office any earlier than we did. Emma just had too many customers that night."

"That's true," Agatha conceded. "And since we didn't want the rest of the town knowing we did business with Emma, we had to wait until the coast was clear."

"Agatha offered to keep watch while the rest of us freshened up in our rooms."

This latest offering came from Sarah Sonnenschein. Per usual, the librarian whispered her comment, and Caroline had to lean forward to hear it.

"So you all went upstairs, and you, Agatha, used your telescope to spy on Emma's visitors."

"I wouldn't call it spying," retorted Mrs. Hagendorf. "Everyone in Rhineburg knows about my telescope. If anyone had seen me in the window, they would have assumed I was stargazing."

"Then you admit you saw Charlie Branch and Professor Littlewort through your scope."

Agatha nodded. "I didn't want to get them in trouble, but the
other ladies said they might be involved in Emma's murder. I thought
if I just described the two of them, you'd figure out their identities on
your own."

"What time did you see them?"

"That part of my story isn't a lie, Mrs. Rhodes. Charlie
arrived at the post office at a quarter past midnight, and it must have
been ten minutes later when I saw the Professor in the alley."

"Did you see either one of them enter the building?"

Agatha shook her head. "The back entrance is not in a line
with my windows. I only saw them go into the alley and come out
again. Then they left, one going up the street and one going down,
just like I told you this morning."

"Who else did you see that night?"

Agatha squirmed in her chair, and Caroline had to remind her
that Chief Moeller already had a list of Emma's customers.

"You can only help them by telling me who you saw. Unless
you do that, every person on that list will be dragged in for
questioning as a potential suspect in the murder."

"How horrible," Agatha murmured. After a moment she said,
"John Meyer arrived right after I set up the telescope. He was
followed by Arch Tillar, the quarry foreman. Next came Albert
Miller and Harry Lee. After they left, Emma turned the lights out in
the post office." She paused and looked down at her feet. "The next
person I saw down in the street was Charlie Branch."

Caroline was acquainted with John Meyer. The baker was
short, fat, and elderly. All three characteristics left him out of the
running as the killer.

"Tell me about Arch, Albert, and Harry. I don't think I've
ever met those men."

"Arch Tillar is sixty-five, and he has emphysema," Emily stated flatly. "There's no way he'd have the strength to kill anyone."

Caroline nodded at the medical librarian. The woman was sharp in an unprepossessing way.

"I take it he's been a patient at St. Anne's."

"I told you I work part time in Accounts and Billing. I must have sent a half dozen statements to his home in the past year, and he always pays after the first one."

With his winnings from gambling, Caroline guessed.

"And the other two men?"

"Albert Miller and Harry Lee share a room at the Rhineburg Retirement Home. Albert's plagued by arthritis, and Harry had a hip replacement in January."

"You've made your point, Mrs. O'Hara."

That left Charlie and Andrew Littlewort as the only two viable suspects. Unless Agatha was leaving someone out.

"Are you sure those are the only people you saw by the post office?" Caroline asked.

Once again, Agatha looked down at her shoes before answering. When she did speak, though, it was with conviction.

"I'm sure of what I've told you," she said.

Caroline suddenly thought of something.

"You said you were going to bet on the basketball games, but you never got a chance. What did you mean by that?"

"Good grief, Mrs. Rhodes. Haven't you figured it out by now?" Eleanor Naumann arched her eyebrows and glared disapprovingly at Caroline. "It was one o'clock in the morning when Agatha finally trooped over to the post office with our money. By that time, Emma was already dead."

CHAPTER 24

Madeline Moeller walked into Professor Atwater's kitchen and pulled a chair up to the table.

"Jake's not home yet," she said as she sat down next to Caroline. "I left a message on the answering machine telling him I was here so he wouldn't worry."

"Looks to me like you're the one doing all the worrying," said Carl. He plunked down a plate in front of Maddy. "Relax and eat your sandwich. Jake's probably busy checking out folks on that list."

"Speaking of the list, Cari, how did you know Agatha and her buddies were on it?"

Caroline laid down her roast beef sandwich and wiped her mouth on a napkin.

"It was just a good guess, Maddy. You told us Jake laughed when Michael showed him some of the names in Emma's records. Then you quoted him as saying, 'What a bunch of petty criminals'. It occurred to me that Jake wouldn't laugh if Teddy Schoen or Garrison Hurst showed up on that list, but he might find it amusing if his gamblers turned out to be elderly women living in a Home for Gentle Ladies."

"You were already suspicious of Agatha."

"You're right, Carl. Agatha's story left a lot to be desired. She said she saw Charlie and Professor Littlewort when she looked out her bedroom window, but she described them just a little too well."

"That's where our little experiment came into play."

Caroline nodded. "When I first looked out Mrs. Hagendorf's window, you were leaning against the lamppost. In the light I could see you fairly well, but when you walked away, you were just a figure moving through the shadows. Agatha's telescope changed all that. Through the scope I could make you out perfectly. That instrument is so powerful I could even see the wrinkles in your forehead."

"It's comforting to know my wrinkles are showing," grumbled the Professor. He slapped three spoonfuls of ice cream on top of an enormous piece of apple pie, and sat down to console himself with food.

"There was another thing that caused me to wonder about Agatha and her friends," Caroline said. "Emma's bookmaking operation was fairly common news by the time they came to see me this morning, yet they never mentioned it at all. It's hard to believe something that sensational wouldn't merit a comment from even one of them."

"Then there was that little slip-up by Agatha when I was admiring the hallstand."

Carl looked up from his dessert. "What slip-up?"

"Agatha told me that Emma advised her on antiques."

"When I was upstairs gathering the other five ladies, I managed to peek into each of their rooms. Every one of them owned at least one really good piece of furniture," added Caroline.

"What's so important about that?"

"Emma invested her money in antiques, Carl. I think she counseled Agatha and the others to do the same. That way their illegal earnings didn't show up on any bank records, and they didn't have to pay taxes on the money. If the day ever came when one of them really needed cash, she could simply sell her investment."

Carl shook his head. "Emma Reiser was one clever woman. She figured out every angle, didn't she."

Madeline toyed with her sandwich. "In a way, I felt sorry for Agatha and the others. They're all making do on Social Security and whatever pensions they have. Who can blame them for trying to hit the jackpot with Emma Reiser?"

"I know what you mean," replied Caroline. "Although I'm surprised you feel any pity for Eleanor Naumann. She's one tough bird."

"I get the feeling she calls all the shots in that house."

"Maybe she did in the past, but I wouldn't be so sure about the future. Emily O'Hara seemed to be in charge tonight."

"She did step up when no one else came to Agatha's rescue," admitted Maddy. "I think I liked Emily the best of all of them."

Caroline nodded. "I only hope she can persuade Agatha to name the other person she saw outside the post office on the night of the murder."

"She saw someone else besides the people she mentioned?" asked the Professor between mouthfuls of pie.

"I convinced of it, Carl. She hesitated twice when I asked her about it, and the second time she gave me some lame reply about being sure of everything she'd told us. That's not quite the same as saying, 'I'm not holding anything back'."

"I wish we could have reached Jake," lamented Maddy. "He could have gone over to Agatha's place tonight."

"I spoke to Emily before we left the house. She promised to get her landlady over to the police station first thing in the morning. I told her I suspected Agatha was holding out on us, and she said she would talk to her. Don't worry, Maddy. Jake will hear the whole story tomorrow."

Madeline looked at her watch. "I guess you're right, Cari. It's almost eleven thirty, and Agatha's probably tucked up in bed already. A few more hours of waiting won't hurt anyone."

That was the first mistake the three of them made.

CHAPTER 25

The next day dawned bright and clear. The forecast was for a sunny morning with temperatures in the mid-seventies followed by increasing clouds in the afternoon. Thunderstorms were predicted for the late evening, but the Festival organizers weren't too worried. Rhineburg's weatherman had been wrong before, and the local celebration had never suffered a rain out. No, they all said. Nothing was going to ruin this year's Festival of Knights.

Caroline was feeling as upbeat about the Festival as those in charge when she arrived on Bruck Green at nine a.m. The Grand Parade wasn't scheduled to begin until ten o'clock, so she had an hour to wander about and select the best spots from which to photograph Carl and the knights.

The procession was due to start at the north end of the Green and travel south past the site of the archery competition. From there, the parade would wend its way through the exhibitors' area, past the Maypole and the fortune teller's tent, and on to the jousting field where a pavilion had been erected at one end for the Duke's entourage. The knights had pitched their own brightly colored tents opposite of the pavilion, while movable bleachers had been placed on both sides of the field for the public.

Caroline decided to take a panoramic shot of the parade as the riders passed the first stand of trees on the route. She wanted to avoid capturing any of the university buildings on the picture.

"This looks good," she murmured to herself as she squinted through the viewfinder on her camera. "Nothing but green lawn and trees."

"And lots of blue sky."

Caroline lowered the camera and turned to find a solemn faced Bricole Gregori standing a few feet away.

"You forgot about the sky," the child said seriously as she walked forward. "It'll show up in the picture, you know."

"I guess it will," Caroline replied. "Silly of me not to think of it."

"Don't feel bad. Lots of people forget about the sky because they're so used to seeing it everywhere." Bricole bent down and picked a blade of grass. "Do you ever get up real early in the morning?" she asked.

"Only when I have to work the day shift. I usually stay up late at night."

"The night's OK," Bricole conceded with a shrug, "but you don't see any colors once it's dark outside. At night the grass is just plain black. Early in the morning it's silvery gray and shimmery."

Caroline laughed. "I think you just made up a new word, Bricole. But I know exactly what you mean. When the grass is wet with dew it sort of twinkles in the sunlight."

Bricole drew back and gave Caroline one of those 'must-I-teach-you-everything?' looks. Then she said quite patiently, "Grass doesn't twinkle, Mrs. Rhodes. Stars twinkle."

Caroline raised her hand. "I stand corrected. By the way, Bricole, how did you learn my name?"

"I asked someone." The child's eyes suddenly widened. "Hey! Do you want to see what happened to the flowers over there? I'd be really mad if they belonged to me."

"Don't tell me the horses have been nibbling at them already," quipped Caroline as she followed the little girl towards one of the paths crisscrossing the Green.

"I think it was squirrels." Bricole tossed the statement over her shoulder and kept moving. A moment later she stopped and pointed to a bed of daffodils lining the walk. "See what I mean?"

Caroline frowned as she stared at a row of perfectly round holes dug in the ground. Next to each hole lay a dead flower still attached to its bulb.

"Squirrels dig up nuts and things, don't they?"

"They do when they're hungry," Caroline replied. She picked up a daffodil and examined it. The bulb was intact without so much as a scratch on its surface. When she checked the other bulbs she found them equally free of marks.

"This feels funny."

Caroline looked over at Bricole. The youngster was crouched on the path next to the flower bed, her hand thrust into one of the holes. Soil buried her arm almost to the shoulder, and as she pulled it out, she grinned up at Caroline.

"These holes are really deep."

Too deep for daffodils, thought Caroline. She tossed the dead flowers back on the ground.

"I'd better find Mr. Branch. He's the gardener here at Bruck, and he'll want to know about this."

Bricole stood up and brushed the dirt from her arm.

"I wish I could go along, but Grandmother will have a fit if she see me with you. She says you're unlucky."

Caroline's eyebrows shot up. "Oh, really?"

"She saw it in the cards yesterday. She says you're headed for trouble, but I hope she's wrong."

"Is she wrong very often?" Caroline asked.

Bricole shook her head. "Hardly ever at all."

The two of them walked back to where they'd met, and Caroline said good-bye to the child.

"Before you leave, would you mind if I took your picture?"

Bricole rolled her eyes. "I guess it's all right. Just don't let Grandmother see it, OK?"

Caroline snapped two quick pictures before the child ran off.

"Having fun?"

Martin waved to his mother as he and Nikki approached from the direction of the university.

"That Bricole is a remarkable little girl," Caroline said as the two came abreast of her. "I don't know what it is about the child, but I feel like I'm under some kind of a spell when she's around."

"Did you see her checking out the artist who did that picture of the Professor last night? Marty and I came along just after he'd started the drawing. We stopped to watch, but I was totally distracted by Bricole. She was fascinated by the man, and kept edging closer and closer until she was standing right next to him."

"The guy was really nice about it," Martin added. "It didn't bother him at all that this kid was practically panting down his neck. He just kept on drawing, and when he was finished, he handed Bricole his charcoal stick. He told her to take it home and draw something."

"I'll bet she did exactly that," said Caroline. "She has an artist's eye for colors and shapes. Maybe she'll be one some day."

Martin checked his watch. "The parade will be starting soon, and the crowd is getting bigger by the minute. We'd better find a place to stand along the route, or we'll end up having to watch it over somebody's shoulder."

The three of them found an open spot near the Maypole. Caroline told the others about her plans for a panoramic shot of the procession, and promised to hurry back as soon as she'd snapped a couple of pictures.

When she arrived back at the north end of the Green, the parade was just getting underway. This morning the trumpeters were in the lead followed by the drummers. All were dressed in black tights covered by long red tunics belted at the waist. Embossed on the front of each tunic was a golden lion in an upright pose.

The musicians were followed by a posse of armed foot soldiers. There were many more in the parade than had been present the night before, and all wore chain mail shirts with attached hoods over leather leggings. The shirts extended to their knees, and over their hoods each man wore a conical steel helmet with a noseguard. The first three rows of soldiers held long spears with leaf shaped heads. The rest bore a variety of weapons ranging from fine edged battle axes to swords, maces, halberds, and spiked flails. All of the men carried round shields covered in leather and rimmed with steel.

Behind that group rode the knights. They were also dressed in mail shirts called hauberks, and their leggings and shoes were made of the same material. Over the hauberks they wore sleeveless cloth surcoats of blue, red, gold, or green imprinted with the knight's heraldic symbols. Each man wore a broad leather belt from which hung a sword and scabbard. Some of the knights wore mail mittens while others were bare handed.

All of the horses were blanketed in long saddle cloths that complemented their riders' colors. The bridle reins were looped through bands of gold or silver material, and some of the horses wore hoods that matched the color of their blankets. Beside each one walked a young squire carrying his master's banner.

Caroline recognized Charlie Branch riding in the procession. He was dressed in a sea green surcoat emblazoned with two diagonal black stripes bisected by a gold leaf. He wore mail mittens and a mail hood, but no helmet.

By the expression on his face, Caroline could tell the gardener had already heard about the destruction of his garden. Charlie's mouth was set in a grim line, and his brow was furrowed in a deep frown. He sat rigidly in his saddle, his hands gripping the reins like they were rods of steel instead of strips of leather.

The man's anger was not only obvious to Caroline. Charlie's horse clearly sensed his rider's emotion, and it reacted in a predictable way. The animal pranced sideways out of line, tossing its head and rolling its eyes each time Charlie jerked on the reins. At one point the horse reared up, nearly throwing the gardener to the ground. It was only when another rider turned to him and said something that Branch seemed to realize he was disrupting the whole parade. He slowly shook his head, then slackened the reins and leaned forward to rub his horse's neck. The frightened animal calmed down almost immediately, and the cavalcade continued across the Green.

When they reached the first stand of trees, Caroline lifted her camera and snapped a picture. She continued photographing the parade as it wound its way past her position on the Green, then she dashed back to join the others.

"I hope the panoramic shots come out all right," she said to Nikki. "I bought one of those throw-away cameras for the wide photos, and used my own for close-ups."

"One of Martin's buddies promised to develop our film at the school this evening. Would you like us to give him yours, too?"

"That would be great," Caroline replied. "It'll save me a trip into town."

The musicians were almost upon them. Martin and Caroline raised their cameras, Caroline focusing on individuals and her son aiming for longer shots of the parade. Both concentrated on the Duke and Duchess as they brought up the rear of the procession.

"Miss Applegate and the Professor look stunning this morning," Nikki commented when the cart bearing the two had finally rumbled past. "Judith carries herself well at normal times, but today she's nothing less than regal in appearance."

"That gorgeous outfit helps a lot," Caroline replied as the three started walking towards the jousting field. "Cobalt blue goes perfectly with her pink complexion and soft silvery hair."

"Carl isn't dressed badly either," Martin remarked. "But I noticed he wasn't wearing a sword over his surcoat like the rest of the knights."

"They probably couldn't find a belt long enough to buckle around him," Nikki giggled.

"Careful, woman. That's my boss you're talking about." Martin wrapped an arm around his wife's waist and squeezed her to his side. "You know what they did in the old days to wenches who made fun of their masters, don't you?" He made a cutting motion across his throat with one finger. "Off with their heads."

Nikki responded to the kidding with a clever retort, but Caroline didn't hear what she said. She'd noticed Morgan Burke leaving the fortune teller's tent, and her attention was focused on the congressman. He'd stopped a few feet from the tent to light a cigarette and was now smoking furiously. Burke was obviously shaken, and Caroline wondered why.

She glanced back at the tent. Mrs. Gregori was leaning on her cane in the doorway. The old gypsy was also watching the congressman, but the look on her face was harder to decipher.

Caroline observed the pair with considerable interest, and as she stood there watching, a third person suddenly came on the scene.

Sid Burke strode towards his father from the direction of the jousting field. He was dressed in the garb of a knight with a sword hanging at his side. His normally handsome features were marred by the presence of an angry scowl, and when he reached the congressman, he leveled a clenched fist at the man. Morgan took a step back, but apparently the boy had no intention of hitting him. Instead, he dragged a dirty plastic package out of the pocket of his leather breeches and threw it on the ground at his father's feet. The boy's head bobbed forward, and he said something to the other man that Caroline couldn't hear. Morgan started to reply, but his son just turned on his heel and stalked off.

A moment later, the congressman bent down and retrieved the package from the ground. He thrust it into his coat pocket, then walked off quickly in the same direction as his son.

Caroline glanced once again at the fortune teller's tent. Mrs.Gregori had backed into the shadow cast by the tent flap, but when she saw Caroline staring at her, she moved forward. Their eyes met, and the gypsy woman slowly shook her head.

CHAPTER 26

In his official role as lord of the manor, Carl had just finished welcoming his guests to Rhineburg when Caroline took her seat in the stands next to Martin and Nikki.

"Everything OK?" Martin asked.

Caroline nodded. "Why are there so many knights and ladies sitting with us in the audience? I thought they'd all be down by the pavilion with the Duke and Duchess."

"They're alumni," Martin explained. "Bruck grads who took part in past festivals come back to town each year for a mini reunion. They wear their old costumes so they can blend in with the current crop of nobility, and when the fun dies down on the Green, they go off to the Blue Cat Lounge to celebrate. Look over there. We've even got a couple of Friar Tucks in attendance today."

"An interesting tradition," Caroline replied before returning her attention to the field. A man in a monk's brown habit had climbed onto the platform and replaced Carl at the microphone concealed near the front of the stand. He gestured to two young men standing off to the side, and the pair came forward. One of the men dropped to his knees before the pavilion while the other took up a spot behind the first.

The monk began speaking in a clear voice that reached every corner of the field. He delivered a sermon on the duties of a knight that included protecting the weak, righting wrongs, and honoring fair womanhood. When he finished, the kneeling youth rose to his feet.

Two other students dressed as squires entered the field bearing a wooden pallet. On the pallet lay a complete suit of armor. As the crowd in the bleachers watched, the three student squires began buckling pieces of the armor onto the knight candidate.

First came a breastplate covered with etched engravings that connected to a plain backplate. These were followed by the tasset, a reversed-'U'-shaped piece that encircled the waist with the arms of the 'U' extending downward over the surcoat to cover the knight's thighs. Hinged plates were strapped to the young man's arms and legs, and metal pads, called pauldrons, were attached to cover his shoulders. Jointed gauntlets were slipped onto his hands, and a metal collar, called a gorget, was tied around his neck. Finally, a visored helmet with four rows of neck-guard plates was placed on the candidate's head.

Due to hours of practice, the dressing of the knight aspirant took only a few minutes. With visor raised, the young man walked up the steps of the pavilion and knelt before Duke Richard of Rhineburg.

Carl rose from his seat and accepted a sword from one of his attendants. He lifted the sword and laid it flat across the youth's right shoulder. In a booming voice, he then solemnly proclaimed,

"In the name of God and St. Michael and St. George, I dub thee knight. Be brave and loyal."

The audience broke into cheers as the new knight rose to his feet and bowed to Duke Richard. He then stepped over to where Duchess Alexandra sat and bowed again. The Duchess nodded graciously, after which she tied a blue silk handkerchief on the young man's helmet as her sign of favor.

The huge crowd cheered again as the knight descended the stairs and an attendant came forward to announce the start of the tourney.

Two mounted knights armed with ten-foot lances and kite-shaped shields entered the field. They were dressed in light armor, and they took up positions at opposite ends and on either side of a short wooden barrier. They waited until the attendant announced their names before kicking their horses into action. Riding at a gallop, they charged towards each other, their lances lowered and their shields raised. Each knight got in a glancing blow as they passed in the center of the field. Neither having been unseated, they turned and charged again. This time the knight farthest from Caroline took a blow to the center of his shield. He tottered in his saddle as he pulled on the reins, and as his horse slowed to a canter, he expertly slid to the ground. He lay there until his squire came running up and helped him to his feet.

"At least he had a soft landing," Caroline said to Nikki. "There must be six inches of straw padding the field."

"They practiced those falls, mom. It's all choreographed."

"That's what the Professor told me. It's a good thing the tips of those lances are encased in wooden blocks, though. A pointed lance could really hurt someone."

"They're made of ash," Martin told her. "They bend easily when they hit the shields, though occasionally you'll see one splinter and break."

A second set of knights was now in position for battle. Once again, one of the men was unseated on the second attempt, but this time he jumped to his feet and drew his sword. The other knight dismounted and took up the challenge. Weapon clashed against weapon as the two circled the field in mock combat. Finally, one of the knights slipped and went down in the straw. His opponent placed his sword against the man's chest, and the supine knight quickly conceded the fight.

After taking the defeated knight's horse and weapon, the victor left the field amid shouts from the audience while the loser stumbled off with the assistance of his squire. They were quickly replaced by two more combatants, and the jousting began again.

Caroline was cheering as loudly as the other people in the stands by the time the fifth set of knights was announced. When only one man rode onto the field, she was as surprised as the rest of the crowd.

"Sir Charles," the attendant proclaimed more loudly as he frowned in the direction of the mounted knights gathered to the left of the pavilion. "Will Sir Charles please take the field."

One of the squires emerged from the pack of horsemen and hurried over to the platform. The boy carried a sea green banner crisscrossed by two black stripes, and he called something to the attendant who in turn relayed the message to Carl. Carl shrugged his shoulders, then waved a hand at his helper as if to say, 'Get on with it'. As he did so, a knight wearing a purple surcoat beneath his armor rode onto the field. The attendant sighed in relief and announced,

"Sir Sidney will replace Sir Charles. Let the joust begin."

"That pennant and those colors belong to Charlie Branch," Caroline told the others.

"It's not like Charlie to back out on his obligations," Martin noted. "I wonder where he is."

Caroline scanned the field for a glimpse of the gardener, but there was no sign of him anywhere. She glanced over her shoulder at the tents set up nearby as changing rooms for the students. Several horses were grazing in the area, but once again she didn't see Charlie.

It was when she turned to look north that she knew something awful had happened. Bricole Gregori was running towards the stands calling to Caroline as tears streamed down her face.

Caroline jumped up and hurried down the bleacher steps. She pushed her way through a knot of people standing near the entrance to the field, and jogged across the lawn to where Bricole had collapsed in a heap.

"What is it, Bricole? What's happened?" she asked as she gathered the child up in her arms.

"Grandma," Bricole sobbed. "I think she's dead."

Caroline transferred the little girl to Nikki who along with Martin had followed her off the field.

"Call the paramedics. Then stay with Nikki," she instructed her son before running off in the direction of the fortune teller's tent.

She was panting by the time she reached Mrs. Gregori's place of business. She pushed back the flap and called out to Maria, but the gypsy didn't answer. A quick look around told her the forward part of the tent was empty. She hurried towards the back where a curtain separated the working area from the Gregoris' living quarters. Flinging the curtain aside, she entered a combination bedroom and kitchen. The light was dim here due to a total lack of windows, but a partially opened flap in the rear wall let in a narrow stream of sunlight that bounced off the waterproofed floor.

"Maria," Caroline shouted as she waited impatiently for her eyes to adjust to the shadows. There was response for several seconds, but then a low moan could be heard coming from just outside the tent. She raced to the rear entrance and tore open the flap.

"Maria."

She knelt down beside the body of Bricole's grandmother and checked for breathing and a heartbeat. There was still life in the old woman, and while her pulse was weak and thready, at least it was still present. Her head was covered in blood from an ugly gash on her forehead, and the skin on her face was pale and clammy to the touch.

Caroline guessed Maria had suffered a heart attack. The laceration must have occurred when she fell to the ground. Caroline placed her fingers on the either side of Mrs. Gregori's head and gingerly searched for signs of further damage. She felt no depression at the base of the skull and no protrusion of bone in the neck. Her hands came away free of blood, which was something to be thankful for. She knew that her simple exam didn't guarantee the absence of a skull fracture or bleeding inside the brain, still she hoped for the best.

She heard the sound of a siren in the distance, and checked Maria's pulse and breathing again. Assured nothing had changed, she made a rapid assessment looking for other injuries. Maria's left leg was shorter than the right, and her foot was turned outward with the toes almost touching the ground.

'Fractured hip,' Caroline thought as she carefully removed the woman's shoe and felt for a pedal pulse. Mrs. Gregori moaned weakly when Caroline ran her hands up the woman's arms and gently probed both shoulders, but her eyelids remained closed.

"You're going to be all right," Caroline whispered in Maria's ear. "We'll have you in the hospital very soon."

With that the ambulance arrived, and the paramedics took over. They connected Maria to a heart monitor and gave her oxygen. One paramedic started an IV drip while the other took Maria's blood pressure and placed a hard collar on her neck. Within minutes they rolled their patient onto a backboard and carried her to the ambulance.

"By the way, we've notified the police about the other body," one of the paramedics suddenly said. "You'd better wait for them."

"What body?" Caroline asked in confusion.

The paramedic pointed to a spot behind her. "That one."

Caroline turned and saw Charlie Branch sitting up against a tree. There was a knife stuck in his chest, and he was very, very dead.

CHAPTER 27

At four-fifteen p.m. Maria Gregori died in the Intensive Care Unit of St. Anne's Hospital. Twenty minutes earlier she had opened her eyes and murmured the word 'mon', but since no one understood what she was saying, the nurses assumed she was speaking in her native tongue. None of them bothered to report it to the policeman standing outside her room, and Caroline would have been in the dark too if she hadn't arrived just as Maria's heart monitor began to alarm.

Since Mrs. Gregori had left no papers indicating her wishes in the matter, every attempt was made by the ICU staff to restart her heart. One nurse began chest compressions while another injected vials of epinephrine and atropine into Maria's veins. A third nurse pumped air into her lungs with a blue plastic bag attached to a mask. When the code doctor arrived, he inserted a breathing tube into her trachea, and the bagging device was attached to that.

Every few minutes CPR was stopped while a staff member checked for a pulse. Each time this happened, the line on the monitor flattened to little more than a squiggle. Round after round of drugs were given, but when fifteen minutes passed with no sign of life, the doctor called an end to the code and walked out of the room.

One of the nurses clamped off the IV line and gathered up the long strip of paper that had recorded Maria's heartbeat. Another cut the intubation tube and gently closed the dead woman's lips. The monitor leads were removed from her chest before Mrs. Gregori was covered with a clean gown and sheet. When all this was done, Caroline was called into the room.

"Her heart was just too weak," one of the nurses told her. "We did all we could."

"I know," Caroline replied with a smile. "It's always hard to lose one, isn't it?"

The nurse nodded mutely and left the room. Caroline moved over to the side of the bed and lifted one of Maria's hands. She stroked the old woman's arm tenderly.

"You tried your best," she whispered. "Don't worry about Bricole. We'll take care of her."

"I'll see to that."

Caroline looked over her shoulder as the voice of another person echoed in the tiny room.

"Hello, Alexsa. I didn't hear you come in."

"I've been sitting in the waiting room." Mrs. Morgan shuffled forward. She leaned heavily on her cane as she stared down at Maria's face. "I owe this woman my life. Now I can repay the debt by looking after her granddaughter."

"Is Bricole an orphan?"

Alexsa nodded. She was about to say something, but just then the chaplain arrived with one of the nurses. The chaplain crossed to the bedside as the nurse drew Caroline aside.

"My name is Amy Wallace," she told Caroline. "Because Mrs. Gregori had no doctor, and the circumstances surrounding her heart attack are unknown, this will have to be a coroner's case."

"I understand the rules." Caroline pointed out Alexsa. "Mrs. Morgan knew your patient much better than I. You'd better talk to her about final arrangements."

Amy waited until the chaplain finished his prayers.

"Do you have a minute, Mrs. Morgan? I need to ask you a few questions."

Alexsa and Caroline accompanied the nurse to the desk where the unit receptionist was waiting with a form. Amy took the piece of paper and turned to Alexsa.

"I'm sorry to bother you with this, but so far the police have been unable to supply us with the names of any family members."

"Maria had no one but Bricole," Mrs. Morgan said. "Her husband's been dead for over a decade, and Bricole's parents were killed in a car accident three years ago."

"No brothers or sisters?"

Alexsa shook her head. "Maria's entire family perished in a concentration camp during World War II. They were among the thousands of gypsies rounded up by Hitler's soldiers during the war." She drew a deep breath before continuing. "Most people think the Jews were the only ones who suffered in the camps, but Hitler annihilated over ninety per cent of the gypsy population of Europe. He pursued them ruthlessly, and most died in his gas chambers."

"But Maria escaped?"

"One of the chambers in her camp malfunctioned. Enough gas spewed in to kill the very weak and the very young, but many others survived. Maria was one of them. Her lungs were badly damaged, but three days later the camp was liberated by Allied troops. Maria was taken to a hospital, and that's where she met her future husband."

"He worked there?" asked a fascinated Amy.

"He was a corpsman assigned to her ward. They married in England after the war."

"No wonder she had difficulty breathing," Caroline remarked. "I'm surprised her heart lasted this long under that kind of stress."

"She was a strong willed woman with an amazing gift for predicting the future," Alexsa replied. "She was never truly healthy, but she was determined to live long enough to see her granddaughter grown and out on her own. Whatever happened on the Green today must have been more than she could handle."

"The police are saying she stabbed Charlie Branch."

"That's ridiculous," Alexsa snorted. She shook her finger at Amy. "Don't you go spreading that story around, young woman. There was no reason on earth for Maria to hurt Charlie."

"He was killed with her sword cane," Caroline reminded Mrs. Morgan. "I noticed that cane the first time I met Mrs. Gregori. It struck me as an unusual piece, but then last night I saw you had one exactly like it."

Alexsa lifted her cane and showed the cobra head to Amy. "Maria gave this to me many years ago. I brought it to the banquet so that she'd see I still treasure her friendship." She unscrewed the head of the cane, withdrew the eighteen-inch blade, and let the other two women examine it. "It's meant to be used only in defense. The Maria Gregori I knew was a gentle woman. If her sword was unsheathed, it could mean only one thing. Maria was being attacked by someone."

"I tend to agree with you, Alexsa. I only wish Maria could have told us what happened before she died. Are you sure she never said a word to you, Amy?"

"Well," hedged the nurse, "she did mumble one word when I was in her room, but I couldn't really understand it. It sounded like she said 'mon', but that doesn't make sense, does it."

It certainly didn't, thought Caroline.

"I guess we can't fill out this form if Mrs. Gregori had no relatives." Amy pushed the piece of paper back on the desk. "If there's no one left to bury her, the coroner's office will do the job."

"I will arrangement for Maria's burial," Alexsa said quietly.
"Dr. Talens, the county pathologist, is an old friend of mine. I'll call
him and find out when the body will be released."

"That's very kind of you, Mrs. Morgan."

Alexsa waved off the compliment. "I must be going. Will
you walk with me, Caroline?"

"Of course."

She accompanied the elderly woman out of the ICU and
down the hall to the elevator, noting as they walked that Alexsa had
shed a good deal of the feebleness that marked her movements last
night. Her shoulders were squared, and there seemed to be new
purpose in her manner.

"How long have you known Mrs. Gregori?"

"We met by accident in England. The war had just ended,
and my husband had to go to London on business. I went along
solely for pleasure, but London in those days was quite depressing
what with all the bombed out buildings and the soldiers everywhere.
I decided to take a train up to Scotland for a few days, and I met
Maria in the station."

"She was traveling also?"

Alexsa shook her head. "She was standing on the platform
next to the train I was about to take. She was crying, and begging
people not to board it. She kept saying she'd dreamed of a crash, but
no one believed her. Finally, a conductor came rushing over. He
threatened to have Maria arrested if she didn't leave the station."

"Did you intervene?"

"Maria was just a slip of a girl back then. I took her by the
arm, and told her to come away. She'd done her best to warn the
passengers, and if harm did come to them, they had only themselves
to blame. We spent the day together waiting to hear the bad news."

"And did the train crash?"

"Oh, yes," Alexsa replied quietly. "They said it was a problem with a switch somewhere down the line. The track didn't quite meet where two lines separated, and the train derailed. Several people were killed, and many more injured."

"But you were safe."

"I believe in second sight. Some people are gifted that way, and Maria was one of them. We became close after that, and we wrote back and forth over the years. When her husband died leaving her nothing but debts, I urged Maria to come live with me. She was too proud to accept charity, though. She went back to her roots, living on the fringe of the gypsy community, and working as a fortune teller. She came here each spring to participate in the Festival as a favor to me."

"And Maria took Bricole in when her parents died."

"She was only four then. Speaking of Bricole, where is she?"

"At my son and daughter-in-law's apartment. They brought Bricole here earlier, and she got to see her grandmother before Mrs. Gregori was transferred to ICU. The poor kid was devastated, but she seemed to sense Maria was dying. She went quite willingly when Nikki suggested they leave."

Alexsa nodded. "If you don't mind, I think I should be the one to tell her Maria's gone. Bricole knows me quite well. She'll take it better if I'm there with her."

"Of course." Caroline wrote down the address of Martin and Nikki's apartment. "Will Bill drive you there, or would you like me to take you?"

"My son is waiting downstairs. There's only one thing I want from you, Caroline. Find out who caused Maria's death. If you do that, you'll also find Charlie's killer."

The elevator doors opened, and Jake Moeller stepped out. He tipped his cap to Alexsa as the matriarch of the Morgan family brushed by him and entered the lift.

"In a bit of a rush, isn't she?" the Chief said gruffly.

"She was a close friend of Maria Gregori, and she's off to break the news of her death to the granddaughter."

Jake rubbed his nose. "I don't envy her that job. That poor little kid has nobody left in the world."

"Not for long, she doesn't. It sounds like Alexsa intends to take Bricole home to live with her."

Jake raised his eyebrows. "Tough job for a ninety-year-old woman."

"Alexsa has tremendous strength of character. She also has a great deal of money. Between the two, she'll get by. So tell me, Jake. What's the situation with Andrew Littlewort? Is Tom Evans going to release him now that Charlie's been killed?"

"Are you kidding? He intends to bring formal charges tomorrow. He's just wrapping up what he calls 'loose ends'."

"You mean he really thinks Maria stabbed Charlie?"

"That's what he says. Several people have testified that Charlie was furious over some kind of damage done to his flower beds. Evans figures the Gregori kid wrecked the flowers, and then Charlie went to the fortune teller's tent to have it out with the grandmother. Supposedly they had an argument, and Maria stabbed Charlie before collapsing with her heart attack."

"Maria was a frail seventy-year-old woman with a bad heart and bad lungs. She didn't have the strength to kill Charlie, much less the personality according to Alexsa Morgan."

"Maria Gregori was a gypsy," Jake said quietly. "That's enough to convict her in Evans' eyes."

Caroline stared at the Chief in shocked silence.

"I know what you're thinking," he said.

"Yeah. All Frenchmen drink, and all gypsies steal," Caroline muttered. "That was one of my grandmother's favorite lines, but I thought that kind of prejudice was dead."

"The term 'gypsy' has gone out of style, Caroline, but the police still do battle with what they now call the Eastern European Travelers Organization. I know all about them because I checked out Maria Gregori the first year she pitched her tent at the Festival of Knights."

"Did you find anything on her?"

Jake shook his head. "Maria was clean as a whistle. Look, Caroline. Tom Evans wants to close the Emma Reiser murder case and get out of town as quickly as possible. As far as he's concerned, whatever happens in Rhineburg is small potatoes compared to the stuff he works on back in the city. He doesn't like small towns, and after last winter, he especially doesn't like our small town."

"But you're not Tom Evans."

"You're darned right I'm not. The way I see it, these three deaths are connected to each other. Evans wants no part in the Branch murder, which is fine with me because now I'm back in control. I can investigate Emma's death any way I see fit as long as I believe it's somehow tied to the murder of Charlie Branch."

"If it helps any, I can assure you Bricole had nothing to do with that flower bed. She knew the bed had been dug up, and she took me to see it this morning, but she thought squirrels had caused the damage."

"And in your opinion they hadn't?"

Caroline shook her head. "No way. Someone used a bulb planter to carefully lift each daffodil out of the ground."

"You mean one of those metal things you push in the dirt, and it pulls out a handful of soil."

"Right. It's a gardener's tool that leaves a round hole just deep enough to bury a bulb. Except these holes were deeper than usual for daffodils. Bricole put her hand in one, and the ground level was over her elbow."

"Maybe Branch liked burying his bulbs that deep. Maybe he figured they were better off that way."

"I had a great garden back in Chicago, Jake, and I never buried a bulb that deep. Besides, Charlie's daffodils had been lifted whole. The flowers were still attached to the bulbs."

"Vandals aren't usually that careful. They like to rip things out so they're totally destroyed." Jake rubbed his chin. "I wonder if there was something else beside bulbs buried in those holes."

"That's exactly what I was thinking. Listen, Chief. I need to do a little thinking. I've heard a lot about Charlie from different people here in town. Some of the things I've heard just don't jive with my impression of the man, but I haven't figured out why yet. One thing I do know. I saw a picture in Charlie's house the night Carl and I took him home from the Blue Cat. Something bothers me about that picture, and I need to go back and take another look at it."

Jake dug in his pocket and produced a key. "You're welcome to search the entire place if it'll help solve this case. Just keep me informed of anything you find there."

"Thanks, Jake. I do have one suggestion for you. Sid Burke was working off a three week punishment as Charlie's helper. Sid had access to the gardening tools, and he sure as heck didn't seem to like Mr. Branch. Yesterday morning I saw his father arguing with Charlie on the Green. Congressman Morgan was probably trying to get Charlie to let up on Sid. I understand the boy is rather troublesome."

"I don't know how Sid ties in with Emma Reiser, but you can be sure I'll have a talk with him."

"Have you found the rune stone yet?"

The Chief shook his head. "Evans figures Andrew threw it away in the woods. We may never find that rock. But Maddy told me all about your visit with Agatha Hagendorf last night. If Agatha identifies Andrew as having been outside the post office the night of the murder, it'll clinch the case for Agent Evans."

"Didn't Agatha come into the station this morning?"

"No. I called her around eight o'clock, but apparently Emily O'Hara drove Mrs. Hagendorf to Newberry for her cousin's granddaughter's wedding. I'll talk to her when she gets back tonight."

"Hmm."

"I have to tell you, Caroline, before Charlie was killed that nutty professor made a good suspect. He had motive and opportunity, and he's got a reputation for a bad temper. He lied to us about being near the post office, although after Agatha fingers him, he may start singing like a bird. As for Charlie, I was on my way over to the Festival to pick him up for a second round of questioning when I got the call he'd been murdered. Apparently Charlie also lied when we talked to him the first time."

"What a mess. You're satisfied, though, that Emma wasn't killed by one of her customers."

"The folks who were placing bets with her? I doubt it. I've got a man checking out some names from Emma's records, and I personally interviewed the four other fellows Agatha told you she saw. I'm positive none of them were involved. Dr. Talens set the time of death between midnight and one a.m., and we now know Agatha arrived there just after one. If she'd called me like she should have, we might have gotten a better jump on the killer. As it is..."

Jake shrugged his shoulders. Caroline knew exactly what the Chief was thinking, and she sympathized with him. She still couldn't figure out who Agatha was shielding, but she was surprised Emily hadn't kept her promise to bring Mrs. Hagendorf to the police station. Maybe the two had thought they'd be stuck with Agent Evans all day and miss the wedding.

"I have to get moving, Caroline. Keep me informed of what you're up to, OK?"

"I will, Chief. I hope your day doesn't get any tougher."

Jake laughed. "It's been a wild one so far. As if I don't have enough on my platter already, one of the students stopped me on the way in here to complain about a missing costume. Somebody lifted his friar's habit from the changing tent, and the kid was hopping mad. I told him to take it up with the Bruck boys. They're in charge of Festival security, thank goodness."

He waved and walked off towards the ICU. Caroline watched him go, a frown settling over her features as an idea entered her mind. She turned and punched the elevator button, suddenly sure she was on the right track.

CHAPTER 28

At five forty-five p.m. Caroline pulled up in front of Charlie Branch's house and switched off the headlights on her Jeep. What had been a beautiful day just an hour ago was fast becoming an ugly evening. Overhead, the sky was crowded with angry gray clouds that skidded eastward and piled up on the darkening horizon. A blustery wind rattled through the branches of the ponderosa pines and stripped the blossoms from ancient forsythia bushes lining the gardener's driveway.

As Caroline started up the walk, a sudden gust whipped the leftover leaves of autumn into little brown whirlwinds that skittered across the lawn and smashed into the side of the house. Fat raindrops splattered the path as a crash of thunder sounded in the distance. Caroline hurried to the door, silently berating herself for forgetting her umbrella.

As she slid the key into the lock, the door seemed to open on its own. Caroline paused, unsure now whether to proceed or retreat to her car. Chief Moeller would never have left the building unlocked, but unlocked it was. That could only mean one of two things. Either someone had entered the house soon after Jake left, or someone was in there now.

A shiver ran down her back as she stared down the hallway layered in shadows. The rooms on both sides lay in darkness, but she remembered there was a light switch was on the right hand wall only a few inches in from the door. She reached in and quietly tripped it.

Nothing happened.

Caroline backed down the path, her heart beating a tattoo on her ribs. Rain pelted her head and shoulders and dripped down her face. She brushed wet hair from her eyes with the back of her hand, then turned and ran to the car.

Safe inside the Jeep, she consciously slowed her breathing and forced herself to relax. She locked all the doors, switched on the engine, and turned the heater on full blast. Then she put the car in reverse and swung backward in a half circle until the headlights, powered up to bright, were pointed at Branch's front windows.

The front of the house leaped into view as the headlamps penetrated the storm. Peering through the arcs made by the windshield wipers, Caroline scrutinized the building for signs of life. She saw nothing, and she was about to look away when a flash of lightening illuminated the yard.

To the left of the house, a figure dashed through the downpour and disappeared behind the garage. Caroline threw the Jeep into reverse and spun the wheel to the right, braking as the nose of the car swung into line with the garage. Straining to see through the dark and the rain, she searched the wooded area that ringed Branch's property.

It was a useless task. The headlights bounced off the trees and revealed nothing more than wet shrubs bent to the ground by the force of the wind. Convinced the intruder had escaped, Caroline gave up and reached for her cellular phone. She dialed the police station.

Ten minutes later, Jake Moeller pulled up in a black and white, mars light flashing, siren turned off. His yellow slicker was streaked with rainwater, but the storm that had caught him in town had already passed over Caroline. She stepped out of her car and greeted the Chief beneath a dark sky still rumbling with thunder.

"Sorry to pull you away from dinner, Jake. When I got here, someone was inside the house. A few minutes later, he ran out from in back of the building and crossed behind the garage. I lost him in the woods."

"Did you get a good look at him?"

Caroline shook her head. "It was pouring rain, and the wind was blowing every which way. I sensed it was a man, not a woman, and he seemed athletic, but not heavy set. He dodged between those trees, and just kept on running."

Jake heaved a sigh. "Let's take a look in the house."

"He must have tampered with the lights," Caroline said as they walked up the path. "The switch in the hallway isn't working."

Jake pulled out a flashlight and shone it through the open door. He motioned for her to wait outside, then he unclipped his holster flap and rested the palm of his hand on the gun butt. Caroline watched as he entered the house and worked his way quietly down the hall. He disappeared for a moment beneath the staircase. Then suddenly the light near the front door flashed on.

A second black and white turned into the driveway and ground to a halt near the Chief's car. A grizzled policeman in his forties jumped out and rushed over to Caroline.

"You OK?" he said in a low voice.

She nodded and pointed to the house.

"Jake went in a minute ago. He got the lights working again."

With that, a lamp went on in the living room, and Jake waved at them through the window.

"I guess we can go in," said the policeman. "Stay behind me."

Caroline followed the man through the door and into the hallway. Chief Moeller was standing in Charlie's den staring at the dozens of pictures on the walls. He turned when she entered the room.

"Wait for us here while we check out the rest of the house."
He motioned to the other officer. "You take the upstairs, and I'll look
out back."

When they were gone, Caroline stepped to the center of the
room and let her eyes wander over Charlie's photo gallery. There was
something about the arrangement of pictures that displeased her, and
she moved closer to examine them.

The Branchs' wedding picture hung where it belonged, as did
the photo of the two of them sitting in their kitchen. But the shot of
Charlie teaching his sons to fish had been moved from its spot in the
corner.

Most people wouldn't have noticed the tiny nail protruding
from the paneled wall. But due to her profession, Caroline had
developed a memory for details, and she knew that the photo now
centered on the adjoining wall had originally hung in this spot.

What picture had it replaced?

She scanned the gallery once again before she came up with
an answer. The photo of Branch and his motorcycle was missing
from the room.

Perplexed, Caroline sat down at the desk to consider the
matter. She brushed aside the pile of seed catalogues still littering the
surface, and rested her elbows on the scarred wood. Propping her
chin on her folded hands, she gazed about the den.

Nothing else looked out of place. The metal filing cabinets
appeared untouched, their drawers closed and locked. A row of
gardening books still occupied one shelf near the desk. On the floor
beneath the shelf rested a pile of paperback magazines.

"Why?" Caroline muttered. She glanced down at the seed
catalogues and suddenly realized something else had been taken from
the room. Branch's scrapbook was no longer on the desk.

"No sign of anyone in the house or outside," Jake Moeller stated as he reentered the den. "If I may say so, you look like a drowned rat, Caroline."

Caroline smiled as she pushed her chair back from the desk. "I feel like one, Jake. Let me find a towel for my hair. Then I want to show you something."

She left him and headed up to the second floor. In a linen cabinet squeezed between two tiny bedrooms she found a couple of well used but clean towels. One she threw over her shoulders, and with the other she dried her damp hair. She quickly ran a comb through it as she descended the staircase.

"Whoever was in here took at least two objects from the house," Caroline told the Chief as she walked into the den. "Let me show you something."

She led him to the corner where the fishing picture had once hung, then pointed out its new spot on the wall. She described the missing photo in detail.

"There was another man standing with Branch by the cycle," she said. "I didn't recognize the fellow, but there was something about him that struck me as being familiar. I swear I've either seen that man, or someone who looked very much like him."

She then told Jake about the missing scrapbook. The Chief scratched his head as she finished her story.

"This is weird," he said. "I don't see any connection between Emma Reiser and these things you saying were taken by the intruder. Maybe we ought to search the house before we jump to any more conclusions. Branch may have moved those objects himself, you know."

Search they did, but there was no sign of the missing photograph or scrapbook anywhere in the place.

"We may as well call it a night," grumbled Jake. "We're getting nowhere here."

"How did the thief get in?"

"A back window was left unlocked. He was probably on his way out the front door when you arrived at the house." Jake motioned to the other officer. "You can go back on patrol, Tim. Keep a lookout for anyone carrying a package about the size of that scrapbook. You never know. We just might get lucky if the guy's still on foot."

Tim nodded and headed off for his squad car. Caroline walked over to her Jeep.

"I'm going home to change clothes," she said. "Do you think the rain's over for the night?"

Jake shook his head. "It's supposed to continue off and on for several more hours. I'm going to stop by Agatha's place and see if she's home yet. I called her right before coming here, and there was no answer."

"That's strange,' thought Caroline as she climbed into the Jeep. Even if Agatha was still at the wedding, one of her tenants should have been home to take Jake's call.

"But everything's strange in Rhineburg lately," she murmured aloud. "Whoever calls this was a sleepy little town is dead wrong."

CHAPTER 29

The phone was ringing when Caroline entered her apartment. She grabbed up the receiver, hopeful it was Carl on the line.

"Caroline? This is Alexsa Morgan. I hope I'm not disturbing you."

"Of course not," Caroline replied as she cradled the phone against one shoulder while peeling off her soaking wet jacket. "How's Bricole doing?"

"I brought her home with me, and my two great-granddaughters are showing her around the house. Jean and Margie understand what the child is going through. They had their own problems handling their mother's death."

Caroline could believe it. Elizabeth Morgan's plunge into an icy river had changed her children's lives forever.*

"Your son and daughter-in-law were kind enough to go back to Maria's tent and gather a few things for Bricole. Tomorrow we'll see to the rest."

"And how are you doing, Alexsa? I know you lost a good friend in Mrs. Gregori."

"At my age, one loses good friends on a regular basis," Alexsa said wryly. "One comes to expect it after a while. Still, Maria was special, and I shall miss her greatly. But I didn't call to talk about Maria. I need to see you, Caroline. Tonight, if possible."

*see A DEADLY LITTLE CHRISTMAS

"What about, Alexsa?" Caroline kicked off her damp shoes and padded into the kitchen. She reached in the frig for a can of cola.

"I have some information about Charlie Branch that may assist the police in capturing his killer. I would like to discuss it with you first."

Caroline hesitated. She knew she should advise Alexsa to call Jake Moeller immediately, but her curiosity got the better of her.

"I just got in, and I'm drenched to the skin from being caught in the rain. Let me change my clothes and grab a bite to eat..."

"I'll have a hot supper waiting for you here. Please come as soon as possible."

"All right," Caroline agreed. "Give me twenty minutes."

She disconnected and immediately dialed Carl's number. The Professor answered on the second ring.

"Where have you been?" he asked. "I've been trying to reach you for over an hour."

Caroline told him about the trip to Charlie's house.

"I wish I'd examined that picture more closely the first time I saw it. I have only a vague memory of the other man's face."

"It's not like you knew you'd need to remember it, Cari."

"That's true," she admitted. She went on to relate the conversation she'd had with Alexsa.

"I wish you could come along, but Alexsa seemed anxious to talk with me privately. I'll call you as soon as I get home."

"Stop by my place instead. I'll have dessert waiting."

Caroline laughed. "I can always count on you, Carl. The sky could be falling, but you'll still make it to the dinner table."

"Hey!" the Professor responded in a hurt tone of voice. "The Duke of Rhineburg had important duties to fulfill today. Unfortunately, satisfying my hunger was not one of them."

A little starvation would have helped the Professor's waistline, but Caroline refrained from telling him so. Instead she said,

"Do me a favor, Carl. Find out everything you can about Sid Burke. I can't stop thinking he's somehow mixed up in all of these murders."

"Sid's a troublemaker, Cari, but I don't see him as a killer."

"I don't have time to explain, Carl. Alexsa is expecting me at her house in twenty minutes."

The Professor agreed to do what she asked, and even offered to call the Archangels for help if necessary.

"Thanks, Carl. I'll talk to you later."

Caroline hung up the phone and went off to change clothes. She slipped into a pair of black corduroy slacks and a gray turtleneck sweater, donned dry shoes, and grabbed a jacket from the closet. Five minutes later she was out the door and on her way to the hospital parking garage.

The roads were almost empty of traffic, and Caroline made it to the Morgan mansion in good time. Alexsa was waiting at the door when she pulled into the driveway.

"Thank you for coming so quickly. Elvira made a pork roast for supper, and I've set a place for you in the dining room."

Caroline followed her hostess down the carpeted hallway that bisected the large house. When they reached the dining room, Alexsa gestured for her to go in.

"There's wine on the sideboard," Mrs. Morgan said. "I'll be back in a moment."

Caroline selected a Merlot from among the array of bottles lining the shelf. She poured herself a glass of the dark liquid and sipped it slowly as she surveyed her surroundings.

The dining room was longer than it was wide by at least twelve feet. Three of the walls were creamed-colored, and they were decorated with groupings of small to mid-sized impressionist paintings. The fourth wall was dominated by a floor-to-ceiling built-in sideboard of carved oak. Open shelves flanked a recessed mirror engraved with fig and grape leaves set above a set of eight drawers.

A Chippendale table surrounded by twelve chairs occupied the center of the room. Ivory candlesticks stood at either end of the table with a centerpiece of freshly cut tulips resting between them. Above the table hung a crystal chandelier composed of cascading teardrop-shaped lights.

French doors at one side of the room led to a flagstone patio encircled by flower beds and low cut hedges. Caroline was admiring a walnut and ebony vase stand placed near the doors when Alexsa entered the room carrying a large covered tray.

"Let me help you with that." Caroline set down her glass of wine and hurried over to the doorway. To the obvious relief of the older woman, she took the heavy tray and placed it on the table.

"I can see you're used to feeding men," she said as she lifted the cover to reveal a plate loaded with mounds of mashed potatoes, red cabbage, and applesauce next to four slices of pork. "This is wonderful, Alexsa, but way too much food for me."

Alexsa waved off the statement as she sank down on one of the dining room chairs.

"It's been a long day, and I doubt you had lunch what with all that happened."

"You're right about that," Caroline responded. She retrieved her wine and joined Alexsa at the table. "I was going to open a can of soup for dinner, but this is a hundred times better. Do you mind if we talk while I eat, or would you rather wait until I've finished?"

Alexsa shook her head. "This will take some time, so go ahead and enjoy your food while I explain why I asked you to come here tonight. I have information about Charlie Branch that may, or may not, be related to his murder. If what I know becomes public, certain innocent people will suffer because of it. But if I hold back, and it turns out the information is pertinent to his death, Charlie's killer could go free."

"It sounds like you're stuck between a rock and a hard place, Alexsa."

"Yes, I am. That's why I wanted to speak to you first." Alexsa chose her next words carefully. "Last winter, you and I made a pact that prevented further tragedy from occurring in this household. At the time, I really didn't trust you to honor our agreement."

"You thought I'd tell Professor Atwater."

The matriarch of the Morgan family nodded her gray head.

"It was obvious to me that you two shared a special bond. I feared that bond would prove stronger than your word."

"I won't deny it was difficult withholding the truth from him, but Carl could never have agreed to the arrangement we made. He would have felt compelled to tell the police."

"I know. Carl has been a good friend, and lying to him was difficult for me also. Still, I had to preserve what was left of my family." Alexsa drew a deep breath. "These past few months have taken their toll. Over time, though, I've learned one thing. You're not only intelligent, Caroline, but you're also someone I can trust."

Caroline put down her fork and looked Alexsa directly in the eye. "I'll listen to anything you have to say, Mrs. Morgan, but don't ask me to withhold information from the police. I have a vested interest in these murders. In fact, I may be partially responsible for at least one of them."

Caroline told Alexsa about her conversation with Charlie the day the rune stone was discovered.

"If I'd kept my mouth shut, Charlie might not have gotten drunk that night and gone off to see Emma Reiser."

"If you hadn't told him about the rune stone, someone else would have, Caroline. I don't believe Charlie killed Emma, and neither do you. Now listen to what I have to say. This story started a long time ago, and it may be more relevant to Charlie's death than that rune stone of yours."

The two women stared at each other in silence. Caroline knew that Alexsa was right about the rune stone. The gardener would have heard about it sooner or later, and his reaction probably would have been the same. She was foolish to blame herself for his death.

"I'm all ears," she said as she picked up her knife and fork.

"Good." Alexsa stood up and went over to the sideboard. She poured herself a glass of Merlot, brought the bottle back to the table, and refilled Caroline's glass. "Last night I told you that Julie Branch worked for me before her death."

"I remember."

"Elvira has always been my regular housekeeper, but Julie came in twice a week to help with the heavy work. She also assisted Elvira at dinner parties and other large gatherings here. I got to know the girl quite well, and when she became ill, I was very concerned. I'd noticed she'd been losing weight, and she seemed distracted and depressed for weeks before she finally took to her bed.

"One day, about a week after I'd heard she was laid up, I drove over to see her. Charlie had gone to work at the university, and Julie was alone in the house. When I walked up the path to the door, I could hear her crying inside. Julie didn't answer the bell, but I let myself in anyway. I found her curled up on the couching, sobbing."

"Poor thing," Caroline murmured.

"Poor thing indeed," replied Alexsa. "She was so upset that I gathered her in my arms and just held her until she stopped crying. Then she began to speak. The words came tumbling from her lips as if she couldn't control them any more. I don't think she meant to tell me the whole story, but once started, she couldn't stop.

"Julie said that Charlie had made a lot of money doing something illegal. She wouldn't go into details, but she kept repeating that he would go to jail if they didn't give back the money. Apparently Charlie believed he was in no danger of being caught. He told Julie he'd hidden the money where no one but he could find it. He was using it to pay for their sons' education, and that really upset her. Julie said she'd never had a head for money, so Charlie paid all the bills and handled the bank account. She assumed they lived as well as they did because both of them were working."

"Julie was a bit naïve, wasn't she?"

"No more so than a lot of wives I know. There are many of them who leave financial matters solely in the hands of their husbands. Then when the men die, these women are up a creek without a paddle."

Caroline grinned at Alexsa's use of the old expression, but the smile quickly faded from her face when she thought of Charlie's scrapbook.

"I offered to repay the money," Alexsa continued. "At first, Julie adamantly refused my help. Then, when I agreed it should be looked on as a loan, she gladly accepted. I took her to the bank that very day and withdrew the sum she needed."

"How did Julie return the money?"

"I don't know. She left town a few days later, supposedly to see her sister in Chicago. When she returned, she was gravely ill."

Alexsa stood up and walked over to the French doors. She stood staring out at the rain that had begun to fall in earnest again.

"I went to see Julie a few days before her death. She was little more than skin and bones by then. That's when she asked me to look out for her husband and sons. I didn't question her about the money, but at one point in the visit, she took my hand and squeezed it. She told me not to worry. No one would be coming after Charlie."

"I've been told Julie died of cancer, but you said it was heart disease."

Alexsa shook her head. "I told you she died of heart trouble, and she did. Julie loved Charlie too much. She couldn't believe he'd deceived her all those years, and when she found out he had, she couldn't handle the pain. Julie turned all the hurt inward on herself. Charlie broke her heart, and she destroyed herself because of it."

Caroline folded her napkin and pushed her chair back from the table. "I think I know why Charlie was killed," she said as she stood to leave.

Alexsa looked over her shoulder. "Charlie's paths of gold," she said quietly.

Caroline nodded. "Jake Moeller has to be told about this."

"Charlie's sons are coming home to bury their father. They should all be in Rhineburg by the morning."

"It can't be helped, Alexsa. They'll have to be told."

"They had nothing to do with it, Caroline. They never even knew, and after all, the money's been paid back."

Caroline hung her head and thought about it for a moment.

"Jake's a good man," she finally said. "Maybe he can figure out a way to handle all this without involving Charlie's sons."

Alexsa turned and gazed out at the rain pelting the patio.

"I leave it in your hands," she murmured.

CHAPTER 30

So Charlie Branch was a bank robber. Caroline shook her head in wonder as she drove to the police station. Now she understood why he kept a scrapbook full of old newspaper reports. They were all about him and the clever ways he had eluded capture.

"Poor Julie," she murmured. She'd probably discovered the scrapbook while straightening up Charlie's favorite room. The whole awful truth had come out, and her life had been turned upside down in a matter of minutes. She'd made amends with Alexsa's money, but that hadn't saved her marriage, or her life. And now Charlie was gone too. What a terrible price to pay for five college educations.

But apparently Branch hadn't used up all his money on the boys' schooling. There was still some buried in the ground beneath his precious daffodils.

Paths of gold. How had Sid stumbled on the truth? Branch had told him, of course. Caroline recalled her conversation with the gardener the day the rune stone was discovered. 'I tell all the boys who work for me, but none of 'em understand. Not even Mr. Smartypants.' But Sid had understood. When Charlie had erupted in rage over the idea of an archeological dig on Bruck Green, Sid must have sensed there was more than a love of flowers involved. He'd lured the gardener to the Blue Cat Lounge, plied him with alcohol, and slowly but surely gotten the man to talk.

Later on at Branch's house, Sid had found the scrapbook. It didn't take a rocket scientist to figure out Branch was the infamous thief. Sid was also smart enough to realize that any investigation on the Green could spell disaster for Charlie Branch. No man buried money in a flower bed unless he wanted to conceal its existence. The police would certainly start asking questions if some rock hound discovered a package of cash stashed beneath a row of posies.

The problem was, there was no time for Branch or Sid to retrieve the money. The Festival of Knights started the next day, and the Green would be swarming with people. While Branch might find a way to work around the crowds, Sid would have no excuse for digging in the beds, unless he attempted the feat at night. Even then, he might not succeed. There were thousands of daffodils lining the paths on the Green, and it was unlikely that in his drunken state, Branch had revealed the exact location of his cache.

Sid must have decided to steal the rune stone from the post office. That would have delayed, if not put an end to, a dig on the university grounds. Caroline suspected Emma Reiser's murder was unintentional. Most likely the postmistress had heard Sid rummaging around downstairs, and had gone to investigate the noise. The boy probably reacted in a panic, hitting her with the stone and then, when he discovered he'd killed her, he placed the body near the steps to make it look like she'd fallen.

After the banquet, Sid had gone to the gardening shed and stolen a tool for digging up the daffodils. When Charlie discovered the mess in the flower bed, he must have known Sid was the culprit. But the Grand Parade was due to begin. Both Charlie and Sid were riding in the procession, so Charlie had to put off any confrontation until after they reached the jousting field. He must have told Sid to meet him near the fortune teller's tent. With most of the visitors watching the combat between the knights, there was little chance their conversation would be overheard.

Caroline pulled into a parking spot near the police station, switched off the engine, and sat thinking about Sid and Charlie. Jake had mentioned that a friar's costume had been stolen from one of the changing tents. She bet Sid had taken it to wear at his meeting with Charlie. He must have known the situation could turn ugly, and he hadn't wanted anyone to recognize him.

But Maria had seen him. With her dying breath, she had uttered the word 'mon'. She'd been too weak to pronounce the last consonant in the word, but Caroline was sure she'd been trying to say 'monk'. Few people thought of friars any more, but everyone recognized a monk in his brown habit.

Maria must have heard the two men arguing outside her tent. Caroline figured the old woman had found Sid fighting with Branch, and in an attempt to scare them off, she'd drawn the sword from her cane. Sid probably grabbed the sword, pushing Maria to the ground in the process, and then stabbed Charlie with it.

It all made sense to Caroline now that she knew about the money hidden out there on the Green. Sid was a troublemaker from way back, and he probably saw an easy chance to make himself a few bucks at Branch's expense. Whether or not he'd bargained on committing murder, she'd never know unless Sid confessed. One thing was for sure. Jake had to be told the entire story so he could go after the young man before anyone else was hurt.

Caroline climbed out of the Jeep and dashed through the rain to the police station. All the lights were on in the pink stone building, and through the large plate glass window she could see Madeline Moeller deep in conversation with Jake's secretary, Annie Holtzbrinck. The two women looked up in surprised when she walked through the door.

"Caroline! We thought you were over at the Morgan place."

"I've just come from there," Caroline told Madeline. "Is the Chief in? I need to talk to him."

Maddy shook her head. "He took off with Professor Atwater about five minutes ago. They're looking for Sid Burke."

"Now what's happened?"

"The Professor arrived here with some information on Sid Burke," Annie explained. "Since it was based on rumor, he wanted to check it out with Chief Moeller before he told you about it."

"What information?" Caroline asked with a frown.

"Michael Bruck heard that Sid was picked up by the Chicago police over winter break. Supposedly he'd had a fight with a guy in a bar there, and the other fellow was injured pretty badly."

"Jake made some phone calls to Chicago and confirmed the story," Maddy said. "Sid would be sitting in jail right now if his father hadn't come to his rescue. Apparently Congressman Burke paid off the victim big time, and the man dropped his complaint against Sid."

"So Sid can be vicious."

"It looks like it," replied Annie. "Of course, Morgan Burke has enough money to pay off anyone he wants. When he sold his daddy's trucking company..."

"The Professor said you think Sid is mixed up in Charlie's murder," interrupted Maddy. "He persuaded Jake to pull the boy in for questioning, and they went to the university together to find him. So tell us. What did Alexsa have to say?"

"Not much, really. She wanted to talk about Maria and Bricole Gregori."

Caroline didn't feel free to discuss what Alexsa had told her in front of Annie Holtzbrinck. She was afraid the news would be all over town in a matter of hours.

"Did Jake get a chance to interview Agatha Hagendorf?"

"Would you believe, she and Emily still aren't home?"

"That's pretty strange, Maddy, unless they're staying over in Newberry due to the storm."

"That could be," agreed Annie. "But you'd think at least one of her boarders would answer the phone. All I keep getting is Agatha's answering machine."

"For some reason that makes me feel very uneasy," Caroline told the two women. "Annie, why don't you call Bertha Meyer. She a good friend of those ladies, and if anyone would know where they are and what they're up to, it would be her."

Annie bobbed her head as she reached for her phone. A minute later she was connected with Meyer's Bakery.

"Hello, Bertha. It's Annie over at the police station. I'm so glad you're home." Annie exchanged views with her friend on the weather, the success of the Festival, and the health of Bertha's family before finally coming to the point of her call. "Bertha, by any chance did you hear from Agatha or one of the other ladies at the Home today? I know Agatha drove over to Newberry this morning for her cousin's granddaughter's wedding, but... What's that, Bertha? The wedding was two weeks ago? Then why would Agatha say... No, I'm sure that was the message on her answering machine. No one else seems to be at home there either. Are you sure you haven't spoken to... No, Bertha, of course I don't doubt what you say. But maybe you forgot... Bertha? Bertha, are you there?"

Annie stared at the phone in shock. "She hung up on me," she told the others. "I can't believe she'd..."

"What did Bertha say?" Caroline asked impatiently.

"What did she say? Oh! Right. Bertha claims she was too busy working their bakery stall at the Festival to keep track of Agatha and the others, but she says that wedding took place two weeks ago, not today. She can't understand why Agatha left that message."

"Something's very wrong, Maddy. We have to get over to Mrs. Hagendorf's right now."

Caroline flew out the door into the rain. Madeline told Annie to contact Jake, then she grabbed her coat and ran after her friend.

"Why would Agatha want to protect Sid Burke?" Caroline called over her shoulder as she headed down Wilhelm to Kaiser Street. "She must have seen him enter the post office the night Emma was killed, but why wouldn't she say so?"

"I don't know," panted Maddy. "Maybe she's afraid of him."

Caroline rounded the corner and cut across the wet street. She took the stairs of the Rhineburg Boarding House and Home for Gentle Women two steps at a time. Not a light was on in the house, and when she rang the doorbell, it echoed back unanswered.

"Agatha!" she called out as she rang the bell again.

Maddy peered through the rain stained glass of the living room window, then turned and shook her head at Caroline.

"I can't see a soul in there. Try the door, Cari. Maybe it's unlocked."

Caroline twisted the knob to the right. She heard a click and felt the door give way under her hand.

"Got it, Maddy. Come on."

The two women entered cautiously. The long hallway lay in darkness, as did the rooms on either side of the entrance, but a light glimmered on the landing at the top of the staircase. Caroline walked over to the stairs and glanced up.

"Anyone home?" she called out.

"Back here," someone answered from down the hall.

Caroline and Maddy looked at each other.

"The kitchen," Maddy whispered. She pointed to a stream of light illuminating the base of a door at the end of the corridor.

Caroline nodded and started walking that way, but Maddy raised a hand to stop her.

"Maybe we should wait for Jake to arrive," she said in a low voice.

They suddenly heard the clatter of dishes coming from the direction of the kitchen. Someone laughed, and soft music floated back to them as a radio was turned on.

"I guess I was worried for no good reason," Caroline said with a shrug of her shoulders. "Come on. Let's go join the others."

She moved down the hall, Madeline following at her heels. When she came to the kitchen, Caroline pushed open the door without hesitation.

"Sorry to burst in on you, but we... Oh!"

"Come in, Mrs. Rhodes. And you too, Mrs. Moeller."

The man in the monk's hooded habit was holding a gun. He pointed it directly at the two women and motioned them to move farther into the kitchen. With his free hand, he turned off the radio.

"That's better. The music helped draw you to me, but I hate distractions when I'm talking." He pulled the hood away from his face and smiled. "Surprised, ladies?"

"Morgan Burke!" exclaimed Madeline. "But I thought you were... "

"My son?" Burke laughed unpleasantly. "Sid may be able to hold his own in a bar fight, but he hasn't got the guts for murder."

"And you do," Caroline murmured.

"It's called self-preservation, Mrs. Rhodes. I've worked too hard to get where I am. I'm not about to lose everything because some stupid gardener would rather bury his money than spend it."

"Charlie was your friend. I saw a picture of you in his house."

"The shot of us standing by the motorcycle?" Burke shook his head. "When Sid said he'd recognized me in the picture, I was afraid you might have also. It's a good thing I persuaded him to break into Charlie's place and steal that photo."

"He took the scrapbook also. Why was that, Congressman?"

Caroline's heart was working overtime, but she knew their only chance to survive depended on the use of delaying tactics. If she could keep Burke talking until Jake and Carl arrived...

"I think we've talked long enough, Mrs. Rhodes. Why don't you and Mrs. Moeller head downstairs now?" Burke motioned with the gun as he opened the door leading to the basement. He circled around them like a sheep dog and herded them towards the steps. "You'll find your friends are all waiting for you. I promised them we wouldn't start the fireworks without you."

Maddy grasped Caroline by the arm, her eyes wide with fear.

"Cari, I can't..." She choked back a sob as Burke poked her in the back with the gun.

Caroline patted her friend's hand.

"We'll be all right," she whispered. "Just do what he says."

She started slowly down the stairs, her fingers clutching the banister for support. A wave of nausea swept over her as she realized time was running out. The university was only minutes away, and the Chief should have been here by now if Annie had contacted him. Maybe Sid hadn't been in his dormitory. Maybe Jake and Carl had driven somewhere else looking for the boy.

"Over by the wall." Morgan pointed to the far end of the basement where a bare light bulb dangled from the ceiling. There on a row of chairs, their hands and feet tied and their mouths taped, sat the proprietor and the residents of the Rhineburg Boarding House.

All six women began to struggle when they saw Morgan Burke with his captives. Agatha Hagendorf made little mewing noises, her worried eyes glued firmly on Caroline's face, while Sarah Sonnenschein appeared ready to faint. The other ladies looked to be in varying degrees of despair as they fought their bonds and uttered incomprehensible words.

"I thought I told you to keep quiet," Burke snarled at the women. He shifted the gun to his left hand and grabbed a folding chair with his right.

"Sit down," he commanded Caroline. He pointed to Maddy. "Get down on the floor and lie still."

The two women did as they were told. Burke walked behind Caroline and quickly taped her wrists together. Then he opened another folding chair and repeated the process with Maddy. When he finished with their wrists, he taped their ankles to the chair legs.

"Now isn't this a cozy arrangement?"

Caroline watched in horror as Burke walked over to a shelf and lifted down a container of gasoline.

"What do you intend to do with us?" she asked.

"I intend to kill you," Burke answered sarcastically as he removed the cap from the container. "This old house will go up like a torch once I light a match to this."

"But you never answered my question. Why did you have Sid take the scrapbook?"

Burke paused and smiled at her. "You read what was in it, didn't you? Do you really believe Charlie was clever enough to pull those jobs off by himself?"

Caroline remembered Annie saying something about Burke's father and a trucking company.

"You were a truck driver too, weren't you?"

"My father owned the company, Mrs. Rhodes, but he wanted me to start at the bottom. Yes, I drove a truck. I was Charlie's partner."

"Did you ride the motorcycle, or was that Charlie's job?"

Burke set down the gasoline container and walked over to Caroline.

"My, my. Aren't you the curious one? You seem to have put two and two together, so I'll fill in the blanks for you. Charlie rode the bike and made all the heists. I simply waited for him at some conveniently quiet spot. When he arrived with the money, I jumped out and dropped the ramp. He steered the bike up into the truck, and off we drove, two innocent fellows with a load of goods to deliver."

"No wonder you eluded the police for so long. But you won't escape them now, you know. Chief Moeller knows that Agatha saw you outside the post office."

That had to be it, Caroline thought as she watched Burke's face contort in anger. Agatha had seen Sid's father that night, but being the woman she was, she couldn't imagine a Congressman killing anyone. She probably thought he was there to place a bet with Emma, so she tried to protect his reputation by concealing his name.

"Sid must have mentioned the rune stone when he called about the picture hanging in Charlie's house. He told you about Branch's 'paths of gold', didn't he? Your son figured out where that money came from, and he knew it would be found if people started digging on Bruck Green. He tried to warn you, didn't he?"

Burke snorted in disdain. He picked up the can of gasoline and started pouring fuel on a pile of rags under the stairs.

"You give that boy too much credit, Mrs. Rhodes. Sid is a whining little fool who comes crying to me every time he's in trouble. If it weren't for his mother, I'd have written him off long ago."

He put down the container and walked back to Caroline.

"The only good thing about Sid is, he's not really my kid. Jeannie was pregnant when I married her. That was a no-no for a kid whose daddy was a big shot politician. I saved Jeannie's reputation, and she repaid the debt by introducing me to the right people."

"So now I know all your secrets."

"That's right, Mrs. Rhodes. But I'm not worried you'll tell anyone. In fifteen minutes this house will be in flames, and you and your friends will be too dead to talk."

"Maybe not, dad."

Burke spun around. He hadn't seen Sid standing on the basement stairs, listening to every word he said. But Caroline had watched the boy creep down the steps and pick up his father's gun.

"Put that down," Burke commanded. "Better yet, give it to me."

Sid backed away from his father.

"I don't think so," he sneered. "Remember, dad, I'm just a whining little fool. Fools do dumb things, and I may do a dumb thing with this gun if you come one step nearer."

Burke recoiled as if he'd been shot.

"I was just talking, boy. Just blowing off steam with these women."

"Before you killed them, right, dad? Like you killed Emma Reiser and Charlie Branch, never even giving them a chance to defend themselves. Well, I can defend myself, dad. Or should I call you 'step-dad'?"

"Now listen, Sid…"

"Put down your weapon!"

All heads turned at the sound of Jake Moeller's voice. The chief stood poised at the top of the stairs, a gun clutched in his hands.

"Jake!" Maddy cried out.

Jake's head jerked in the direction of his wife. In that split second, Morgan Burke recovered from his surprise and lunged forward. He caught Sid's hand and dragged the gun away. Then he spun the boy around, caught him by the neck, and pointed the weapon at his head.

"You've got him," said Jake as he lowered his own gun and ran down the stairs.

"No, Jake! It's not Sid!" screamed Caroline.

"Shut up!" yelled Burke. "Stop right where you are, Chief Moeller, or I swear I'll kill him."

Jake halted a few feet away from the Congressman.

"What's going on?" he asked in confusion.

Burke tightened his hold on Sid's throat.

"Stay back!" he shouted as he pulled his son towards the basement door leading to the back yard of the house. He fumbled with the handle, then pushed the door open with one foot. He leaned into Sid and shoved him forward. The boy collided with the Chief as Burke turned and bounded out the door.

He ran right into the arms of Michael Bruck.

CHAPTER 31

.   "Sir Sidney of Rhineburg."

Sid Burke spurred his horse into a gallop and, to the applause of the spectators, joined a half dozen other knights on the jousting field. He extended his left arm, raising his shield above his head as he bowed to the people in the stands.

The Festival herald continued announcing names until the center of the field was filled with brightly dressed horsemen, squires bearing banners, drummers, trumpeters, and pages, and a full company of armed soldiers and archers. When the entire group was assembled, they fell into line and circled the makeshift arena. To the continued cheers of the audience, they came to a halt in front of the main pavilion where the Duke and Duchess of Rhineburg stood waiting.

"Good people of Rhineburg," Carl called out. "You see before you the bravest of the brave. These knights have acquitted themselves well both on and off the battlefield, and we honor them here today."

Another cheer arose from the crowd, and Carl raised his hand for silence.

"Our great poet Chaucer described a knight as valorous, prudent, and meek in his bearing. It is our hope that these virtues were witnessed by all who visited us this week. We invite you to return to our fair land at the same time next year when we will once again bestow knighthood on one of our own. And now, my friends, I declare a close to this great tournament and to the Festival of Knights. I bid you, return to your homes in harmony and peace."

Caroline stood and applauded along with the rest of the throng in the bleachers. People seemed reluctant to let the celebration end, and when they finally exited the stands, many of them wandered back to the area where the crafters and artisans were closing down their booths.

"They don't want to leave yet," she commented to Martin and Nikki as they made their way down to the field.

"It's always like this on the last day," Martin told her. "Reality can seem pretty dull after you've lived in a fairy tale world for a week."

"But it's different this year," Nikki reminded him. "How often has murder intruded on the Festival of Knights? I think folks just want to unwind today. It's like they're shell shocked. They need to remind themselves that Rhineburg is really a safe place to live."

Martin wrapped an arm around his wife. "If that's what you want to think, honey, go right ahead. But you're being naïve, you know."

"Now why would you say that?" Nikki asked crossly as she pushed him away. She stalked over to a picnic table and sat down. "Give me two good reasons for your cynical attitude."

Martin looked to his mother for support, but she only raised her eyebrows in response.

"OK," he sighed as he settled down across from Nikki. "Reason number one. Emma Reiser's funeral. Reason number two. Charlie Branch's funeral."

Nikki's eyes narrowed. "Explain," she demanded.

"You attended both of them, Nikki. Did you see any real sorrow expressed at Emma's funeral? And outside of his sons, was anyone really mourning the loss of Charlie?"

"Lots of people came to both services."

"Lots of people came to the Festival of Knights, also."

"Oh, Marty! How can you equate the two?"

Martin gazed up at Caroline again. This time she decided to step in.

"What Marty's trying to say is, neither Emma nor Charlie had any true friends here in Rhineburg. People knew Mrs. Reiser either as their postmistress or as their bookie, but not as the person she really was." Caroline paused, searching for the right words to express her thoughts. "Emma lived a secret life up on the second floor of the post office. There wasn't a person at her funeral who admitted ever being invited upstairs."

"People attended the services out of curiosity, Nikki," said Martin. "The same goes for Charlie's funeral."

"Julie Branch was well liked by the women I talked with, but everyone said Charlie was a loner. He was protecting a secret also, and secrets have a way of isolating people from those around them."

"What an awful way to live," said Nikki. "I'd hate to die without leaving even one person to grieve for me."

Caroline thought of Maria Gregori. Her funeral had been sparsely attended compared to Emma's and Charlie's, but those who were there had loved and respected the woman. Sorrow had forged a bond between Alexsa Morgan and little Bricole Gregori. They were inseparable now, and both would live happier lives because of it.

"Here comes the Professor," said Martin. "Mrs. Moeller and the Chief are with him."

Carl had exchanged his royal robes for street clothes. He looked more at ease in his plaid shirt and corduroy pants, and Caroline commented on the fact when he greeted her.

"Can't say I'm sorry to be done with that costume," he replied. "It weighed a ton, and it was much too warm for this weather."

"I thought you looked great in it," said Nikki. "Very regal and authoritative."

Carl stroked his beard to hide his pleasure. "It did fit me quite well," he purred.

Martin rolled his eyes. Fortunately, the Professor didn't notice.

"I thought all the costumes were beautiful," remarked Madeline. "I just have to study up on all this medieval stuff so I know what the decorations stand for."

"The decorations?"

"You know what I mean, Professor. The symbols on the shields and banners."

"Those are called devices, Mrs. Moeller," explained Martin. "Back in the old days, knights had a custom of emblazoning devices on their shields and surcoats so their followers could find them on the battlefield. The surcoat was the original coat of arms."

"How interesting. So tell me what some of those devices mean."

"It's pretty complicated," laughed Carl. He turned to Martin. "Did you notice Sid Burke altered both his costume and his shield?"

Martin nodded. "On the first day of the tournament, Sid wore a surcoat with two diagonal bands crossing his upper torso. His shield was painted with the same device. He must have removed one stripe, though, because today his costume and shield bore only the band crossing from the upper left to the lower right."

"Sid's new device is called the 'bend sinister'. People used to consider it a sign of illegitimacy."

"It must have come as quite a shock to Sid when Morgan said he wasn't the boy's real father," said Caroline. "Tell me, Jake. How does Sid stand with the law?"

"Morgan confessed to everything," Jake replied. "He did ask Sid to steal the picture and scrapbook from Charlie's house, but he didn't give him the real reason why. He told the kid he'd hardly even known Charlie, but he said he'd be embarrassed politically if the man's thievery became public knowledge."

"Do you think Sid really believed that?" asked Carl.

Jake shrugged. "I think he did at first. Sid admitted to calling Morgan the night of the murder. He told him about the rune stone and Charlie's obsession with the flower beds. He also told him what he'd seen in the den. Morgan asked Sid to burglarize the house that same night, and apparently Sid did go. But he got scared off when Branch walked outside and saw him hiding by the garage."

"Charlie must have been on his way to the post office."

"I think so, Caroline. Branch never saw Emma, though. Professor Littlewort has finally admitted to being at the P.O. He had second thoughts about sending the rune stone to the museum, and he went there in hopes of getting it back. He saw Charlie, and Charlie saw him. They both lost their courage and ran off.

"Evidently Morgan arrived only minutes after those two left. He broke in and found the stone, but Emma heard him and came downstairs. He claims he hit her in a moment of panic."

"What happened to the rune stone?" asked Caroline.

"Morgan threw it in the river when he drove out of town. Evans has his people looking for it. Maybe they'll get lucky yet."

"What about the time I saw Burke talking with Charlie?"

"Morgan was angry that Charlie had been dumb enough to talk to Sid. He wanted Branch to stay away from his son. He also wanted to know what Charlie had told the police."

"Remember the night of the banquet when I said someone was watching us? That was Sid," said Maddy.

"His father was upset that Garrison Hurst asked you to investigate. He told Sid to follow you and learn anything he could."

"Alexsa showed me her swordcane that night. She said it was just like the one Maria had."

Jake nodded. "Morgan set up a meeting with Branch. He claims it was only to talk, and things got out of hand, but I suspect he attacked Maria first in order to get her cane. Alexsa called me today. She talked with Bricole, and the kid says she saw a monk go into her grandmother's tent. She thought he was a customer, so she stayed away. Then she heard Maria call for help. By the time Bricole found her out back, the monk had disappeared."

"Burke stole the friar's habit from the changing tent."

"Right, Martin. He hung onto it because by that time he knew he had to kill Agatha Hagendorf and the others." Jake turned to Caroline. "When Sid told him you and Maddy were going to see Agatha, Morgan decided to follow you. He saw you in the window with the telescope, and he watched as the Professor walked up and down the street. He figured Agatha had spotted him the night of the murder, but he couldn't understand why she hadn't told me about it."

"He went to the house after you left, and Agatha was pleased as punch to see him. She thought he was going to explain what he was doing at the post office with Emma, but instead he forced her into the basement and tied her up. Agatha didn't go quietly, though. Before he knew it, Morgan had a whole bevy of women on his hands. He really did panic then, and he left them all tied up in the basement while he went back to his motel to plan his next move."

"The following day he stole the habit and killed Charlie."

"Yes, Caroline. He kept the habit because he had to return to Agatha's place in the daylight. With the hood hiding his face, he thought no one would recognize him if he was seen."

"You still haven't told us where Sid stands in all this," said Carl. "Will he be charged as an accessory to murder?"

"Not in Emma Reiser's death," responded Jake. "Tom Evans says there's no evidence to prove he knew what his father intended to do. Sid is cooperating, but I'll have to talk with him a few more times before I decide whether or not to charge him in Charlie's murder."

"I really don't think he was involved," argued Caroline. "I saw him confront his father that morning, and he was very angry with Morgan." She told Jake about the package Sid had thrown at the congressman's feet.

"Sid's explained all that, Caroline. He was the one who dug up the flower bed on Bruck Green. He unearthed some of Charlie's loot from the bank robberies, and he claims that's when he first suspected his dad was lying to him."

Caroline shook her head sadly.

"Maria told me there was something wicked in the air here in Rhineburg, and it seems she was right."

"I wish you'd listened to her, mom," said Martin. "You almost got yourself killed again."

"Don't worry about her, Marty," said Carl. "Cari's just fine. As for life in Rhineburg, it'll get back to normal in no time flat."

A big smile spread over Jake's face. "Not for me, it won't. Michael Bruck found information on Emma's computer about a Newberry bank safety deposit box. Evans got right on to it, and this afternoon he called to say he'd found Emma's will. Seems like Mrs. Reiser left all her worldly possessions to the city of Rhineburg."

"That's wonderful, Jake," said Caroline. "Does Mayor Schoen know about this?"

"Oh, yeah," Jake laughed. "When I showed it to him, he was ecstatic. He started right then and there making plans on how to spend the money. He didn't mention giving one red cent to the police department until I pulled out the list of Emma's customers. When he saw his name in bold letters right up at the top, he changed his tune real quick. It looks like I'm getting two more officers and a brand new squad car. Plus a raise for Annie Holtzbrinck."

Caroline gave the Chief a hug.

"That's the best news I've heard today, Jake. But if I were you, I'd hold out for a few more perks. Ask for something really outrageous, like an all-expense-paid vacation with your wife."

"Sounds good to me," piped up Maddy. "I wouldn't mind a couple of weeks cruising the Caribbean."

"Neither would I," agreed the Chief. "Of course I wouldn't leave Rhineburg unprotected. I'd appoint Caroline interim Chief of Police, and Professor Atwater could be her second-in-command."

"I like that idea," said Carl enthusiastically. "We could...."

Caroline put her fingers to his lips and firmly shook her head.

"Don't even consider it, Professor. Our days as detectives are over. From now on we stick to what we do best. It's teaching for you, and nursing for me."

Carl looked crestfallen, but he brightened considerably when Caroline suggested the group drive into town for dinner.

"Remember," she added with a twinkle in her eye, "Duke Richard hasn't had a bite to eat since lunch. The poor man's likely to keel over if we don't hurry up and get a menu into his hands."

Carl grinned from ear to ear. "I knew there was a thread of compassion running through that diet-conscious soul of yours, Cari." He linked his arm in Caroline's and started towards the parking lot. "How about burgers and beer at the Blue Cat Lounge? While we're eating dinner we can discuss a case I read about in the Newberry newspaper. It seems this fellow walked into the bank and..."